DARK REFLECTIONS

A NILE GHOST STORY

CRISTINE COURCY

SMASHED HOUSE PUBLISHING LLC

WWW.CRISTINECOURCY.COM

For my mother.

CONTENTS

THE HOUSE

I dreamed about her on the car ride there.

That should've been my first clue that moving to Martin Isle, the paranoid hotspot of America, would be a nightmare.

I didn't dream anymore. Not a single one for the past seven years. I took meds for that. My prescription for a dead-sister-less sleep was the only reason I tolerated my psychiatrist. Okay, not entirely true. I depended on her. After all, therapy was critical in ensuring that I didn't end up like my father...a drunk, in and out of mental hospitals.

And the dreams I had? They would drive anyone insane. So, when I drifted off to sleep on the way to the island and came face to face with my dead sister, I should've made Mom turn around. I should've said something.

But I didn't.

Why would I? I knew what it would do to her. And it's not like we had any other options. Housing was limited, and our budget even more so. A matchbox apartment in some ancient old house on an island full of freaks was all we could afford.

So, I just chalked it up to the fact that I'd had the box clutched in my hands and my neck bent in *The Shining* for half the trip and shrugged it off. That's a scary book. And plus, I don't usually touch the thing. The box, I mean. I definitely don't open it. I just keep it...stashed away in a drawer or in the corner of the room...and I never touch it. Honestly, I hate the thing. But I have to keep it. It's all I have left of her. And it's the least I could do.

So, really it only makes sense that I'd have a nightmare about her...for the first time in seven years...

We got off the ferry boat and turned right down a back road that curled along the shore and up a cliff. Apple Shore Road...I think. Then we took a left onto the mile long driveway. The road bumped and dipped with so many potholes it was impossible for us to avoid them. All the way up a huge hill, we were jolted and banged around inside the tiny car. By the time we reached the top, my newly straightened teeth were aching—along with the rest of my bones. And there it was: the Rosecrest House.

It looked like it had dropped from the sky and crumbled a bit from the landing.

Not crumbled...more like shattered.

The old Victorian was huge but in complete shambles like it was literally as decrepit as Queen Victoria's corpse. Shutters dangled like loose teeth. Shingles were missing and the pale-purple paint was peeling. And this...this was supposed to be my new home? I gritted my aching teeth.

"Well, come on. Don't you want to see your new room?"

I glanced at Mom with an eyebrow raised.

She gave me a rueful sigh and shook her head. She shoved open the car door, and it creaked and squealed in protest. "Would it kill you to look on the bright side for once, Hannah?"

Yes...yes, it might.

I threw open my own door, which groaned louder than my mother's, and slammed it shut. I stood in the gravel driveway, the box held out in my hands like a bomb, and stared up at the house. It had a wide wooden staircase that led up to the porch, which wrapped around the front and to the left. There was a rickety second wooden staircase that zigzagged all the way up the right side of the house like a poorly constructed fire escape, leading to a tiny rooftop porch and a small door almost too far up to see. In front of the house, separating it from the stoney parking lot, was a huge tangle of dead plants.

Mom, purse in hand, trudged up the winding path that cut through the dying wall of thorns and branches and up the porch steps to the front door. I didn't move, combat boots dug firmly in the gravel. Maybe if I refused to go inside, Mom would be forced to tell the old lady there'd been a mistake...we can't live here...she can't clean your house...

But we had to live here. We had nowhere else to go.

And she had to clean the house. It was a condition of the lease to lower the rent.

I sighed and followed after Mom. It was the least I could do.

The door opened just as I made it up the stairs. An old woman appeared in the doorway with a small polite smile. She wore a huge sun hat that dipped down over half her face. Her neck was weighed down with thick ropes of beads. Peacock feathers dangled from her earrings.

She spoke in a soft Mid-Atlantic accent as she asked, "How may I help you?"

Mom blinked, clearly as taken aback by the old lady as I was. She recovered quickly. "Yes, ma'am. I'm Elizabeth Green. This is my daughter, Hannah. We're here—"

The old lady's eyes widened, and her face warmed. Her eyes flickered toward me before returning to Mom. "Oh, my, yes!"

She clasped her hands around Mom's and then took mine as I hastily shifted the box under my arm. Her hands were as soft as her voice but weathered and a bit shaky. "My name is Barbara Blake. Apologies. Please, come in...I was just heading out to the gardens... is it really Friday, already?"

The woman threw open the door and ushered us inside. "Welcome to Rosecrest. One of the oldest houses in Nile...and *that's* saying something."

"'Nile?'" I mouthed to Mom.

"I'll show Miss Hannah to her room, and then I can give you a tour—show you what I'll be expecting of you, yes?"

I blinked into the entryway and squinted as my eyes adjusted to the dim. It was like the house had been drained of all color except for a muted gray-purple, which washed over everything. A few feet from the front door, lining the right wall, there was a staircase that led up to what appeared to be an apartment. To the left of the staircase was the narrowest of hallways, illuminated by several old, cloudy glass lamps. It was a strange hall in that it didn't lead anywhere—instead, it stopped at the same point as the staircase, abruptly in a dead-end. I squinted harder. There was a large black sheet hanging on the back wall. The black sheet seemed to be draped over something, hiding it from sight. I frowned as I looked at it, feeling that nagging sensation in the back of my mind, like it was familiar...and then I remembered.

My dream.

"Hannah!" Mom prodded my arm with her finger.

I flinched, eyes darting away from the sheet. Mom nodded to the left of us; there was a door with the number two on it. Our apartment. Casting one last look at the sheet at the end of the hallway, I followed Mom and Ms. Barbara into our new 'home.'

"My rooms are up those stairs back there...the whole remainder of the house is yours...the stairs outside lead up to young Elijah Grunvald, and the stairs out back leading to the cellar are the Sawyers'..."

"The whole remainder...? Your advertisement said simply two bedrooms with access to—"

"The kitchen, yes, well..." Barbara smiled back at Mom as she led us, arms wide, through the living room and into a sitting room and out through a kitchen. She hesitated in a doorway, her arms falling to her sides. "I find that if I go into too much detail about the amenities...I don't care for the sort of folks who turn up to call..."

Our silence prompted her to add, "I prefer to surround myself with a humbler kind of person...the sort who don't turn their noses up to small spaces...don't you, dear?"

Poor people. They were called poor people.

Barbara showed us to a second staircase that led up to the second floor and yet another hallway, if possible, even more narrow than the first.

"Now, Ms. Hannah's room is this one all the way down at the end..."

Barbara held out a delicate hand to me as she pushed open the door with a soft creak. "In you go, dear." She placed her hand gingerly on my arm and guided me inside.

"The whole of the house is yours to explore...just not up that first staircase in the entryway, mind. And don't touch the black sheet in the hallway."

And they left me alone.

The room...my room...was the same drab gray-purple color as the foyer. Like the color of a faded bruise...depressing. And painful. There were two long windows that stretched the length of the wall. The dusty curtains framing them were a pale-purple paisley pattern that hurt to look at. The view would've been okay, if not for the old wooden railing of the balcony outside, blocking most of it. The only furniture in the room were the small bed, a short dresser, a tiny wicker wastepaper basket, and a large round mirror above the dresser. As pathetic as it was, I was grateful for the furnishings...it wasn't like I had anything better. Everything I'd had...we'd sold. What was the saying? Beggars—take what you can get?

I dropped the box on top of the dresser, grateful to let go of it, before looking around the room. I sighed and tossed my bag in the corner. The floorboards creaked and groaned as I crossed the room and dropped onto the bed, which screeched underneath my weight. I bounced a few times, testing the squealing springs. Painful. But I'd slept on worse.

I went back to the dresser and checked my reflection in the mirror. The long drive through the mountains and the boat ride across the lake to the island had done a number on my appearance. I looked a lot older than my seventeen years...tired...haggard. Once I read a medical journal that explored the concept of stress and aging. I'd had enough stress to age me decades. My eyeliner had smudged from the stuffy car ride, I had dark circles rimming my brown eyes, and my hair was tangled and matted from the ferry ride. Gross. I smoothed a finger underneath each eye and ran my hands through my hair.

"Do you need a comb?"

I flinched and sucked in a breath between my teeth. A girl had somehow appeared behind me in the mirror. I whirled around, my dark hair fanning out and swatting her in the face.

"Excuse me?"

The girl smiled serenely. "Your hair. Do you need a comb?"

I raised an eyebrow dubiously, still trying to figure out who this girl was and what she was doing in my room. "Uhh...no."

The girl nodded, her white-blonde hair swaying with her as she rocked back and forth on her heels. "Then I wouldn't stand too close to that mirror if I were you... If you're done with it, that is. You shouldn't ever watch yourself through looking glasses. You never know who might look back."

What? I blinked at her. She was the oddest girl I'd ever seen. She had a white swim cap, with little plastic flowers stuck on the sides, pulled over her head like a beanie. She wore a jean jacket, with planets embroidered all over it, coupled with bright-yellow leggings and a thin orange scarf wrapped around her waist like a belt. Not to mention her lilac galoshes.

"Right. Thanks." I glanced toward the door, wanting nothing more than to run out of it, but manners kept me frozen in place.

"I'm Lacey..."

"I'm—"

"You're Hannah Green," she said, as though I might not know. "My daddy told me all about you. He's Ms. Barbara's handyman. Chuck McGregor is his name."

"Right."

"Come on...I'll introduce you to your neighbors." Lacey grabbed my hand and pulled. She was surprisingly strong for such a small person. Lacey led me through the hall and down the twisting stairs, and weaved us around the rooms, all the while mentioning random things about the house. ("Rosecrest used to be a bed and breakfast." "There are giblies in the floorboards." "The servants had a secret staircase to the attic." "Watch out for the dust bunnies, they bite.")

By the time we made it out of the house, I was desperate to be back inside, alone. But before I could think of a way to untangle myself from her, Lacey tugged me all the way up the teetering makeshift fire escape to the tiny door at the top.

The door looked like someone had ripped it off a child's treehouse and stuck it to the side of the Rosecrest. Beside the odd little door was a large bell like the kind they rang at malls during the holidays. Lacey pulled its giant cord which set off a chorus of obnoxious clangs.

There was a crash from inside. Someone let out a yell as a cat yowled in pain. There was a hiss and a yelp. Then whoever it was let out a string of swears and ripped open the door.

A guy of no more than eighteen bent through the doorway, leaning out to glare at the both of us through fogged-up glasses.

"*I told you not to*—" He snapped, angrily swiping a finger over his lens to see us better. "Oh, hey, Lacey...sorry. I thought you were Damien."

Lacey rocked back and forth on her heels with a sweet smile on her face. "That's all right, Elijah. I've brought your neighbor to meet you... This is Hannah Green. She just moved here."

He ducked underneath the doorframe and straightened.

I held out my hand with a polite smile. How had I let this girl take me up here? Elijah wiped his hand on his shirt before giving mine a good shake. It was still sweaty. I flexed my fingers, fighting the urge to wipe them on my jeans.

"Elijah isn't from Nile, either...his family moved here from Europe."

I raised an eyebrow, looking at Elijah for confirmation. He didn't have an accent.

He shrugged and mumbled, "I was little...my mom's from here..."

"Elijah is an inventor," Lacey said.

Elijah's tan face reddened with clear embarrassment. "Oh, no, I'm—I work down at the docks...well, sorry, you're new to Nile... it's, uh, the *east* ferry dock...just down the road, off Route 2?"

"He's an inventor," Lacey said again.

"Tinker...really."

"He makes machines. He's going to make me one that can detect EMF."

I looked at Lacey. "EMF?" Seriously? Any small notion I had had of Lacey and I becoming friends vanished quicker than proof of a UFO.

Lacey smiled dreamily, completely oblivious to my skepticism. "Electromagnetic—

"Fields...right..." I murmured coolly. This girl wasn't just odd...she was nuts. I shifted awkwardly where I stood, anxiously thinking up an excuse to leave.

"Lacey, listen, I got a lot of work—" Elijah started.

"I need to get back—" I muttered.

"For the fair—" Elijah added.

"Let's have a tour!" Lacey announced brightly as she moved past Elijah, ducking underneath the doorway and disappearing into his apartment.

I looked at Elijah who shrugged and held out a hand for me to go first. Groaning inwardly, I slipped inside.

The whole apartment was filled with steam. Elijah hurried to open a window and instantly the hot fog cleared, leaving me cold with goosebumps trailing my arms.

The space was small. Cramped. The size of the apartment Mom and I had expected to be forced into. This was it. There was only one room, aside from the bathroom, which was a narrow door slapped up against the back wall. The windows were slanting inward from the left which gave me the uncomfortable claustrophobic sensation of being crushed. Like the trash compactor in Star Wars. There was a small kitchenette set shoved against the left corner that looked like it could've been made by Mattel and a couch that seemed to be serving as a bed, judging by the pillow and blanket tangle on top of it. To the right of the bathroom, shoved against the back wall, there was a bookcase stuffed to the seams with books, which seemed to be spilling out in stacks on the floor. Several machines were scattered around the living space, one of which seemed to be responsible for the steam. There was a workstation pushed against the left wall beneath the slanted ceiling and open window and another flimsier worktable shoved between two machines in the middle of everything, bent beneath the weight of a computer with a monitor like a box. There was no TV.

While I studied the decor, Elijah scrambled around the room, tucking old socks behind couch cushions, shoving wrappers into the giant black trash bag in the corner, and hastily dropping dirty dishes in the sink as Lacey walked in a small circle, admiring the space.

"Where did you hide her this time, Elijah?" Lacey peered into the sink where Elijah had just dropped an empty mug.

Elijah looked at me.

Lacey waved a dismissive hand. "Oh, Hannah won't tell."

"Bathroom..." he admitted.

"Who?" I glanced at the narrow door.

Elijah moved to open it, and a black cat bolted out, mewing

indignantly as though highly offended to have been shut in such a place.

"Ms. Barbara is allergic…"

"So she says…" Elijah muttered.

"She doesn't allow cats in the building." Lacey scooped up the cat and held it to her face. The cat nuzzled her, purring contentedly.

"If you could keep this to yourself…" Elijah pushed his glasses up the bridge of his nose and fiddled awkwardly with the frames, avoiding my eyes. "I had a heck of a time getting her to rent this place to me as is…and I…well, I don't have many other options…"

I didn't answer. Instead, I moved toward the book lying open on the worktable. It was an anatomy book…highlighted and annotated. Thoughtfully. I looked back at Elijah with new respect. "Are you a med student?"

He hurried over to the table and shut the book. "Oh, nah…I just…"

"Tinker?" I suggested with a small smile. Clearly, he didn't have the money for med school. I felt for him. I didn't have that kind of money, either.

"He had a scholarship…but—"

Elijah cleared his throat. "Lacey, have you introduced her to the Sawyers yet? I bet she'd like that…"

Lacey blinked, her sweet smile still in place. "All right."

The Sawyers lived down a set of stairs around the back of the house in what used to be the cellar. I could still see where the cellar doors had been ripped off to give the place a more welcoming, less-dungeony appearance. But before Lacey could tug me down the stairs to meet them, there was a loud roar at our backs. We twisted in the grass as a guy on a dirt bike sped around the side of the house and came to a sharp stop just feet from us.

"Hi, Peter." Lacey paused at the top of the stairs. "What are you up to today?"

I pulled my hand from Lacey's grasp and crossed my arms over my chest, feeling extremely awkward to be caught holding hands with anyone, let alone someone like Lacey.

The guy—Peter— leaned back on his bike as it rumbled pleasantly underneath him. He raised his voice over the engine as he said, "Looking for you." Peter lifted his helmet off his head, revealing a mop of golden hair and a kind, handsome face. "Mom was wondering if you and your dad wanted to come over for dinner tonight."

Lacey hopped a bit where she stood. "Daddy can't come. He's leading a campfire night at the Inn. But I'd love to." She turned to me and held onto my arm. "Would you like to come, too, Hannah?"

"Uhh...no...I—"

"We live right down the road..." Peter's smile crinkled his blue eyes.

"Please!" Lacey smiled, too, (again,) and I couldn't help but wonder if her face ever hurt from smiling all day long.

"We have horses..." Peter's grin broadened just before he tugged his helmet back on.

I opened my mouth to say 'no' and said, "Sure."

Lacey bounced up and down.

Peter revved his dirt bike and rode off.

I should never have left the car.

THE MIRROR

We didn't make it to the Sawyers. Instead, Lacey disappeared to find her father with a promise to pick me up just before dark. I'd tried to leave myself a way out, explaining that I hadn't asked my mom, but Lacey simply smiled. "Either way, I'll be here for you, Hannah."

Great.

And somehow, despite all my introverted instincts to the contrary, I found myself sitting on the porch steps of the Rosecrest, the sun setting behind the house, watching Lacey peddle up the hill through the dusk on a pink bicycle with a white basket strapped to the front, covered with plastic daisies. Except...I squinted my eyes. They weren't daisies. They were doll heads.

Lacey pulled to a stop in front of the house. She was wearing a helmet with a headlight, rain boots (canary-yellow this time), and pink rubber gloves. She seemed to notice my stare because she said seriously, "You never know when you might need to catch a champlet."

"Right...uh..."

"Elijah has a bike you can use—it's there...under the stairs... yup." She smiled her serene smile as I emerged from the staircase, hair covered in cobwebs, with the bicycle in hand...thankfully without a basket.

I hopped on, and we headed down the road with Lacey's headlamp to guide us. At the end of the driveway, we turned left and biked in silence to the sound of the waves hissing against the rocks just down the bank below us. After a few minutes, we turned left (again) down another long driveway that cut through the woods, and Peter's house came into view...only it wasn't really a house. It was more like an estate with stables and horses and shiny, expensive cars tucked into a three-car garage.

"Peter's very rich. All the Blanchards are. His mother is a doctor. And so is his stepfather, Keith. He's not a Blanchard...his last name is David...but I'm sure he's just as wealthy," Lacey murmured, as we skidded to a stop in front of the house. We propped our bikes, and I followed Lacey to the giant double doors.

She leaned forward and pressed a gentle finger to the doorbell. Inside, dogs barked, and one let out a long howl.

Lacey giggled. "That's Squirrel."

The door opened.

Peter struggled to hold back a dog as big as a bear and keep the door open at the same time. "Hey, sorry—I forgot to ask—do you —mind dogs?"

I cracked a smile. "Love them."

"Good," Peter puffed. He released the beast, and it bounded out of the door. Then he jumped on me in a huge hug. I was tall... but this guy was just as...

I nuzzled into his furry face as his huge pink tongue licked the length of my cheek. I laughed and shoved him down, and he headed for Lacey to do the same to her...only Lacey was a foot shorter than me and much smaller, so the goofy thing knocked her over, sending her headlamp flying.

"Jeez, Squirrel...you're gonna kill her." Peter bent down to help Lacey up and bellowed over his shoulder into the house: "*Courtney, call the dog!*"

"SQUIRREL!!"

Immediately and with as much enthusiasm, the dog bounded back inside.

Lacey brushed off her leggings as I handed her back her headlamp.

Peter waved us through the door. "Well, that's Squirrel...the other knuckleheads are in the back..."

The house was beautiful. It was like stepping into a Pottery Barn. I half expected to see price tags dangling from the lamps. And yet, it wasn't stiff or uncomfortable. It was lived-in. Homey. Warm and bright and cozy. But the thing I loved most? It reminded me of my house. My *real* house in the mountains. Our home before my sister was taken and my daddy went off his meds. That (and the delicious smells of whatever Peter's mother was cooking) made all my regrets about coming fade away.

Or rather—what Peter's stepfather was cooking.

"Mom can't cook to save her life." Peter snickered through a bite of baked mac and cheese.

His mother, a short, slim blonde woman with a kind face like her son, sat to my left at the end of the table. She scoffed in mock indignation as she hid a loving smile behind her water glass.

"My daddy doesn't like cooking..." Lacey murmured thoughtfully from my right.

I smiled slightly. "My mom is the same...if I wasn't here, I'd be having a lukewarm TV dinner on a tray. Really, thanks so much for having me."

"We're glad you came." Peter's stepfather, Dr. David, nodded to both Lacey and me from the other end of the table. He was tall, dark, and handsome—to the extreme. Like a younger Idris Elba, complete with the accent.

Peter's sister, Courtney, was across from me. I felt her eyes moving over my face as I chewed.

"Where are you from?"

I swallowed thickly and looked at her. She had honey colored hair that curled prettily around her face. Her eyes were a deep cerulean blue. I considered her for a moment, wondering how much of myself I wanted to give her. "A little town up in the mountains..." I answered vaguely.

Courtney nodded, her eyes sharp and critical. "You haven't heard what they say about Nile have you?"

"Courtney..." Her mother scolded. "I hardly think this is dinner conversation."

I'd heard. "Martin Isle is—"

"Nile," Courtney corrected me. "You live here now; you might as well call it what we call it."

"It's supposedly one of the most haunted places in the country..."

Courtney nodded. "And do you know what they say about that house you're staying in?"

"Courtney Ann," Dr. David said sharply.

Courtney shrugged and pushed her food with her fork. "Just asking..."

I watched her, trying to decide how to take this obvious hostility. She glanced up at me with narrowed eyes.

"The most haunted place is actually Bird Island..." Lacey replied seriously. "Elijah Grunvald is building me an—"

"Oh...Elijah!" Dr. Blanchard put down her glass, giving Lacey her full attention. "How is he doing these days, Lacey?" She smiled ruefully as she took a sip of her water.

"He's doing very well, Ms. Blanchard. He's building—"

"I think about him a lot these days..." Dr. Blanchard looked from Lacey to me with a sad smile. "What with his sister and all... it's so good of Ms. Barbara to rent him that room when he's still so young...not barely eighteen, is he, Keith?"

"Just." Dr. David nodded over his water glass.

Courtney scoffed and looked darkly at her plate. "May I be excused?"

She didn't bother to wait for an answer. Courtney grabbed her plate and stalked out of the dining room.

Dr. Blanchard made to follow her, but her husband held out a hand. "I'll go," he said gently. Then he excused himself with a kind smile to Lacey and me before he left the table and headed after Courtney.

Dr. Blanchard sighed. "Don't mind Courtney, dear. She's been struggling lately."

Peter's cheeks grew pink as he gave me an apologetic wince. "Her best friend used to live in the Rosecrest House...she had—"

"Peter." His mother shook her head.

Peter shot his mother a pained, pleading look, but she simply shook her head again.

Dr. David returned to the table with a small smile that didn't reach his dark eyes. "She'll be all right."

I stared down at my plate as an awkward silence settled around the table, punctuated by forks scraping plates.

"When she's not working at the hospital, Ms. Blanchard writes books about half-naked men," Lacey said suddenly.

I raised my eyebrows and stifled a snicker. Dr. Blanchard snorted into her water glass. Peter and his stepfather exchanged glances, right before we all dissolved into fits of laughter, save for Lacey who looked around the table, smiling politely.

"Sorry for my sister," Peter said for the hundredth time as he walked Lacey and I to the stables.

I inhaled the sweet smell of the barn and moved to pet the cream mare with the black mane. She snuffed my hand, and I smiled. Her velvety muzzle tickled my palm. I patted her neck as she leaned over her stall to sniff my pockets.

"Don't worry about it. Really. It's okay. Some people get too wrapped up in the whole paranormal activity thing..." My face fell. No one knew that better than me.

"Her friend had to be committed to a psych ward," Peter explained quietly.

My fingers stiffened in the mare's mane, and my palms grew slick with sweat. I wiped my hands on my jeans and tried to focus my attention on the muzzle nudging my side.

"Don't say 'psych ward,' Peter." Lacey pressed her forehead against the head of a chestnut mare and looked deep into the horse's dark eyes. "You should say a behavioral health facility, actually...or a psychiatric hospital, if you like. But never 'psych ward.' Maple Leaf House is its name."

Peter nodded respectfully. "Sure...sorry, Lacey. She's a patient at the Maple Leaf House. And it's been hard for Courtney. Her friend—Desiree Lapierre—she doesn't want to be there. Her parents won't see her. And the—what do you call them, Lace? Doctors? They barely let Courtney visit her because when she does, Desiree gets upset that she can't leave with her. And I know that doesn't give her an excuse to be a brat to you, but—well, she's normally not like that. If that makes sense..."

I shifted where I stood. It did make sense. And I understood where Courtney was coming from. More than I would ever say. Instinctively, I reached out and touched Peter's shoulder. "I wasn't judging her. I just—it bothers me when people talk about...you know, things that aren't real. Like ghosts and monsters and stuff."

Lacey turned her head so that her cheek still rested against the chestnut mare. "Ghosts are very real. And champlets...and mermaids...and..."

I kept my mouth shut and focused on the horse in front of me as Lacey continued to name random things, half of which she'd probably invented herself.

Peter chuckled. "I don't know about ghosts, but my mom swears by the Nile Witch."

I raised an eyebrow. "*The* Nile Witch?"

"Yup. Charlotte Grey. The Nile Witch. Anytime either of us has the flu—Mom zips over to grab a tonic. She gets her cards read at least once a week. And she can't get enough of her love potions." Peter snickered.

My eyes widened, and my hand fell away from the mare.

Peter laughed. "Keith isn't my first stepdad, you know...although he *is* my favorite, so far...and has lasted the longest...like, going on six years?"

"Wow." I chuckled despite myself. "Lacey said your mom was a doctor..."

"She is. A heart surgeon, actually." Peter grinned and gave me a playful nudge. "Just because you believe in science doesn't mean you can't believe in other stuff, too." Peter shrugged. "And trust me...the Nile Witch's stuff *works*."

I scoffed and shook my head. Placebo effect. Obviously.

"What is it, Hannah?" Lacey murmured, blinking serenely up at me with her large hazel eyes.

I scrunched up my face, trying to decide how much of myself I wanted to give them. I pivoted the conversation. "What do they say about the house?"

Lacey and Peter exchanged glances. There was silence, and then Peter said, "People think it's the house. But it's not the house. It's the mirror. It's cursed."

It was dark by the time I made it home. Lacey was kind enough to escort me back up the road to Rosecrest so I wouldn't get lost. And I had to admit, her headlamp came in handy. I waved good-bye, watching Lacey's light disappear down the driveway, and then tucked Elijah's bike back in place beneath the stairs.

I trudged up the porch steps but almost fell backward with a sharp gasp.

There was a large shadow sitting on the porch.

A lighter flicked on, illuminating Ms. Barbara's face as she lit a long cigarette. I released the breath that had caught in my throat in a low hiss.

"God, you scared me, Ms. Barbara!" I clutched at my chest as my hammering heart began to slow, and I stomped up the rest of the steps.

"Oh, Hannah, I'm so sorry." Ms. Barbara gripped her cigarette between her lips and held out a hand in the darkness for me to hold.

I let her squeeze my hand. "It's all right... What are you doing out here?"

Ms. Barbara pointed to the door. "Flick on the lamp, dear, so we can see each other...there, that's a dear, yes, just twist it."

Ms. Barbara smiled as the front lamp popped on, casting a yellowy tinge over the both of us. "I was looking at the stars... I have a fondness for them, you know. Beautiful. Like specks of glass. Don't you think?"

I returned her smile and glanced up at the night sky. "I do..." Before I could stop myself, I added, "I used to want to be an astronomer. When I was little, I used to chart the stars...in an old notebook." Stop. Talking. Now.

My cheeks burned, and I stared down at my boots.

"Well, dear, I think that's just lovely. You've a sharp mind, haven't you? Your mama was going on and on about how brilliant you are, and I must say, it's refreshing to see a young lady with her nose in a book instead of sucked into a phone. With her mind on the world and not on the boys. Why, most girls your age sit for hours in front of the looking glass, lost in their vanity. Not you, huh?"

I nodded, unsure of how to respond to any of that. "Well, I better head inside..."

Ms. Barbara smiled as she rocked back and forth on her rocker, but before I could get my hand on the door, she asked, "What did you make of Miss Lacey?"

I blinked. "Uhh..."

Ms. Barbara laughed, and her eyes sparkled. "She's something else...but you mustn't be too hard on her. She's had a rough time of it."

I nodded as though I understood.

Ms. Barbara seemed to know I didn't. "Her mama and sister passed away a few years back. It's just her and her daddy these days, and he's always working. I think she takes comfort in her imagination. You'll have to indulge her, dear."

I nodded again. This time I did understand. I knew what it was like to lose a sister...and a parent. I thought of Lacey and her soft, gentle smile and made a mental note to not be so...me... around her.

"Did she tell you about the house?" Ms. Barbara asked softly, her voice trailing off as she stared up at the sky.

I hesitated.

Ms. Barbara chuckled lightly. "Well, whatever she said...don't touch the sheet on the mirror in the hallway."

GOSSIP AND GHOST STORIES

I couldn't stop thinking about it.

The sheet was covering a mirror.

That simple fact scratched at the back of my brain like a fingernail. For I'd known there was a mirror behind the sheet. I'd seen it in my dream. It was only a coincidence, of course. I had years of therapy to hold up that truth: dreams are just dreams. But I still couldn't stop thinking about it. Every time I passed through the house, it felt like the thing was looming over me like a monster lurking at the end of the hall. I should've asked why it was covered...maybe that would've helped. But I didn't. I refused to stoop so low as to play into whatever lunacy these Nile islanders believed.

And I said as much when Lacey, Peter, and I were in the Ferry Dock Diner a week later.

"Not even...like, God, or angels, or anything?" Peter asked over the top of his mug of hot apple cider, clearly amused at my resistance.

"Well...maybe God..." I grinned indulgently. Peter had easily become one of the highlights of this whole move. And I had to admit, Lacey, especially. As much as she was odd, she was genuine and joyful, with a good heart so much like my sister. I was glad she wandered into my room and made me her friend.

"So, which school are you going to?" Peter asked around a huge bite of his sandwich.

"Which school?" I gave him a funny look. "Don't districts determine school?" I'd moved around enough to know this was true.

Lacey shook her head serenely. "Nile children get to choose because there isn't a high school on the island. Peter goes to the private school in town, but I go to one of the rural public schools—both are on the mainland. My mother went to my school…" Lacey sipped her cider from the top of a tower of teacups glued together. She'd brought it from home in her satchel. ("I made it myself.") I tried not to stare as I hid my smile. The sight of her in her bottlecap sunglasses sipping daintily from a homemade stack of cups was too much.

I cleared my throat. "Well, I'm homeschooled, so I don't have to decide."

"Pshh. Lucky. We head back next week." Peter started piling our plates as the waitress came over. "Here you go, Rach."

"Thanks, dude…" The waitress tucked a strand of inky-black hair behind her ears as she gathered as many dishes as she could carry. She clicked her tongue ring against her teeth. "Are you still having your party this weekend? I only ask because Cole said he's not going to make it…I might not, either, if they keep calling me in…" she grumbled as she glared over at the large, beefy manager seated at an empty table, tapping away on his phone.

"Oh—yeah, party's still on. Sorry, Rachel—this is Hannah. She just moved here. She's homeschooled."

Rachel smiled and nodded in greeting. "Some friends of mine are homeschooled. They live off Adam's School Road, down Grey Lane. Do you know—oh, shoot." She flinched as the manager bellowed at her from behind. "Yes, hang on! Sorry, guys. I gotta get back to work." She rolled her eyes apologetically and hurried back to the kitchen, snapping back at the manager who yelled at her from the corner.

Lacey frowned thoughtfully. "She's quite angry for a cheerleader."

I looked back at Rachel as she shouted retorts at the barking manager, taking in her dark eyeliner, tight black shirt, and bright-red baggy pants, zigzagged with way too many zippers, and I smiled.

"Petey Blanchard..."

The three of us turned in our seats as a short girl with an upturned nose squashed into a pudgy face stomped up to our table. Ignoring both Lacey and me, she pouted at Peter. "Why haven't you invited me to the party, yet?"

"Er...well, you know it's never really invite-only..." Peter stumbled over his words, clearly trying hard not to hurt the girl's feelings.

The girl poked his shoulder. "You know I'm teasing."

Peter forced an awkward laugh as he scratched his head, his golden hair falling into his eyes. "Uhhh...Portia, this is Hannah... she just moved here."

Portia's pale eyes slid to mine. Even though she was standing over me, we were practically nose to nose. Her mouth curled nastily. "Don't tell me...you moved into the Rosecrest House? Wow." She snorted. "Good luck."

"Excuse me?" I eyed her coolly.

Portia grinned. "You couldn't *pay* me to live in that place. They say a girl *died* in the house—that you can still see her in the mirrors...not to mention that mainlander girl who went crazy last spring." She shook her head with a dark giggle. "Yeah, I'll say it again: good luck with that." She turned to Peter. "I expect you to text me the party details, Petey." She gave him a raunchy wink and walked away.

Lacey watched her leave with a sad shake of her head. "She's quite rude for a person with such an unfortunate nose."

Peter caught my eye, and we burst out laughing, nodding in agreement. But as rude as she was, I couldn't help but think of the mirror in the hallway hidden behind the sheet.

That night, as I helped Mom fold Ms. Barbara's laundry, I was still thinking about it.

"Mom, did someone die in this place?"

Mom's brow crinkled, but she didn't bother to look up. Her hands continued to fold. As I watched her, I realized how tired she looked. Stress had aged her, too. Plus, she was overworked and dead on her feet. Not only was she caretaking Rosecrest for Ms. Barbara, but she had also gotten a job at the west ferry dock and was often working double shifts from sunrise until late into the evening.

"Not that I know of...why?"

I shrugged and continued to fold. "Just rumors..."

"Well, if anyone would know, Ms. Barbara would be the person to ask..." Mom wiped her forehead with the back of her hand. "Okay, I'm going to run these upstairs and—"

"I'll do it." I offered.

Mom looked at me and smiled gratefully. "Okay...I'll nuke us some dinner, and we can watch a movie?"

"Sure. Just don't start without me."

As the biggest apartment in Rosecrest, we were the only unit with a washer and dryer hookup. Ms. Barbara had made it clear, in addition to cleaning her rooms, we'd be responsible for a laundry service for the other tenants, herself included. There wasn't a laundromat in Nile. The closest one was on the mainland over an hour away. It wasn't a big deal, though. Laundry was easier than trash duty...for which we were also responsible.

I stacked all the folded clothes into the basket and left our apartment, pausing in the entryway. It was dark. All the wall lamps lining the dead-end hallway had gone out except for the last one... the lamp right before the covered mirror. Its ill, yellowy light shined above the black sheet like a spotlight. I hurried to the stairs, making a mental note to change the bulbs.

The stairs groaned uncomfortably underneath my feet. What if they gave way? Would I fall right into the Sawyers' apartment? I gripped the laundry basket firmly in hand as I made it over the final step, onto the landing, and knocked on Ms. Barbara's door.

"Ms. Barbara? I have your—laundry..."

The door creaked open, and light spilled into the dark stairwell. The rich aroma of beef and onions seeped through the cracks, making my mouth water.

Ms. Barbara threw the door open as wide as her smile. "Come in, come in, Hannah. I was just about to have dinner... Laundry, yes, thank you. The bedroom is in the back...if you'd be so kind as to tuck them away in the drawers for me, dear?"

"Yes, ma'am." I gave her a smile and tried not to stare as I moved to the back of the apartment. It was like walking back in time. Or into that old 60s drama about the men. The entire living room was styled like a rerun of Bewitched with paisleys splashed on the carpets and strangely shaped couches. There were even beads dangling from the lamps. And a curtain of beads hung from Ms. Barbara's bedroom doorframe. I stuck a hand through and parted the strings as I passed through the doorway.

I found the dresser, put the clothes in their appropriate drawers, and left the room quickly. It was awkward rummaging through the old woman's things. When I made it back out into the living room, Ms. Barbara was busy in the kitchen.

"Have a good night, Ms. Barbara..." I gave her a slight wave, wishing I had come up with a way to ask her about the dead girl.

Ms. Barbara turned from her crockpot. "Are you hungry, dear? Have you ever had boeuf bourguignon?"

I hesitated by the door. "No, I—"

Ms. Barbara slapped her dish towel onto the counter and waved me over. "Oh, you must try it...it's a beef stew...come see? I've had it cooking all day and—mmm—the smell is enough to make your mouth water, isn't it?" She wrapped an arm around me and pulled me toward the top of the crockpot. "What do you think?"

"Uh..." Mom was waiting for me downstairs...but if I could get Ms. Barbara talking, maybe I could ask her about the girl. And the stew smelled good. My stomach growled. I wouldn't stay long. I dropped the empty laundry basket by the door and walked back over to the pot.

"The mashed potatoes are next. Why don't you fetch them?"

Obediently, I went to the pantry and looked for a box. There weren't any left. "Ms. Barbara...I think you're all out of mashed potatoes..."

The old woman laughed. "No, dear, the potatoes are right there."

My cheeks burned. Oh. *Real* potatoes...

I grabbed the sack and brought them to the counter.

"Now take the peeler—yes, and—like this, yes. That's great, Hannah."

I smiled. Slicing the skin off the potatoes was surprisingly satisfying, and I set to work feeling strangely content.

Ms. Barbara joined me, and the two of us eased into polite conversation over the peels. Once the conversation moved to Rosecrest, I took my chance. "I was with Peter and Lacey down at the Ferry Dock Diner, and this girl seemed to think Rosecrest is haunted..."

Ms. Barbara's peeling slowed as her jaw tightened ever so slightly. She made a soft 'mmm' sound but made no comment.

I tried again. "Did a girl really die in the house?"

Ms. Barbara looked up at me, her eyes sharp. Startled, I slipped on the potato and sliced the side of my thumb. I gasped and dropped both the potato and peeler onto the counter, squeezing my hand as blood oozed from under the flap of skin I'd flayed. Some dropped onto the potatoes, blossoming like little red flowers in the white-yellow flesh. "Shoot. I'm sorry, Ms. Barbara..."

"Oh, don't be..." Ms. Barbara murmured, her eyes kind and sympathetic. "Head into the bathroom, and I'll get rid of these. They weren't necessary anyways. Go give your finger a wash. There's some bandages and antibacterial ointment under the sink."

Holding my hand out, I did as I was told.

The bathroom was just before Ms. Barbara's bedroom. I flicked on the light and stifled a sharp breath. The sink was directly across from the door, illuminated beneath the two skylights. The bathroom was ordinary...but there was something missing. The mirror was gone. Removed. There was no mirror above the sink. Only a bright rectangular shadow on the wallpaper where one used to hang. I forced myself to enter the bathroom and practically ran to the cabinet underneath the sink, heart pounding. I scrambled for the bandages and cranked on the water.

"Missing something?"

I flinched and whirled around.

Ms. Barbara's tall, slender frame filled the doorway, her face smiling.

"What?" I asked loudly over the thud of my heartbeat, deafening in my ears. My nostrils flared as I tried to steady my breathing. Why was I freaking out? So what, if she didn't have a mirror in her bathroom? It wasn't strange. Not *that* strange.

"The antibacterial ointment, dear... Are you all right, Hannah?" Her smile slipped, and her weathered face crinkled with concern.

"Uhh…" I turned back to my hand and the water stream. I fumbled with the soap and began to lather my hand. The soap burned. I sucked in a sharp breath. "Yes, I'm fine. No antibacterial needed. It's just a flesh wound…" I tried to joke but my voice came out thin and high.

"All right…well, dinner's almost ready…" Ms. Barbara said hesitantly.

I dried my hand and taped my skin flap down with the bandage. "Actually, Ms. Barbara, I just remembered; my mom is waiting for me downstairs with a movie…so, I don't think I'll be able to stay…" I forced a smile as I switched off the water.

"Oh…well, all right, then, dear…" Ms. Barbara murmured softly.

I left quickly, taking the stairs two at a time, and nearly tripped on the last stair. The single lamp light at the end of the dead-end hallway flickered over the black sheet as I hurried to our apartment door. I fumbled with the doorknob, all the while feeling like something would rip off the sheet and charge at me through the darkness.

I wrenched it open and slammed it shut. Then I flicked the latch and leaned my back against the door as an added precaution, heart still pounding, breathing still labored.

"Hannah?" Mom called from the couch in the living room. "What took you so long? The corn dogs are getting cold."

I couldn't sleep. I laid in bed, waiting anxiously for my sleep meds to kick in, waiting to drift off to the calm, dreamless sleep I'd grown accustomed to over the years…but I couldn't.

The huge mirror above the dresser, like a giant black hole in the wall, kept drawing my gaze. The moonlight spilled onto the floor to my right, casting shadows and reflecting strangely in the glass.

There was no such thing as ghosts. Or monsters. Or…or

anything else these 'Nile' people might come up with. And I wasn't about to let them get to me, especially after everything I'd been through with my sister...and my father.

I was Hannah freaking Green. Logical. Reasonable. Sane.

I tossed and turned, rolling in a ball of blankets. Now, not only was the mirror irritating me, but thoughts of my father had wormed their way into my brain. That was the last thing I needed.

Hannah Green. Restless. Bothered. Annoyed.

With a furious groan, I kicked my way out of the tangle of bedding and snatched my hoodie off the floor. I needed to get out of the house. Clear my head. I yanked my hoodie on and crept silently through the apartment so as not to wake my mother.

The floorboards creaked the whole way down the hall, down the stairs, and through the rest of the house. The apartment door even creaked as I shut it.

I hesitated in the entryway.

The final lamp had died. The sheeted mirror was now hidden within the depths of the dark, dead-end hallway. I couldn't move. For one insane moment, I was sure that if I did, something would attack me from the shadows.

Ridiculous. I was being completely ridiculous.

Despite myself, I gulped a quick breath of courage and bolted for the front door. I threw it open, slammed it behind me, and scrambled onto the porch.

The cool September night hit me like a dunk in the lake. Slowly, I relaxed and breathed in the chilly breeze as it pressed against my face. The moon was high, leaving a blue tint over the fields along the driveway. At the bottom of the hill and across the road, the lake glowed with its own white moon, reflected in the shimmery gray-navy water that mirrored the sky. The forests on either side of the Rosecrest clearing and the mountains across the lake were all black shadows in the darkness.

Beautiful.

The island was beautiful.

"Can't sleep, either?"

I clapped a hand over my mouth to smother my shout. In the dark beside me, Ms. Barbara sat in her rocker. I hadn't even noticed her.

"Err. No..."

Ms. Barbara nodded sympathetically. "It's hard sleeping in a new place. I never could stand the thought of it. We moved into this house when we were little...and I haven't ever left."

"We?"

Ms. Barbara chuckled. "I wasn't always a lonely old woman, my dear. In fact, my sister is coming in a few days..." Her voice hardened as she added, "She wants to put me in a *home*—you know, one of those old retirement communities?" She shook her head, her silver hair shining in the moonlight. "I told her, I said, 'Sandra, I'll die first. And happy to do it. Rosecrest House is *my* home...' She's not going to get me out of this house, I promise you..." Ms. Barbara trailed off.

I cleared my throat, and, in an effort to change the subject, I blurted, "I'm sorry I couldn't stay for dinner." I sat down on the steps and leaned my back against the post. I stared up at the sky, increasingly embarrassed I had been spooked by an empty bathroom wall and suddenly grateful for her company.

"Oh, no worries, dear...I expect it had to do with the missing mirror in the bathroom?"

I glanced at her as she flicked a lighter and lit a cigarette.

"I thought so..." She nodded as she blew the smoke off to the side and away from me.

I waited for her to explain, but she didn't.

The silence stretched uncomfortably long.

Then she spoke so suddenly I flinched at the sound. "I didn't want to answer you before...when you asked about— Well, you see, there was a young girl who lived here just before summer, and she came to me, like you, wanting to know about what had happened in this house...and I made the mistake of telling her.

She became very distraught and had to be taken away shortly after..."

"Desiree Lapierre?"

Ms. Barbara nodded again. "So, you see why I didn't want to answer your question?"

I turned slightly so I was facing her. "Ms. Barbara...don't take this the wrong way—but I don't believe in any of that...stuff. So, you can tell me whatever you want. I'm not going to lose myself over it."

Ms. Barbara's smile was illuminated by the ember of her cigarette as she said, "That's right...your mama said you were going to be a doctor. No room in your mind for ghost stories?"

"Try me."

"The history of the house goes back nearly to the founding of Nile. At one time it was a family home, then it became an inn, and then it was later turned into apartments... When I was about your age, my family was invited to live here by an old woman named Kathleen Murphy. Even then there were rumors all around Nile of the Rosecrest House, you see. So, one day I asked Ms. Kathleen about it. She said, a long time ago, a family with two young daughters moved into the Rosecrest House. On a dare, the girls wandered down old Grey Lane and met the Nile Witch... The girls became twisted by her dark magic and began using the dark arts themselves. You see, dark magic is a poison that corrupts even the gentlest of souls, and, eventually, one sister murdered the other in the hallway of the Rosecrest House at the foot of the mirror. Then she sealed her sister's soul behind the glass. Now, they say that anyone who looks at the mirror will be cursed, forced to live a haunted life, and be forever changed, tainted by the evil of the witch. Ms. Kathleen said whatever I did—to never pull the sheet off the mirror in the hallway. And especially not the one in the attic."

I hesitated, my lips shut on the one question I wanted to ask the most.

"So—I'm telling you, just as Ms. Kathleen told me: don't uncover that mirror."

"Did you?"

Ms. Barbara sucked on her cigarette. The ember burned bright. She stood slowly, her hands clutching the arms of the chair for support. She tossed her cigarette off the porch. "Stay away from the mirror."

SPACEY AND GHOST GIRL

"It's common knowledge not to stare into a mirror for too long. They are doorways to one of the four Waking Realms. I'm not surprised," Lacey murmured matter-of-factly as she hopped from rock to rock along the shore, the lake gently rolling in to lap at her orange polka-dotted rain boots.

I smiled at Lacey as her arms swayed in the air with each hop. "Does *anything* surprise you?"

Lacey stopped mid-hop, balanced on one foot. She thought for a moment.

Before she could answer, the rev of Peter's dirt bike distracted us both. We looked up the bank just in time to see him park on the road above us. He slid down the steep hill, helmet in hand.

"Lacey—your dad's been looking for you. He's up at Ed's." Peter smiled as Lacey let out a small gasp. She quickly slipped from the rock and splashed through the water to the shore. She took my hand and pulled me toward the bikes we'd left discarded on the hillside.

"Hurry, Hannah! I've been waiting all summer for this!" Lacey cried, breathless with excitement as she pushed her bike up the embankment.

I shot a dubious glance at Peter as I lifted Elijah's bike. "Are you coming?"

Peter shook his head. "I'm on my way to the lake house. Courtney needs my help with the set up."

"Lake house? You have a *second* house?" I repeated as we hiked up the steep slope to the road. "And what do you have to set up?"

"The party." Peter tugged his helmet over his golden mop of hair, muffling his voice. "It's our annual end-of-the-summer party. You're coming, right? I have a whole 'meet the new kid' theme going on..."

My foot slipped off the pedal as I mounted the bike. "What?!" I demanded incredulously.

Peter's laugh sounded through the helmet. He jumped on the dirt bike and kicked it alive. "Kidding."

The engine roared, and he sped down the street.

I glared after him, not at all amused and half hoping he'd get pulled over for riding the stupid thing on the street.

"Hannah..."

"Right, sorry, Lace...let's go."

The trip to the machine shop was a bit of a trek. First, we had to bike up and down the looping, sloping Apple Shore Road. Then we had to bike along Route 2, the only highway (and main road) on the island. According to Lacey, at the northern tip of the island, Route 2 led to a draw bridge to Canada. I wasn't so sure. But because it was the only highway (and main road) through Nile, it was extremely busy, with car after car zooming past us, sending violent blasts of air at our bikes which threatened to tip Lacey in particular over into the ditch. We passed field after field until the highway slowed to a couple dozen miles an hour as it headed toward 'main street,' which, according to Peter, wasn't actually its own street, as it was still technically Route 2, but instead was simply a small strip of shops on either side of the highway, miraculously with a sidewalk along one of them. The only sidewalk anywhere in Nile.

Edwin Martin's shop was positioned just before 'main street,' in the middle of another field, down a long stretch of gravel road. Lacey and I waited on the side of the highway for the dozens of cars to pass before we were able to cross the street to the shop.

The building looked like a giant warehouse with an even bigger garage opposite it. Lacey parked her bike beside the front door of the shop, and I did the same. She didn't bother going through the glass door with an 'open' sign hanging from it. Instead, she took me around the side of the building and called into the open bay, "Mr. Martin?"

A man stuck his head out from underneath a bright-orange sports car and smiled up at her. "Your daddy's in the back. I hope you like it."

Lacey was bouncing on her heels with excitement. "I *know* I will, Mr. Martin; thank you, thank you so much."

Lacey didn't bother to introduce me. Taking my hand, she tugged me into the heart of the machine shop.

The place was neat and orderly yet, somehow, still cluttered with stacks and stacks of stuff. My nostrils flared at the mix of steel and gas and grit as we weaved through the narrow paths between the piles of part boxes and various machines. Lacey stopped abruptly at the sight of a large burly man with a huge, bushy beard. His hands were the size of tree stumps as he tinkered with a wrench on an overhanging pipe. His limbs were like logs. His whole body was like an oak tree. Or a weeping willow, what with his hair falling all over the place. At any rate, he seemed too big to be. And yet, there he was... I looked from the giant man to the small, delicate Lacey, and my eyes popped.

"Daddy...do you have—"

The man looked down, and his dark eyes crinkled beneath all the hair. "It's in the box over there..." His voice was soft with a thick burr that made me blink. "Mrs. Martin just dropped it off. Where've you been all day, lassie?"

Lacey didn't answer. She dropped to her knees beside the box and gingerly lifted the flaps.

I shifted where I stood and awkwardly held out a hand. "I'm Hannah Green, Mr. McGregor. It's nice to meet you."

"Oh, yes." Mr. McGregor lowered his wrench and stuck it on the belt slung around his thick hips. He hastily grabbed a cloth and wiped his hands before grasping mine with both of his giant ones. I was prepared for my fingers to be painfully crunched together, but Mr. McGregor was gentle as he held my hand. His strange hazel eyes, so like Lacey's, found mine. "It is a pleasure. My absolute pleasure, Miss Hannah. Thank you for being such a good friend to my Lacey. She talks about you quite fondly, she does."

A loud gasp caused both of us to turn toward Lacey, who had sat back on her heels and was staring wide-eyed at the contents of the box. Slowly, she reached both of her hands inside and pulled out a strange set of metal rings with an arrow floating in the middle, like a crude compass with no directions.

Her father chuckled as he took out his wrench and went back to tweaking the pipes. "I'm glad you're happy, my lovely. Ah, and you best tell the Blanchard boy to be more careful on that bike of his... He's going to get in trouble one of these days."

"Isn't it beautiful, Hannah?" Lacey murmured, placing it carefully back in the box.

"Sure," I agreed, though I didn't know if anyone other than Lacey would think the old thing 'beautiful.'

"What is it for?"

"Finding ghosts..."

That night, Lacey and I pedaled our way through Nile to Peter's lake house for his back-to-school party. Neither of us wanted to bother our parents for a ride, so we took it upon ourselves to get there. Plus, I was eager to explore deeper inside the island. Peter's lake house was all the way on the opposite side of Nile—the west shore...literally off West Shore Road. It took us a good hour or so to get there, and though I was happy to see the island, my calves were burning by the end of it, and I was grateful we weren't heading back home until morning.

By the time we got there, the party had started.

The house itself was huge: a massive log cabin with giant windows overlooking the lake, only a few stone steps from the porch. The property was positioned on an embankment, and the steps leading to the lake simply dropped into the water. There was no beach to be seen, only feet of grassy cliff. To the right of the house, there was a large yard the size of a small soccer field. Dense forest surrounded everything like a giant black wall, blocking out the moon and half of the stars.

There were kids everywhere. Kids over in the yard starting a bonfire, laughing and joking and splashing each other with gasoline. There were several different groups huddled together by the water, a few of them tossing firecrackers into the lake. And judging by the outlines moving past the illuminated windows, there were dozens of kids inside the house itself.

Lacey led me through the jumble of cars parked every which way in the gravel driveway, and we propped our bikes up against the side of the porch. Elijah's bike had somehow quickly become mine. As though Lacey could hear my thoughts inside her head, she said, "Elijah's not coming."

I squinted through the twilight at the shadows of kids moving all over the place. "Why don't we head inside?"

Lacey nodded in agreement, and the two of us headed up the porch steps, only to hesitate at the door. "Should we knock?"

"I'm not sure." Lacey pursed her lips to the side and stared thoughtfully at the large door knocker. "I've never been to any of Peter's parties before..."

"Ugh." Someone groaned from behind us. "*Puh-lu-eaaase* tell me Petey didn't invite you people."

Portia elbowed her way between Lacey and me and then shoved open the heavy door. She was quickly followed by another girl who looked like an overgrown insect. The girl buzzed a bit as she snickered, "What are *you* doing here, Spacey? Don't you know the Carnival of Nightmares doesn't come to Nile?"

Portia howled as she pulled her friend inside and slammed the door in our faces.

I glanced at Lacey, who, for the first time since I'd known her, looked sad. Underneath the glow of the house, her pale cheeks colored as she looked down at her purple jelly shoes. "They...well, the girls like to give me nicknames...for fun. It's all for fun." She took a quick breath as though she couldn't catch it. "I think I'm going to go...head home... I should check the champlet traps..."

I put my hand on her shoulder. Lacey blinked her shining hazel eyes as she looked up at me. I smiled at her. I didn't understand her and thought half of what she said was lunacy, but Lacey was the kindest, gentlest of creatures, and I'd be damned if I let anyone damper her spirit. "The champlets will be there for you tomorrow. Peter is expecting us. And I can't stand this without you, Lace. I need my best friend."

Her face warmed and the light burst back into her. "Best friend? Am I? I've never been the best of someone's friends before..."

I laughed and pushed open the door. This time, I tugged *her* by the hand, and Lacey followed behind me, bouncing on her heels once more.

We couldn't find Peter in the house. And we just narrowly avoided Portia and her friend, who were hovering around some boys playing pool in the den. We were just about to give up and go back outside when Peter's sister, Courtney, spotted us heading for the front door.

"Where are you going, Hannah?" she called from the couch. The living room that had once been full of chatter suddenly quieted as if all the kids could feel the tension filling the room. The only sound was the crackle and snap of the fire in the giant fireplace.

Begrudgingly, I stopped. Lacey bumped into me, stepping on my heel. "We're looking for Peter. Do you know where he is?"

Courtney stared at me. She twirled her thick blonde braid around her fingers as her crossed leg bounced up and down. Her eyes never left me. "Have you seen her yet?"

I chewed the inside of my cheek, biting back the bitterness from my words. I didn't trust myself to speak, for I knew I wouldn't be kind. I tried to remind myself that she was hurting—lashing out...but it was hard. Really hard.

"Who?" a guy asked from the loveseat across from her.

Courtney didn't take her eyes off me. "Hannah moved into Rosecrest."

The entire room turned to stare at me. A few girls gasped, and some of the boys started muttering to each other. My face grew hot.

"How can you *sleep* in that place?" a girl with deep-red hair breathed sympathetically.

"How long did Desiree last?" a guy asked Courtney.

"She saw her within a week...but I don't think Hannah's taken the sheet off, yet."

My nostrils flared, and my heart began to pound. "I hate to break it to you all, but ghosts aren't real, so—"

Some of them, Courtney and a few girls excluded, laughed in that cruel way only a pack of teenagers could laugh. My jaw tightened.

"I've been in the Rosecrest House many times and haven't felt anything unusual..." Lacey murmured thoughtfully. "It's Bird Island you need to watch out for—"

"How can you hang out with Spacey Lacey and *not* believe in ghosts?" a girl quipped nastily.

"Psh— Don't you know, Kaitlyn?" Another girl snickered. "They're too busy taking notes on Champ sightings and stargazing for UFOs to worry about ghosts..."

Lacey smiled patiently and opened her mouth, probably to explain all about champlets and the difference between aliens and alions, but I took her by the arm and pulled her toward the door, slamming it on the laughs that followed us into the dark.

I wanted nothing more than to hop on the bike and leave, but I wasn't about to give any of them the satisfaction of driving me out. Still seething, I led Lacey toward the grassy edge and looked out over the black lake.

"You're angry...why?" Lacey asked softly as we stared out over the water. The light sloshing of the waves churning against the rock was calming, and I took a deep breath.

"It bothers me...when people act like things are real...when they aren't."

Lacey tilted her head. "Why?"

I struggled with how to explain it. How much to say. "It's dangerous."

I couldn't see her clearly in the dark, away from the light of the lake house and the fires. But I could tell her lips were pursed as she stood quietly pondering.

I sighed heavily. "My dad used to—"

"Hey! I've been looking for you guys all over the place!"

Peter came up behind us and passed us each a sparkler. Lacey's eyes widened in delight as the glow cast on her face. She skipped through the grass, weaving the sparkler through the air like a fairy with a magic wand.

I held mine over the water and smiled despite myself as the sparks showered into the soft hissing waves below.

"Are you having fun?" Peter asked.

"Err..." I stared at the sparkler as it died.

Lacey made her way back over with the dead metal stick in hand. "Not so much fun, Peter...no."

"Well, looks like I found you just in time, then." Peter looped his arm through mine and pulled me toward the front of the house. Lacey giggled and skipped beside us. And from that point on, Peter made sure we had enough fun to make up for the whole summer. He rounded up a group of his friends and got to work.

First, we all took turns racing four-wheelers with huge spotlights through the woods. And then he grabbed a rowboat and flashlights, and we all went night swimming in our clothes. But when Lacey spooked everyone with a matter-of-fact comment about Champ, Peter moved us inside for a movie in the home theater room...after making everyone take turns tossing their clothes in the drier. ("Mom will kill me if I get the furniture wet.")

The home theater room was awesome. It was three different levels of plush cushions and bean bags in front of a giant screen that took up the entire wall. There was even a little snack bar with oversized boxes of every kind of candy and a popcorn machine. I tried to focus on the movie, but in the dark of the theater, my thoughts kept drifting back to the mirror.

When the movie was finished, Peter started corralling us all to our sleeping quarters. Boys were in the living room downstairs; girls were upstairs in the bedrooms... Peter was chivalrous like that.

Lacey and I found a room with two of the girls from four-wheeling...Rachel, the punk cheerleader/dock waitress, and her best friend, Aubrey, a blonde waif of a girl with sad doe-eyes and a kind smile. But when we'd all claimed beds and sleeping bags and couches, Portia and her friend shoved their way inside the room just as Rachel was shutting the door. ("I can't sleep with doors open—it freaks me out.")

Rachel gave Portia an irritated look as she muscled past her. "Sure..." Rachel said dryly. "Come on in..."

"Everywhere else is full," Portia sniffed snootily. "Oh, great, looks like we got stuck with Spacey and Ghost Girl," Portia muttered loudly.

Her friend buzzed behind her as Portia scurried to snatch up my sleeping bag.

I raised an incredulous eyebrow. "Seriously?"

"Oh, was this yours? Too bad. I win."

"You *win*?"

Portia smiled, her squished nose flaring. "I always do. So, you might want to think twice about getting too close to Petey Blanchard."

Aubrey looked anxiously to Rachel, who glared at Portia and held the door wide. "Why don't you leave now before I tell Peter you both need rides home?"

Portia smirked, her pointed piggy nose high in the air. "Why don't *you* leave, Rachel? Shouldn't you be on the *boys'* floor, anyway?"

Aubrey gasped.

Rachel only rolled her eyes at the insult. "Out, Portia."

"'Out?'" Portia snickered cruelly. "You mean, like *you* are? Congratulations, by the way."

Aubrey reached for Rachel's hand and tried to pull her back, away from Portia. But Rachel stood her ground. And she didn't flinch.

The room fell into an awkward silence, the kind of silence only a hateful bigot can cause.

Portia grunted indignantly. "Fine. I don't want to spend the night in the same room as *her*, anyways." She jutted a pudgy thumb at me. "That curse is contagious. I'd watch it, if I were you, Rach... Although, you're friends with witches, so—"

"What curse?" Aubrey asked softly. Her voice was gentle and

her demeanor delicate, like an elf or a fairy. Her beautiful face crinkled in concern.

Portia smiled greedily. "Hannah lives in the Rosecrest House."

Rachel, still holding the door, scoffed impatiently. "Here we go."

Aubrey's eyes widened. She looked from me to Rachel.

"See?" Portia snorted. "Aubrey gets it."

I felt my temper rising. This was enough. "What is with you people? There's no such thing as ghosts...curses...or anything else."

Lacey nodded loyally. "It's Bird Island that you need to be careful of...remember, Aubrey, when we went—"

A wide smile curved darkly on Portia's round face as her small watery eyes watched me carefully. "If there's no such thing, why don't you take the sheet off the mirror? Desiree told everyone all about it. She took the sheet off and was committed within a day—"

"A week..." Aubrey breathed. "It was a week. She jumped out the hallway window in the girls' dormitory at Martin House..."

At that, Rachel grabbed both Portia and her insect friend roughly by their arms and shoved them toward the door. "Out."

Portia tossed the sleeping bag at me. "Fine."

Then she giggled as Rachel continued to shove her through the door, and her friend buzzed behind her. Rachel gave her a final shove as Portia called back into the room. "Take the sheet off, Hannah. Prove me wrong."

Rachel slammed the door and twisted the lock. "God, I hate those two." She glanced grimly around the room. "Let's get some sleep."

Lacey climbed into bed with Aubrey as Rachel stomped her way toward her sleeping bag muttering angrily. Discreetly, I dug into my backpack and pulled out my sleep meds. I tapped out a pill and noticed with a guilty pang, I was low and hadn't ordered more. Making a mental note to do that first thing when I got back to the apartment, I pressed the pill into my palm and slipped out of the room, mumbling something about the bathroom.

It didn't take long to find the kitchen downstairs. I just had to hurry through the living room, stepping over several boys bundled in sleeping bags, scowling as I dodged discarded backpacks and catcalls whistled my way. Down the hall and to the left, there was a glow spilling out into the hall from the kitchen. Blue refrigerator light mixed with warm stove light. The sound of hushed voices made me pause, still hidden in the dark of the corridor.

"Here, Court—it'll help." There was a dull thud as the refrigerator shut.

"Nothing helps," Courtney muttered so low I had to strain to hear. "And it definitely doesn't help that that girl had to move in—Peter's like *obsessed* with her and all I can think about—"

"Is Desiree?" the other girl asked gently.

Someone sniffed loudly.

"It's my fault...the whole thing."

"Courtney—"

"No. It *is*, Morgan. I dared her to do it. She took the stupid sheet off because of me. It's my fault."

Suddenly feeling incredibly uncomfortable about lurking in the shadows, I cleared my throat loudly and hurried into the kitchen.

I gave a small wave and forced a smile. "Sorry—just getting a snack."

Neither of them said anything.

The girl, Morgan, had two spoons in one hand as her other hand rubbed Courtney's back.

Courtney looked awful. Her blonde braid was falling out, and her face was blotchy and shining with tears in the yellow light of the stove. There was a pint of unopened Chubby Hubby ice cream sitting between them.

I could feel their eyes as I went for the refrigerator. I grabbed the first thing I could reach and quickly left the kitchen. It wasn't until I made it back to the bedroom that I realized I'd grabbed the remnants of a stick of butter. Awesome.

I debated for a moment which would be worse: the nausea that I'd suffer from taking my meds without food or the moral disgust I had at the idea of eating raw butter. Rolling my eyes, I shoved the butter in my mouth, crushing the wrapper into my jeans pocket. I swallowed the pill dry and hurried back into the room.

Everyone was quiet, although Lacey murmured softly in her sleep. I knew it was her because I distinctly heard the word 'bull-bos.' I laid down on the couch, pulling the sleeping bag up to my chin. As I waited for the meds to kick in, I found myself thinking about Courtney. My opinion of her had instantly softened. I knew better than anyone what it felt like to be weighted down by guilt.

No.

I would not go there.

Especially not before I fell asleep. What if I dreamed of her again?

I looked over at Rachel. She was using her backpack as a pillow. I counted the pins and keychains that decorated her bag until I finally drifted into a restless sleep.

5

BAD LUCK

Sunday morning seemed to come late to the lake house. The sun barely managed to stream through the thick woods that engulfed the house, so the room slowly became tinted in a strange cool light as I watched. I hadn't slept well, instead, tossing and turning most of the night. But at least I didn't dream.

Lacey and I went home early while everyone else was still sleeping. She had to help her daddy at the Charlebois Inn, a bed and breakfast vacation resort for rich people who wanted to experience Vermont. And I had to get home, too. Sunday was grading day, so it was the last day to hand in my schoolwork. Plus, with Mom at her day job, I was expected to take over most of the Rosecrest House cleaning duties, and, according to the big chart Mom had stuck up on the wall, it was trash day.

Great.

As soon as I got home, I pulled out my schoolwork. I had a few tests and last-minute tweaks on some essays to finish. It didn't take long. Then I packed up my school stuff, tucked my papers in the folder for Mom to grade, and headed outside to the cans with our trash.

The sun was high and unusually hot for September as I

surveyed the cans with my hands on my hips. Flies buzzed around the bags. The smell made me crinkle my nose. Both cans were overflowing with a week's worth of garbage from the four different apartments. How was I going to lug them all the way down the mile-long driveway for the dump truck? Groaning, I tossed our bag onto one of the cans and gripped the handles of each.

It was a bumpy, sticky, stinky trip to the side of the road. I must have hit at least half the potholes along the way. For every hole I swerved, I slammed into another, dropping a trash bag and throwing it back on every couple feet. By the time I made it to Apple Shore Road, I was a sweaty, smelly mess. I positioned the cans properly along the roadside, but before I could trudge back up the driveway, a hot pink car came over the hill. The car slowed and stopped in the middle of the road beside me.

Courtney Blanchard.

She rolled down her window and raised an eyebrow. "Are you okay?"

My cheeks grew hot as I realized how gross I must look. "I'm fine, thanks." I turned to leave.

"Wait...Hannah—do you want a ride?"

I glanced over my shoulder with a skeptical stare.

Courtney had the decency to blush. She brushed her golden curls back from her face. "Okay, okay—what I really wanted to say was: I'm sorry."

I turned back toward her and let her finish.

She bit her lip as she furrowed her brow. "I'm sorry for the way I've been treating you. And *really* sorry that I let everyone gang up on you and Lacey last night. Please, hop in? We can grab a bite at the snack bar or something...I'm not normally such a jerk. You can even ask Lacey."

I considered her for a moment, impressed with her apology. "Lacey and I had plans to grab an early dinner at the snack bar tomorrow at four... You can meet us there if you like."

Courtney gave me a small smile. "Sure...thanks, Hannah."

Then she drove away, leaving me in a cloud of dirt road and wishing I'd waited to take the trash out.

When I made it back to Rosecrest, it was well past lunch. I still had a few hours until Lacey would be done at the Inn. I'd never realized how dull my days had been without her. Although I didn't believe in champlets, it was fun jumping over rivers and wading through ponds to look for them. It had even been fun making fairy houses, but I wouldn't admit it if you asked me.

Somehow, restless and desperate for something to do, I found myself at Elijah Grunvald's door and ducking underneath the doorframe into his apartment. He was bent over one of his machines and looked up as I walked inside. He smiled and wiped his glasses on his shirt, before pushing them back up the bridge of his nose.

"Sorry about the door... This is really just a remodeled attic." He left his work and walked over to the tiny kitchenette. The cat darted out from a table and got caught between Elijah's feet. Elijah's foot came down on the cat's tail. It yowled loudly and scrambled underneath the couch as Elijah stumbled a bit and cursed loudly. "Mangy thing! It's always getting underfoot..."

I laughed. "'It?' Does *it* have a name?"

"No...it doesn't," Elijah replied, his back to me as he reached into a cabinet for two mugs.

I raised an eyebrow but didn't bother pressing the issue.

Elijah glanced back at me. "Coffee? Oh—how was the party? I was going to go, but I had to work late." He shrugged and powered up the coffee machine. "Sugar? Anything?"

I made a face, and Elijah chuckled. "Black it is."

"The party was fun...for the most part." I smiled as Elijah handed me a steaming mug.

He leaned back against the kitchenette counter with his arms crossed, regarding me curiously. "Explain?"

I took a sip, the rich earthy taste warming me inside and out. "Well, everyone on this island seems obsessed with ghosts. It's...frustrating."

"Ah..." Elijah reached for his cup and drank deeply as though stalling for time.

I put my mug down on a side table by a large steel machine. "You don't believe this place is haunted, do you?"

"No. I don't believe in ghosts, or champlets, either." Elijah smiled over his mug. "But it doesn't ruin my day when Lacey asks me to make her ghost detectors or champlet sonar." He held up a finger. "I won't do Champ sonar, though. That's still technically illegal."

I couldn't help but smile. My heart felt lighter than it had since the party. "I guess I take things too seriously, huh?"

"A bit..."

I ran a hand through my hair and sighed. "Did you know Desiree Lapierre?"

Elijah hesitated. "Yes."

"They say she uncovered the mirror and went insane."

Elijah nodded.

"Do you think that's what happened?"

Elijah put down his mug and thumbed his suspenders. "It's what she says happened."

I shook my head, my temper rising. "It's all ridiculous."

"But why does it bother you so much?" Elijah studied me as he added, "If you don't believe in any of it, who cares if *they* do?"

I didn't answer. I thought of Courtney crying in the kitchen over her friend. And despite myself, I thought of Daddy. I wanted to say: because it's hurting people. But instead, I asked, "Do you have a video camera?"

Ms. Barbara had a habit of sitting out on the porch at night. So, I waited. I waited hours up in my room with the weak, yellow lamp light mixing unpleasantly with the dull gray-purple until I heard the creak of the front door vibrating through the bones of the house. And still I waited, my breath held silent in my chest, as I listened for her light footfalls and the groan of the stairs as she headed up to her apartment.

This was it.

I grabbed the video camera off the nightstand, slipping my hand in the strap. I already felt stupid, but this was the best idea I had. The only way to clear Courtney's conscience and shut Portia's face.

As I moved through the house, I pressed the red record button and held the camera up. The closer I got to our front door, the harder my heart seemed to pound.

Slowly, I unlocked the door and slipped out into the hallway. I debated flicking on the lamps. (Fortunately, I'd changed the bulbs that morning.) It was dark with only blue moonlight falling through the clouded windows of the front door. I squinted through the black. The sheet looked like a figure, a person or creature standing at the end of the hall. Like it was waiting for me to move before it charged out of the shadows.

I scoffed at myself. I needed to get a grip. My hand tightened on the video camera, before slapping on the light switch. The lamps blinked on with soft pops. And there was the sheet. No creature. No figure. Just a black sheet over an old mirror.

I held the camera up and hurried down the hall. Not because I was afraid—but I didn't want Ms. Barbara to see me. The last thing I wanted to do was upset her, but I had to put a stop to all these rumors.

My feet slowed the closer I got to the mirror. I didn't realize how big it was from the other end of the house... It was so tall. I swallowed thickly and reached my free hand up to take hold of the sheet.

And I pulled.

The sheet billowed to the ground, casting dust down like a

cloud of gray snow. I coughed and blinked into the mirror, nearly surprised to see myself. It was just an ordinary mirror. I frowned at my reflection as I pointed the camera at the mirror and scanned the surface with the lens for the record to clearly reflect: just a mirror.

The house groaned, reminding me very sharply that I shouldn't be there. I clicked the camera off and placed it carefully down on the floor. I grabbed at the sheet, struggling to cover the mirror.

I couldn't.

It was too tall. I couldn't reach it. No matter how high I tossed it, the sheet simply slipped down the length of the looking glass, fluttering like an oversized bat.

This was bad.

I needed something.

I flicked off the lights to hide my crime, flinching as they went out with another pop. I hurried through our apartment, grabbed a kitchen chair and ran it to the hall. I pushed it up against the wall and stood on top of the seat, but somehow, despite my height, the top of the mirror was still just out of reach.

A ladder.

I needed a ladder. Elijah could have a ladder...or a broom. A broom? I ran back through the house and returned with a broom.

Squinting through the dark, I prodded the sheet with the handle. Gripping the broom in one hand, I pulled myself back onto the chair. The mirror was cold, and I tried my best not to touch it as I stretched up high. The glass was black and empty, my reflection dark and faceless, as I leaned up to cover it. No. It wouldn't reach.

My heart pounded, my eyes blurred with frustration, as I stretched and reached and tried, over and over, and still couldn't hook the sheet. What would happen in the morning when Ms. Barbara saw what I'd done? Would she fire Mom? Would she kick us out?

No. I wouldn't screw this up for us when Mom had worked so

hard to find us a place. I *had* to hook the sheet. Gritting my teeth, I shoved the shaft up once more. My heart stalled in my chest as the mirror rattled against its hanging.

"No!" I leaned my weight into it, the cold glass burning my skin as I held it in place against the wall. I dropped the broom, and the sheet billowed down with it. I gripped the sides of the mirror, my face a breath away from the dark reflection. Closing my eyes, I pushed the heavy thing back in place.

It snagged. Panting, I moved back, teetering a bit on the chair, and looked it over, smoothing back the tears from my cheeks.

But then my heart stopped. As though in slow motion, the mirror slipped and dropped to the floor.

Glass exploded everywhere.

6

THE VIDEO

I should've gone to Ms. Barbara.

I should've told her what happened.

But I didn't.

In the dark of the hallway, in a blur of panic and stomach knotted with shame, I swept up the glass and tossed every last shard into our kitchen trash can. Then I draped the empty mirror frame with the black sheet and hung it back on the hooks, hoping it would look as ominous as ever...a black sheet hooked on an empty frame.

No one would know.

But, as I tucked Elijah's camera under my arm, picked up the broom and kitchen chair, and stared back at the black sheet through the darkness, I knew that *I* would know, and it would haunt me much longer than any seven years of bad luck ever could.

The next morning, Lacey stopped by early on her way to the bus stop. I was a twitchy, jittery, guilty mess when I opened our apartment door and hurried her inside, as though the air of the entryway might whisper my secret.

"Hey...did you have breakfast?" I led her into the kitchen. "We have...cereal...just cereal." I opened the cabinet revealing the nearly empty cupboard.

Lacey blinked her large hazel eyes and scrunched her mouth up into a pouty frown as she watched me. "What's wrong, Hannah?"

I hesitated. Then shrugged. "Nothing, just tired." Which was true... I'd tossed and twisted in the covers all night, tormented by guilt and dreams of shadows in shattered mirrors.

Lacey made a small 'hmmm' noise. "Well, I just wanted to make sure we were still meeting at Kip's Snack Bar after school... It's closing this weekend...end of summer, and all."

"Sure...four, right?"

Lacey watched me closely. "Are you sure you don't want to talk about the mirror?"

"What?" I demanded, my voice high and thin.

Lacey furrowed her brow and twisted her platinum-blonde hair around her finger. "You said you had a plan to put the ghost stories to rest; I thought it might help to talk about it..."

"Oh, right... Well, I'm not too worried anymore..."

"I would be," Lacey said as she bounced toward the door.

I hurried after her anxiously. "Why?"

"If there *is* a ghost—ghosts get meaner as they rot." Lacey gave me a light hug. "See you at four." And then she was gone.

I spent twice as long as usual to finish my schoolwork. I was too distracted. And I was late to pick up Ms. Barbara's laundry...and it was bathroom day.

Awesome.

I gathered the cleaning supplies, dumped them in the laundry basket, and hurried out into the hallway, not daring to glance at the black sheet. I took the stairs two at a time as they whined and groaned in protest. Taking a shaky breath, I rapped lightly on Ms. Barbara's door.

"Ms. Barbara, I'm here for your laundry—and bathroom."

There was a rustling noise from inside, a scurrying as though she were in a hurry to get to the door. My stomach twisted uncomfortably. What if she'd heard me last night? What if she knew?

The door flew open, and Ms. Barbara smiled. "Good afternoon, dear. I was expecting you a lot sooner..." She was wearing her large gardening hat. Her thick silver hair was twisted in a fat braid. She looked at me and frowned thoughtfully. "Hannah? Is that...*glass* in your hair?" She reached toward me.

I stepped back, hastily shaking my head. I propped the basket on my hip and ripped my fingers through my dark hair. "I don't feel anything," I lied. "Probably a trick of the light."

"Hmm..." Ms. Barbara's frown slipped back into a kind grin. "Well, I was just heading out for a walk...would you care to join me?"

I followed her inside, the laundry basket full of cleaning supplies still on my hip. "Oh, that's all right, Ms. Barbara. I should get started..."

She gave me a small rueful smile. "Very well, dear. Make sure you don't lock the door. I don't have my key." She went to leave but hesitated. "Hannah?"

"Yes, ma'am?" I held my breath.

Ms. Barbara studied me for a moment, her delicate hand on the door. "Did you sleep all right last night?"

"Yes."

Ms. Barbara's perfectly shaped eyebrows furrowed. "I had nightmares all night... I was almost certain—well, never mind..." Her warm smile brightened her face, and she nodded to me before disappearing out the door.

I exhaled sharply.

Time to clean.

I set up in the bathroom and got to work. I scrubbed and wiped and organized every inch of the place. Then I went from room to room, straightening her things, sweeping the floor, dusting the furniture, and gathering all the trash around the apartment as I went. Then I rounded up her laundry and headed back down the stairs, my arms full with the overflowing basket and cleaning supplies.

I got the laundry going and then waited an hour to switch it. By the time I'd finished, brought it back up to Ms. Barbara's, and put it all away, it was time to get ready for the snack bar.

I hurried upstairs to my room and grabbed fresh clothes from my dresser. I checked my reflection in the large round mirror hanging on the wall. It seemed silly to shower before a thirty-minute bike ride. I tugged on fresh jeans and a new T-shirt, grabbed a hair tie, and pulled my hair into a high ponytail. I felt something hard. Sharp.

I gripped it between two fingers and slid it out of my hair. It had pricked the pad of my thumb, and a tiny trickle of blood ran down my hand. Glass.

Something moved in the corner of my eye. I looked up and gasped slightly at the sight of my own reflection staring back at me. Ridiculous. I chucked the shard into the wastepaper basket and left the room.

When I got outside, Elijah was getting ready to leave for work. He waved me over and said in a low voice, "How'd it go last night?"

"Err..." I glanced uneasily back at the house.

"Well, I'm off to the docks—I'll be home tonight if you want to talk." He hopped in the cab of his truck and pointed at me. "And I haven't forgotten—you still have my video camera."

I forced a smile and gave a small wave as he pulled out of the parking lot and drove away, down the driveway.

"He's an odd one, that kid."

I flinched at the unfamiliar voice and whirled around. A little man in a cowboy hat and boots was standing just in front of the porch steps, almost hidden by the dying bushes, with an indulgent grin cracking his face. I hesitated, unsure how to respond to a strange little man lurking in the bushes.

"Yes..."

The man tipped his hat and spoke with a gravelly Southern drawl. "We haven't had the pleasure of meeting yet... I take it you're Miss Hannah?"

My muscles relaxed, and I hurried forward, bending down a bit to shake his large hand. "Mr. Sawyer?"

"Yes, ma'am." He smiled as he looked up at me. "My wife hasn't been feeling too well these days. She's been stuck in the house...otherwise, she'd have found you by now."

"I'm sorry to hear that..." I murmured awkwardly.

He waved a hand and headed toward the driveway to his car. "Feel free to come calling. I'm sure some company would brighten her spirits. I'm off to the Martin stables...Don't be a stranger, Miss Hannah."

The ride to Kip's Snack Bar was an easy one. I was now relatively familiar with the island and had a mental map of the general layout. The nice thing about living on an island: all roads led to the water, so it was pretty impossible to get completely lost.

Lacey was already at a table with a giant, dripping ice cream cone. Courtney's pink car was in the parking lot, and she was in line ordering food. I set Elijah's bike next to the picnic table and sat down.

Lacey smiled as she licked her cone.

"Is the whole island here?" I quipped looking around at all the people. It was mostly adults and younger children because most of the island teenagers boarded at the private school through the week.

"Courtney's here," Lacey murmured.

"Yeah—she wanted to talk...so I told her to come."

Lacey nodded. "I talked to her at school today. She felt bad for being mean to you."

I glanced over at Courtney. She was ordering now. "I thought she and Peter went to the private boarding school?"

"He does...and she did. But she switched this year." Lacey turned her head sideways and caught a sticky drip with her tongue. "Because of Desiree."

Courtney grabbed her food and hurried to our table. "Hi."

"Hey."

There was an awkward quiet.

Lacey frowned slightly. "This feels uncomfortable."

Courtney groaned. "I know. *I know.* It's my fault... I'm sorry for the way I came after you about the—the house."

I nodded. "It's okay. You already said sorry. I get it. Peter said it's hard for you."

Courtney nodded, running her fingers through her hair. "You just—you remind me of her...Desiree. You look a lot alike and—"

Lacey inclined her head thoughtfully. "Desiree liked to smile. Hannah doesn't like to smile."

I laughed. Courtney gave Lacey an indulgent smirk before clearing her throat and continuing, "She was—*is* my best friend, and the house...the mirror—changed her. It hurt her. She was new to Nile, and she didn't understand. Anyways, it was my fault. So, yeah. I'm sorry. Again," she finished.

I tried to give a sympathetic head nod but felt I was failing. And based on the reproachful look on Lacey's face, I was. I cleared my throat and tried again. "See, I don't...I just don't believe in any of that stuff. But I *am* sorry your friend—isn't well. And I'm really sorry you feel that way. I know how it is to feel responsible."

Courtney rolled her eyes and a few tears spilled onto her cheeks. Lacey patted Courtney's hand.

Courtney smiled gratefully at Lacey before turning her attention to me. "I'm not looking for sympathy. I'm trying to *warn* you, Hannah," Courtney said in a low voice. "There's something *wrong* in that house. I was mean before—but the message is the same. You need to be careful. Peter cares about you, and I don't want my brother to deal with what I'm dealing with now."

"There's nothing wrong with the house, Courtney. And it wasn't your fault your friend had a psychotic episode and had to get help."

She scoffed, shaking her head as more tears leaked from her eyes, streaking her eyeliner.

"No, seriously. I'm telling you. I—" I bit my lip struggling to hold in my secret but couldn't stop myself. "I pulled the sheet off the mirror last night."

Courtney's eyes widened, and she sucked in sharply.

"I couldn't take all the gossip about it," I snapped defensively. "It was driving me crazy, plus...I overheard you in the kitchen. About the dare. And it's really not your fault what happened. You shouldn't blame yourself for something that didn't have anything to do with you."

There was a heavy silence.

I kept going. "And I videotaped the whole thing. You can watch it for yourself. Nothing bad happened. No ghosts. Nothing." I chewed the inside of my cheek, purposely neglecting to mention the fact that I broke the mirror in the process.

Courtney's whole demeanor changed—going from cool and confident to shrinking and scared. She shook her head, her words coming out in a soft rushed panic, "Oh, no...no...no. Hannah, this is bad. This is *bad*. What are you going to do?"

I frowned. "I told you. I'm fine—nothing happened. When we get back, you both can watch the DVD when I return it to Elijah. Proof that it's all just made up. I mean—I'm sorry your friend is struggling, but it isn't because of the house. Or the mirror. Or you," I added firmly.

Courtney's eyes continued to leak as she exchanged glances with Lacey. Lacey, though not as disturbed as Courtney, looked at me uneasily. "I think it would be good for Courtney to see it..."

"I'm not going in that house," Courtney breathed.

Lacey smiled reassuringly and squeezed Courtney's hand. "Maybe Hannah could bring it to your house, then? I think it might help you feel better about what happened to Desiree... because whatever happened, like Hannah said, it wasn't your fault, Courtney."

We decided to watch it at Lacey's. Courtney's mother was having a launch party for her newest book, so her house was out. Lacey lived along Apple Shore Road, too, but all the way at the end of it in a cabin at the Charlebois Inn.

She led us inside her home with a shy smile. "Daddy is closing down the grounds now...so he won't be home for a while. I've never had people over before."

Lacey's cabin was pretty much the same on the inside as it was on the outside. The room was a combination living room and kitchen with a small table for two and a kitchenette only slightly bigger than Elijah's. There was a large couch in front of an ancient TV with knobs on the box and tinfoil bunny ears on top.

Lacey pointed to the TV, and I set it up. "There's a DVD player—yes, right there. Should I pop some popcorn?"

Courtney, still tugging anxiously at her hair, shrugged as she eyed the TV like it might jump up and attack her at any moment.

I popped the DVD into the player and twisted the dial on the TV.

Lacey went to turn off the lights, but Courtney stopped her. "Lights on. Keep the lights on. Please."

The three of us dropped down onto the couch.

Lacey pressed play on the remote, and the video started.

"Did you have to record the whole house?" Courtney grumbled as we watched my slow, bumpy descent down the stairs.

Lacey whispered, "Can you hear that?"

I strained my ears. "No?"

Lacey blinked thoughtfully. "It sounds like whispers."

Courtney moaned. "*What?*"

"I'm probably just breathing heavily." I stared at the screen, struggling to hear what Lacey was talking about.

We watched me approach the front door and hesitate in the hallway. The pop of the lights made the three of us jump.

"Here, see... I'm going to pull it down, and you'll see the whole thing..."

The black sheet engulfed the camera.

It was all we could see.

We heard me cough, and then the mirror flashed on the screen.

Courtney sighed in relief and then laughed lightly.

Lacey commented thoughtfully on the dust.

And I stared at the dark reflection in the mirror, that wasn't my own.

CASSANDRA SAWYER

"Rewind that! Where's the remote? Lacey!" I snatched the controller out of her hands.

Courtney's voice was high as she watched me fumble with the buttons. "What's wrong?"

With shaking hands, I held the remote out and pushed play. I stared at the screen, refusing to blink, as I watched myself move toward the mirror.

"Hannah..." Courtney hesitated. "You were right—nothing happened. It was just a mirror. Like you said."

I watched as the sheet fell. I squinted at the dark reflection as the camera scanned the surface of the mirror.

I paused it.

It was me.

Only me.

"I—I thought I saw...something else." I should've felt relieved, but all I felt was unease.

Gingerly, Courtney took the remote from my outstretched hand. "It's dark...but it's you, Hannah. There's nothing else there."

I glanced at her, almost bemused. She gave me a gentle smile. I looked at Lacey who nodded encouragingly.

"Right." I forced a smile that didn't reach my eyes.

Courtney turned to Lacey. "Can we watch a Disney movie now?"

Lacey bounced to the TV stand and began digging through old VHS tapes. "How about *Cinderella*?"

"Perfect. I'll pop the popcorn." Courtney headed for the kitchenette.

And we spent the rest of the evening binging on cartoons and carbs. But despite the laughter that quickly filled the cabin, I couldn't shake the feeling that I'd seen something in that mirror.

Someone.

Of course, I couldn't sleep that night. Instead, I twisted in the blankets until I was tangled and found myself casting cool glances at the mirror hanging above the dresser like a giant black hole in the wall.

Soon, it was almost dawn. I rubbed my tired, itchy eyes as the distant muffled sound of Mom's alarm clock chirped down the hall. Acting fast, I rolled out of the bed and moved past the mirror without bothering to check my tired and frumpy appearance. Mom had seen worse. I hurried down to the kitchen and started the coffee machine. Then I poured two bowls of dry cereal and two glasses of milk. I filled her favorite mug. Then I waited.

It wasn't long before Mom came down the stairs. At the sight of me, she smiled, lighting up her tired face. I hadn't seen her much lately. She was pulling double shifts whenever she could. She looked exhausted and worn down. My heart ached for her, and guilt seeped into my stomach. She worked so hard to keep us in a decent home, and all I'd done to thank her for it was pour two bowls of stale cereal and snuck around, breaking the landlady's stuff.

"Well, this is a pleasant surprise. Thank you, sweetheart." Mom poured a small splash of milk on her cereal and toasted me with a spoonful. "How was your day yesterday? I missed you."

I poured milk on my cereal and scooped up a bite. "I met Lacey and Peter's sister at the snack bar...Kip's? Then we went to Lacey's and watched a few movies."

"That sounds like fun." Mom smiled warmly. "And Ms. Barbara said you did a great job with the housekeeping. Thank you for picking up my slack, Hannah. With the job at the dock, it's hard to find time for anything else. It helps. A lot."

I shrugged. "You know I'm happy to do it...it's not like I have anything else to do around here."

Mom looked down at her cereal. "I'm sorry, Hannah—"

Aghast, I added hastily, "Oh, no, Mom, I didn't mean it like—"

She shook her head. "No, it isn't fair...none of this has been fair to you...and I'm so sorry I let us get in this situation."

"It's not your fault."

Mom rolled her eyes and dabbed them lightly with her fingertip.

"It's *his* fault," I said without daring to speak his name. "And you know it."

"He may have made some bad choices..." Mom shook her head again and looked at me sharply. "But don't you ever excuse my mistakes. And you need to learn from them. You never—"

"Never put my financial security in someone else's hands," I finished for her.

She blinked and a sad smile slid onto her face. "You have it memorized...I just hope you take it to heart."

I took a deep breath. We'd come so close to mentioning Daddy...I had to talk to her about it. "The people here...they believe all kinds of things."

Mom snorted into her mug as she drank. She set it down and nodded. "That they do."

"Why did...I mean—how did he get into all that...you know, supernatural stuff?" I stared pointedly down at my cereal, watching the little puffs dissolve in the milk.

"He was desperate to find someone, even some*thing*, to blame for Rebecca," Mom said shortly.

At her name, my stomach twisted, knotting painfully. My heart tightened. I gritted my teeth.

Mom put down her mug and brought her bowl and glass to the sink. "I'll see you later, I hope? Or do you have more plans with your friends?" She returned to the table for her coffee mug and a bright smile on her face. But I could see the sadness shine in her dark eyes.

"Uhh...I'm not sure." I bit my lip and tried again. "Why did he..." My words failed underneath Mom's piercing stare.

"Why the sudden interest in your father? If you want to get in touch with him, I think I—" Mom snatched her purse off the counter and began digging through it.

"No, no...it's not that...I just...I was wondering how someone starts getting into that kind of thing," I finished quickly.

Mom lowered her purse. She sighed heavily and rubbed her temple. "Hannah, you know there is no such thing as monsters. You should understand this better than anyone by now." She bit her lip, concern lining her face. "Are you afraid of the house, is that it?"

"No, I—"

"Are you taking your medicine at night?" she prompted, her voice a bit high.

"Yes, of course—"

"Did Ms. Barbara tell you that ridiculous ghost story?" She rolled her eyes to the ceiling. "That's it, isn't it? I'm so sorry, sweetheart." She shook her head as she slammed her purse back down on the counter and hurried over to give me a hug. "I should've told her that it might trigger you..."

I stiffened. "Does Ms. Barbara know about Rebecca?"

Mom pulled back a bit so she could meet my eyes. Chocolate brown to chocolate brown. Rebecca had golden, caramel eyes...like Daddy. My eyes prickled and itched. I blinked and squinted slightly, refusing to cry.

"No. She doesn't know about Rebecca. So, if she said something insensitive, it's my fault, and I'm so sorry, sweetheart."

No. It was my fault...really. "What ghost story did she tell *you*?"

Mom rolled her eyes and made a goofy face. I managed a small smile. "Just that there was a girl who lived here once—broke a mirror and—"

I flinched as Mom's phone went off. She had alarms set every half hour so she wouldn't be late. My heart thudded in my chest. I could feel the beat of my blood in my palms. I clenched my fists.

"Anyways—" Mom kissed me on the forehead. "I love you. Be good. And the Sawyers and the boy upstairs—Elijah Grunvald, that's it— Oh, did you know his father owns the *Free Press*?" She waved a hand. "Sorry, point is: everybody needs their laundry done, so if you could get that taken care of for me, sweetheart? Thank you. I'll see you tonight!" She walked out the door and shut it sharply behind her.

I went down for the Sawyers' laundry first. The steps were steep and dark. I was strongly reminded of the fact that it was originally a cellar...not an apartment. And as I pressed the doorbell, I was incredibly grateful this was not *our* apartment.

The door creaked open. A woman peeked through the gap in the door chain.

"Yes?" Her voice was high as though she were trying her best to be polite but couldn't quite hide her irritation.

"Hello, Mrs. Sawyer? I'm Hannah Green from upstairs. Uhh...my mom sent me for—"

"Oh, the laundry!" Mrs. Sawyer shut the door, slid the chain, and let me in with a wave of her hand. "I'm so sorry, Hannah...Yes, please. Call me Cassandra. The laundry is in the bag..." She clasped her hands together and gestured to the large sack propped up against the couch.

The apartment was unlike anything I'd ever seen before. The furniture was wooden and cozy like in Lacey's apartment, but instead of lamps, there were candles. Tall tappers and short thick ones and tiny circular ones. But that wasn't the strangest thing: there were plants. Everywhere. It was as though I'd walked into an underground forest. Like the plants were simply growing wild all over the place. The sunlight streaming in through the small rectangular windows lining the walls hardly seemed enough to feed them all...and yet they were thriving: lush, leafy, and green. And it was hot—no, *humid*. I glanced up, checking for signs of rain.

Mrs. Sawyer—Cassandra—smiled and ran a delicate hand through her long, dark-red hair. She was dressed in a black lace dress that wouldn't look out of place at a Renaissance fair. And I noticed with a jolt that what I'd thought was a scarf around her neck was actually a thick black snake. It wrapped itself lazily around and around Cassandra as she continued to smile.

I realized that I was staring and hurried to grab the laundry bag, hugging it to me like a giant teddy bear.

"How do you like Nile?" she murmured with an amused glint in her green eyes.

"It's...fine." I shifted the bag awkwardly and then added sincerely, "The island is beautiful."

Cassandra nodded knowingly. "The people can take some getting used to...I moved here when I was your age. I lived on East Shore North. Up by the Kennedy farm? I left...joined a circus...and met Huckleberry. He oversaw the horses." She grinned, her eyes sparkling at the memory. Her face suddenly darkened, and she frowned. "I still don't know why I ended up back here."

I fought the chuckle that tickled the corner of my mouth. "Do you need anything else? Mr. Sawyer said—"

"Call him Huck, Hannah," Cassandra said, smiling once more.

"Uhh...Huck said you weren't feeling well."

She nodded. "Oh, he would be telling people that, wouldn't he? I'm fine...my sight's been acting up since you moved in...that's all."

I inclined my head. "Do you need glasses?"

Cassandra laughed lightly. It sounded like tickling bells. Her laugh made me smile.

"Something like that..." She studied me for a moment. An amused twitch tugged at the sides of her lips. "Wait here...I have something for Lacey." She turned around and hurried through the forest of plants and out of sight. I craned my neck to see where she'd gone. She might've disappeared into another room, but there was no way I could tell. Her voice called back to me, "You'll give it to her, won't you?"

"Sure."

Cassandra emerged through the greenery with a beaded bag. "I knew you were friends." She draped the strap over my head and lightly cupped my face with her hand. Her touch was warm and gentle and motherly. I fought the instinct to close my eyes.

"Don't be a stranger, Hannah."

I dropped the Sawyers' laundry bag off in our living room and then hiked up the fire escape to Elijah's apartment.

"Door's open!" he shouted over the bangs and shudders of his machines.

I ducked inside and immediately pulled the strings on my hoodie, hiding my nose. Smoke, thick and hazy, clouded the room.

I pushed the door back open and began to fan the smog. "Open a window!"

"What? Oh, yeah..." Elijah stood back from his tinkering and ran a hand through his dark hair as he surveyed the room. "I guess it is a bit smoky in here, isn't it?" He took his glasses off, wiped them on his shirt, and tucked them into the breast pocket.

I'd opened all the windows before I went to stand beside him. "Just a bit...what are you working on?"

"Something useless...pointless...for the fair. It's this Friday...the inventor's expo. I got work off so I could...you know. The prize is a scholarship and...well, anyway..." Elijah's voice trailed off, and he looked over at me. "Did you need something?"

I loosened my hoodie from my face revealing a small smile. "Your underwear."

"Oh, my under—what?" Elijah blinked at me, a dark blush bruising his tan cheeks.

I laughed. "Your laundry. Where is it?" I scanned the room, noting the socks and shirts strewn about the place. "Ahh. I see. It's all over the place..."

Elijah smacked his forehead. "Right. Okay, just give me a minute...grab a coffee and a book, if you like...this may take a minute to sort out..." He hurried around the room gathering his clothes into a basket.

I made my way to the overstuffed bookshelf. The cat was draped over the top of it, her head rested on a small pile of books, and her eyes, bright yellow slits, watched me suspiciously. Her tail twitched as I got closer. I eyed her warily. "Don't jump on my back or anything, Cat..."

Slowly, so as not to spook it, I sat down and shuffled through a stack of books on the floor. "You really should come up with a shelving system... Tolkien does *not* deserve to be on the floor." I took the book and tried to wedge it onto a shelf. My breath caught. "I can't believe I didn't notice this."

"There. All there. Uh, notice what?" Elijah came over with his arms full of clothes.

I rolled my eyes as I sat back on my heels and looked up at him. "Look." I pointed to the wall—which wasn't a wall—behind the bookshelf. The cat jumped down from the shelf and rubbed against my side, before trotting quietly away.

Elijah blinked and bent his head closer. "Is that a—?"

"Door. It's a door. How did *you* not notice this?" I heard the irony before I said it.

Elijah shook his head and dropped the rest of his laundry into the basket. He sank to his knees beside me, his hand on the bookcase. "It was here when I moved in...the bookcase..."

I pulled on the shelf. It wouldn't move. It was nailed to the door.

Elijah and I exchanged glances. "Does it lead into Ms. Barbara's rooms?"

"No...she's on the second floor. You're on the first and second." Elijah stared at the door. "My apartment used to be the attic...so, it must lead to more of the attic..." He dropped his hand and shrugged. He slid the basket toward me. "Take your time bringing it back." He snapped his fingers and pointed at me. "Don't think I've forgotten about that video camera."

I frowned. "You don't want to move the shelf?"

Elijah stood up and brushed off his pants. "Ms. Barbara probably sealed it off because she has a bunch of old stuff in there. Old people are pack rats; however glamorous and well put together they may appear...they are all secret hoarders." He gave me a wink and then slid his glasses back on his face.

I didn't want to give up so easily. A secret door? Hidden behind a bookcase? But I didn't think I'd be able to convince Elijah to trespass so blatantly. Maybe if I mentioned it to Lacey, she could convince him. Lacey had a way of talking people into things without even trying. I sighed, plucked up the basket, and said goodbye.

I finished the laundry, dropped each load off at its respective owners, and spent the rest of the day scrubbing the porch and mowing the lawn. It was a cool September afternoon, and the wind whipping up from the lake made it colder. I shivered hot from the labor, cold from the weather, and freezing from my cool sweat. I looked up at the house and blinked.

The sunlight had reflected in such a way I thought I saw....

And again, it looked like someone was standing in Ms. Barbara's window. But it was just a trick of the light against the glass. It was then that I realized I hadn't seen Ms. Barbara since the morning after I broke the mirror. Was that just yesterday? I switched off the mower and massaged my temple. Either way, I made a mental note to stop by once I'd showered. Just to make sure she was okay...

As I was putting the mower back under the porch, Lacey came up the drive with a bucket, a net, and a fishing pole. She had on a striped orange raincoat and her bright-pink galoshes and a soft smile on her face. "Make sure you put your hair up...things may get messy."

Lacey went up to Elijah's while I ran up to get changed. I didn't bother to shower. Instead, I got on some new jeans, a clean top, and a new hoodie out of the dresser. I grabbed my brush and a hair tie, looking pointedly deep into the big round mirror as I swept my hair up high on my head. Just an ordinary mirror. I frowned slightly as I noticed my eyes.

They were dark.

Too dark.

I leaned over the dresser, eyes wide, staring deep into them. My chocolate eyes looked almost black. I leaned closer, shivering slightly in the drafty room. My nose pressed against the cold glass.

I gasped.

Blood poured from my nose, dripping down my pale face.

"Great," I muttered. I moved away from the mirror and headed to the bathroom. But right before I hurried out of the bedroom, hands cupped underneath my chin, I could've sworn I saw myself smile.

MIRROR MESSAGE

Down at the creek, as I helped Lacey snag a thin piece of pickle onto her hook, I tried to forget about mirrors and focus on yobas.

"What are yobas, again?" I jabbed the hook into the pickle.

Lacey giggled. "They are kind of like frogs...but more like fairies."

"And they like pickles?" I asked, barely hiding my amusement.

Lacey nodded. "Oh, yes."

"What are we going to do if we find them?"

Lacey tilted her head, her silvery hair falling to the side underneath her rain hat. "Hmm...I think we will know what to do when the time comes," she said sagely and dropped the pickle into the stream with a plunk. As she watched the bobber drift along the water, she added softly, "My sister knew more about yobas than I ever did."

I stiffened and glanced sideways at her. A tear slid down her small, pointed nose and fell into the creek. I took a shaky breath. "My sister thought there was an owl outside our window. That it would come and visit us at night."

Lacey looked up at me in soft surprise. "I didn't know you have a dead sister, too."

Her words packed a punch. I inhaled sharply as my eyes prickled. I watched the bobber spin as it bumped into a rock. "It's hard to talk about her."

Lacey nodded sympathetically. "My father used to feel that way...but I disagreed. I felt it was crueler *not* to talk about them. So, I take comfort in telling their stories. Sometimes, she follows me to the creek and down to the lake. And if I listen really closely, I can hear them. Cassandra helps me talk to them, but with the EMF I'm going to prove to Daddy that—" She stopped and gave me an apologetic smile. "I'm sorry, Hannah. I know you don't like to talk about this kind of thing."

"No, it's just I forgot—" I lied quickly. "Cassandra had something for you—I left it in my room when—" I got the bloody nose. I remembered my black eyes...and the manic smile I saw. *Thought* I saw.

"Oh, look!" Lacey pointed down into the water.

I bent over and peered into the stream. A small tadpole was swimming just beneath the surface. Lacey laughed in delight, and I smiled despite myself. But then my smile slipped as I saw the dark reflection in the churning water. A girl like me, but not me, with a smile that pulled up as though hooked to the corners of her black eyes, revealing rows and rows of razor-sharp teeth. I gasped as I lost my footing, slipped on the edge of the bank, and fell into the icy water.

"Hannah!"

Lacey tossed her pole aside and helped me out of the creek. My heart raced. My lungs sputtered. I couldn't calm down. My eyes kept darting to the water. Lacey's small delicate hands held me firmly by the shoulders, and she sat me down on the grassy bank.

"Hannah. You're having a panic attack, Hannah...look at me... yes, that's right. And take slow, deep breaths," Lacey murmured, her wide hazel eyes inches from my brown eyes...or were they black? I blinked rapidly, trying to focus on Lacey's soft words. What was happening to me?

"Let's head back to the house."

I shook my head furiously. No. Not yet. I did not want to go back.

"Lacey...do you think there's something wrong with the house?" My breathing was coming in rattling gasps and gulps like a fish out of water.

Lacey bit her lip before she whispered, "Did you see her, Hannah? In your reflection?"

I lied. I had to lie. "No."

Lacey sighed as though she were disappointed. "I don't know what's wrong with the house...but I know Desiree does."

"Courtney's friend..."

Lacey nodded. "Maybe we should go visit her?"

No. No way. My thoughts became clearer and my heart steady. I inhaled deeply, finally coming to my senses. "I'm fine. I just let all this haunting talk get to me. Sorry for ruining the yoba hunt, Lacey."

Lacey opened her mouth, but closed it slowly, then gave me a sad smile. "I'm here for you..." And with that, she picked up her pole, straightened her rain hat, and headed back through the clearing and into the woods toward Rosecrest with me hurrying to keep up.

As soon as we made it back, I made sure to hand over the beaded bag before Lacey hopped on her bike.

"This is perfect!" Lacey exclaimed in her soft, awed whisper as she looked over the beaded handbag. "Don't you think it's perfect?"

I nodded with a weak smile.

"I'll see you tomorrow?" She slipped the bag over her head and patted it neatly in place at her side. The ornate beaded accessory looked strange on top of her striped raincoat. "What day is it? We're all going to the fair on Friday. And Courtney said Peter wants to meet us for lunch on Saturday...but I think I'd rather go mermaid watching on Elijah's boat."

"It's only Tuesday, Lace."

"Right. Well, whatever happens—Fair on Friday...and remember..." She kicked up her kickstand. "I'm here for you."

"I know where you live." I waved as she started off down the driveway.

I shivered, still wet and cold from my dunk in the river. Hugging myself, I waited, rooted to the spot, until Lacey disappeared from view.

"That sounded like a threat."

I turned, hands on my hips, and squinted up at the fire escape. Elijah was leaning over the balcony grinning as he pushed his glasses up the bridge of his nose. "Why are you wet?"

I smirked at the obvious observation and made one of my own. "Why are you out in the sunlight?"

He hurried down the stairs to meet me. "The sunlight? Did you forget I work down at the docks?"

"In the evening..." I said with a sly smile.

"True...perhaps I do need to get outside more..." Elijah shrugged and stuck his hands in his pockets.

"Oh—your camera." I snapped my fingers. "I'm sorry, hold on."

"Oh, no, that's all right—I was kidding about...okay..."

Ignoring him, I grabbed him by the hand, tugged him inside, and into the apartment.

I left him standing awkwardly in the living room while I ran up to my room for the camera. I hesitated in the hallway only briefly before snatching the camera off the dresser and heading back downstairs.

My pace slowed. Elijah wasn't alone...

Ms. Barbara.

My grip on the camera tightened. It was ridiculous to be

nervous. It's not like she'd demand to see the video camera. Or watch the footage...

I put a smile on my face as I entered the living room. Relief washed over Elijah's face.

Ms. Barbara grinned at the sight of me. She was wearing one of her best sun hats and purple dangly earrings. "Ah, Miss Hannah. I stopped by to say hello and was so happy to see Mr. Elijah here, too."

Elijah mumbled something as I handed him his camera back.

"Is that a tape recorder? Are you kids messing around down old Grey Lane?" Ms. Barbara gave Elijah a sharp look.

He blushed scarlet and adjusted his glasses. "No, ma'am. Hannah, err, well—I've gotta get ready for work..."

He held the camera close to his heart as he gave her a little bow and left.

Ms. Barbara shook her head. "That boy..."

There was a short silence before I remembered my manners. "Would you like some water or something?"

Ms. Barbara smiled. "No, dear. I just came to make sure you were all right."

"All right? Yes...I'm fine." I twisted my dark ponytail and realized I must look strange. My hair and my clothes were still damp and slightly drippy. Had she seen me fall into the creek? "Lacey and I were down at the river..."

Ms. Barbara smiled indulgently. "Her sister used to love to play in that old creek...wonderful memories." She sighed and stood. "Well, I just wanted to stop in for a moment before I'm off..."

"Are you going somewhere? I didn't know you had a car?" I inclined my head.

"Oh, my baby sister is picking me up shortly..." Ms. Barbara made her way to the door, and I hurried to open it for her. "She's trying to put me in a retirement home, remember. But I told her— I said, 'Sandra, those places are for old people. Do I look old to you?'" She laughed lightly, but her eyes were hard.

"She can't *force* you—can she?"

Ms. Barbara waved a hand. "She seems to think so...but we'll show her. Won't we?"

"If I can do anything to help..."

She reached up a bejeweled hand and gently patted my cheek. Then she gave me a roguish wink and headed out into the hallway. She stopped at the door, resting her hand on the doorknob as she turned back to look at me.

I fought the urge to glance to the left...the urge to make sure that the black sheet was still in place, still concealing my crime.

"Now, I'll be back late...so don't be waiting up now." She wagged a weathered finger at me. The rings on her fingers glittered in the dusty sunlight. "And you tell your mama, I appreciate all of her hard work." Then Ms. Barbara smiled. "And remember...don't touch that mirror."

Again, I couldn't sleep.

My meds were almost out, and I had resorted to cutting them in half. And unfortunately, half the dosage wasn't helping much. I couldn't shut my brain off. Thoughts of the face—the girl with the black eyes and hungry smile continued to flash in my head. I laid there in the dark, the covers pulled up to my chin, staring into the black...trying to judge if the dark shape lurking in the corner was a shadow or a trick of my eyes. My heart hammered against my ribs: a wild thing, trapped in a cage. My breathing was labored as I willed myself to exhale as silently as I could. What if there *was* something? Something waiting...just out of sight, hidden in the black, waiting to grab me? I couldn't think like that. Not again. It'd been years since I'd been afraid of things crawling out from the dark. I knew better now.

I blinked.

Did that shadow move from the corner to the wall?

Was it darkness or a creature leering over my bed?

I gripped the covers, refusing to reach out, telling myself it was all in my head. I wanted to turn on the light, but the light switch was past the door. And if I passed by the door, that dark archway, what might jump out and grab me with a monstrous growl?

And the mirror above the dresser—hanging there ominously. Like a black pool of water, reflecting the weak, waning moonlight that dripped in through the curtains. It had to go. The mirror. In the morning, I would take it down.

I scowled in the dark as my cheeks burned. I was letting all the Nile nonsense get to me...turning my head. I was losing it just like my father. But he had a disorder. I was just being impressionable. Pathetic. There were no such things as ghosts or cursed mirrors or any of it. It was all in my head. I wasn't afraid. And I wasn't waiting until morning.

I threw off the covers and stomped across the room. Ignoring the flighty feeling in my chest as I rushed past the doorway, I grabbed the mirror and pulled.

It wouldn't move.

I shivered. I was nose to nose with the shadowy reflection. I pulled and pulled. It wouldn't budge. Why couldn't I get the mirror off the wall? My breath fogged up the glass as I struggled to yank it from its hanging.

And then...

I heard it before I saw it: the slow, squeaky lines stuttering down the mirror.

YOU'RE NEXT

COFFEE CURES

I released the mirror and backed up. Mind reeling, I tried to process what I was seeing. Make logical sense of what I was seeing. It wasn't real. I was hallucinating. I swiped at the condensation on the mirror, smearing the words, erasing the message. My breath was coming fast and panicked. I needed air. To clear my head. I ran from the room, out of the apartment, out of the house, and outside into the night.

I didn't stop at the porch. I just kept walking down the driveway, the gravel grinding painfully underneath my bare feet. Away. I wanted to get as far away from the Rosecrest House as I could.

I found myself at the ferry dock. The diner was closed, but the ticket booth was open. The parking lot was nearly empty. Only a handful of cars were waiting for the next boat. The wind whipped violently against my oversized T-shirt and pushed through my pajama pants. I shivered and crossed my arms against the cold. I hadn't thought to grab a hoodie, let alone a pair of shoes. The only sound, apart from the whistling wind, was the hissing of the waves as they rushed to meet the rocks below.

I walked up to the window of the ticket booth. A guy about my age sat slumped over in his seat swiping at his phone with a dazed expression on his face. I frowned, waiting for him to notice me. He didn't.

"Excuse me."

He jumped, locking his phone quickly, and sat up straight. "Yeah?" he drawled.

"Is Elijah here?" I asked.

The guy gave me a mystified expression and said stupidly, "No. He's on the boat."

He turned back to his phone.

I raised an eyebrow. "Thanks for your help..."

I went down to stand by the loading dock as the ferry lights inched slowly across the lake. Several minutes passed. I spent the time collecting myself. Calming myself. Reasoning with myself. And by the time the ferry docked, unloaded, and I waved Elijah over, I was fully in control of my thoughts once more.

He jogged over to me, his glasses sliding down the bridge of his nose and his dark hair blown to the side by the wind. He put his hands on my shoulders and searched my eyes. "Are you okay? What's wrong?"

I realized then: me, pajamas, bare feet, hair whipping every which way—I must look insane. I tried to laugh it off. Think of a sarcastic joke to quip. But all that came out was: "I couldn't sleep."

Elijah cocked an eyebrow as he sputtered on his words.

I waved him away and held myself tighter against the cold. "I'm sorry. I wasn't thinking. I'll see you tomorrow."

Before I could turn to leave, Elijah cursed under his breath, stripped off his jacket, and draped it over my shoulders. "No...I— err...listen, I have a break coming up. I'll take it early. We can grab a coffee from the breakroom and—yeah, come on."

Then he led me onto the boat. The metal of the ship was so cold against my naked feet that it burned with each step. As we entered the cabin, a blast of hot air hit us in the face. They had a heat fan set up in the corner, aimed at the door. It didn't work very well. There was still a chill hanging in the air. But the floor wasn't nearly as painful, though still pretty cold.

Elijah hurried to the cabinets and began to brew two mugs of coffee, passing me one quickly. He gestured to a small table with chairs, and we sat down. I crisscrossed my legs, tucking my feet underneath me for warmth.

He sipped his coffee quickly. He paused briefly to open his mouth to speak, but then he thought better of it and took another sip instead.

I eyed him warily. "Is coffee your solution to everything?"

Elijah grinned. "Most things. If it's really complicated, I'll cook a big breakfast."

I managed a small smile. Calmed by the coffee and Elijah's company, I took a deep breath. I couldn't do it. I shut my mouth, clenching my teeth together. I couldn't go down that road again—admitting to seeing things that weren't possible.

Elijah hesitated. "You know...you can tell me anything and I—well, I won't—"

"I used to have nightmares," I blurted. My cheeks burned, but I kept going. "When I was little, I had trouble discerning the night terrors from reality. Then my sister...died...which led to a series of psychological evaluations and a sleep prescription. I've kept it together for seven years..."

I paused and shrugged, feeling defeated. "I think I'm letting all of this Nile superstition get the better of me..."

Elijah's mug slipped a bit in his grip. He pushed his glasses farther up on his nose.

Surprising both Elijah and myself, I kept talking. I couldn't stop. I had kept quiet for so long; it was a relief to get it out. To let it out. It was cathartic. "My dad has bipolar disorder...when my sister—*after* my sister—he went off his meds and had a psychotic break...he spiraled into a manic depression...which led to para-normal delusions...coupled with an extreme case of alcoholism. I haven't seen him in years. Currently, he's still off his meds and in and out of mental facilities." I took a deep breath. "Please, don't say anything."

Elijah drank deeply from his mug.

"I feel like I'm going crazy," I said bluntly.

Elijah scrunched up his face into a thoughtful pout as he nodded his head.

"Words of reassurance would be great...if you have any," I added dully from over the brim of my mug.

Elijah cleared his throat and stared down at the coffee in his hands. His fingers drummed against the mug. "I don't think you're going crazy, Hannah. And if your father has bipolar disorder, you'd know the symptoms of mania better than anyone. So, you wouldn't be asking me, you'd know already, right?"

I ticked off the most common symptoms on my fingers. "Increased activity. Rapid speech. Exaggerated self-confidence. Don't apply." I took a sip from my mug. I didn't mention sleeplessness, racing thoughts, or poor decision making...and in rare cases, hallucinations...which one could argue...

"Right," he said firmly. "I think..." He hesitated.

"What?"

"Honestly?" Elijah cocked an eyebrow. "I think you shouldn't have taken off that sheet."

I rolled my eyes.

Elijah shrugged. "You can scoff all you want. And I'm the last person in Nile to believe something crazy, but I remember what happened to Desiree Lapierre."

"Right." I rolled my eyes again. I was getting tired of her name. "She took off the sheet and was committed a week later. Courtney told me. *Everyone's* told me."

Elijah frowned at my dismissive tone. "She was haunted. Tormented. Everywhere she went she saw the same girl."

I picked up my mug, brought it to my lips, and put it back down again. "She saw a girl?"

Elijah nodded grimly. "They were having a sleepover at the house. Courtney and Desiree. Courtney dared her to pull off the sheet. Then she started to see it. She called them 'dark reflections.' Of a girl—all over the place. Everywhere she went."

"It's not real." I shrugged. "She saw a girl...and if I *thought* I saw a girl...that's because it's some messed-up manifestation of ourselves. Psychological delusion, not supernatural phenomenon."

Elijah raised his mug to me. "Well, whatever it is, I don't think it's bipolar disorder, Hannah."

I spent the rest of the week keeping my mind busy. When I wasn't doing schoolwork or the housekeeping chores that I'd taken over for Mom, I was spending time with Lacey or hanging around Elijah's apartment while he banged away on his machine. And if I wasn't with them, I was exploring the island on Elijah's bike. I figured if I could just keep busy, I'd stop obsessing about mirrors and dark, menacing reflections. But it didn't help...and I wasn't sleeping well.

And it showed.

Friday morning, I stumbled out of bed with Mom's alarm and met her at the table. I felt her critical gaze, but it wasn't until I tried to pour coffee into my cereal that she cried out in alarm.

"What are you—did you not sleep last night? You're dead on your feet!" Mom wrenched the coffee pot from my hands and smoothed back my hair from my face to feel my forehead.

I tried to make up a believable excuse, but all I could manage was a few mumbled words about reading late. I'd also run out of my meds and the order wouldn't be filled until next week. But I couldn't bear to bring *that* up.

"You know how important sleep is for you, Hannah." Her voice was high and teetering on panicked. "Have you been dreaming again?"

Guilt dropped into the pit of my stomach like a stone as she cupped my face and searched my eyes, looking positively distraught.

I forced a smile and squeezed her wrist. "No, Mom. They haven't come back." It was true...kind of. I took a deep breath. "I just ran out of—"

"You ran out?" She stepped back from me, stricken as though I'd slapped her. "Did you order more? How could you be so irresponsible, Hannah?" Mom's face fell with disappointment, and her dark eyes misted. She threw her hands up in a defeated shrug. "Don't you remember—"

"Yes, okay? I get it," I snapped. My shame only fed my anger, and I lost control. "Of course, I ordered more! Do you think I want to go through all that again? Dreaming horrible things? Confusing reality? Disappointing you over and over?"

"Hannah..." Mom blinked, eyes threatening to spill.

But I couldn't stop. "How do you think it is for *me*? Knowing that it's my fault our family's broken? Knowing if it hadn't been for my messed-up head, not knowing a dream from real life, Rebecca might not have—and Daddy wouldn't have—" My voice died in my throat.

Mom wrapped her arms around me. She squeezed so tight the air left me. "I'm so sorry, Hannah. I'm so sorry," she breathed into my hair as she stroked it softly. My body stopped shaking, and slowly I started to relax again as she continued, "I'm sorry I reacted that way...when you said you'd run out of— It just brought up a lot of stuff from..."

"I know. I know," I mumbled. It brought her back to when Daddy went off his meds. He didn't want to sleep anymore after Rebecca was taken. I had a different approach—dreamless sleep was all I'd wanted to do since.

Mom held my face in her hands and smiled a watery smile. "Just know, you are *not* irresponsible, and I'm so very grateful for everything you do around here. I mean, gosh, we wouldn't be able to keep this apartment without you."

I forced a smile. "I'm sorry I—"

Mom shook her head. "No need to be." She kissed my forehead. "Well...anyways, you better not stay out too late at the fair tonight. And try to get some sleep or no boat tomorrow." She ruffled my hair and brought her dishes to the sink. "I'm working late again. Overtime. We might actually be getting somewhere..."

"That's great, Mom."

Mom nodded with a smile. "Oh, and I'm grading the week's work on Sundays, remember. Not Friday anymore, so you have a bit more time. Don't forget, your first research paper is due at the end of the month. Did you pick your topic?"

"Not yet...but—"

"You better get to the library, then; it's by the school—" Her alarm blared, and she clicked it off. Then Mom kissed me quickly on the cheek and hurried to the door. "I'm late, sweetheart. I'm sorry. Sunday, I expect you to make room for me in your schedule! Grading and then movie marathon, you and me." She pointed at me with a smile that was too tired to reach her eyes. And then she was gone.

I sighed and shoved my uneaten cereal away from me. Maybe someday we'd be able to afford a decent breakfast. Sausage and pancakes drenched in real syrup. My stomach growled painfully.

The Nile library didn't look like any library I'd seen. It was a tiny little house that had once served as the Nile schoolhouse in the 1800s. The place had stayed the same since then, but over the years of adding more and more newly released novels, it appeared to have outgrown itself. It was cramped and stuffed as though the whole building had been constructed out of books and simply collapsed in on itself. The few shelves in the room were exploding with books, much like Elijah's bookcase, but even worse, with stacks upon stacks lining the floors, some paperbacks on top of the bookshelves themselves, and some even tucked into the tiny rectangular windows cut into the top of the walls. But unlike Elijah's collection, it didn't suggest feelings of cozy, obsessive love, but rather neglect and abandonment, as though it were the island's abandoned book disposal. Yes, that's exactly what it was—a hoarder's den, but instead of garbage: books.

I had to turn sideways to inch my way through the dusty shelves and around a tight corner to the librarian's desk, which was almost completely hidden by piles of more books. There was a large, bulky computer monitor plopped on top of the desk. A plump, ashen woman with thick, oversized glasses and wild gray hair sat staring at the screen.

I cleared my throat.

She didn't look up.

I frowned. "Excuse me?"

Her eyes slid away from the screen and found my face. She fixed me with a bored, disgruntled stare. The thick glasses made her droopy eyes too large for her squishy old face.

"Hi. I'm here to set up a library account? My name is Hannah Green." I handed the woman a copy of our lease from my backpack.

She wrinkled her nose as she looked down at it, as though I'd just handed her something indecent. She passed it back to me slowly.

I took it back with a polite smile and put it back in my bag. "Thank you."

Her beady eyes squinted up at me suspiciously as she pulled a fresh paper card from a drawer and scrawled my name down, her movements even slower than before.

"Why aren't you in school?" Her gravelly voice grated on my ears.

I tried not to wince as I took the card from her.

I pursed my lips into a tight smile that probably looked more like a grimace. "Homeschooled..."

The woman scoffed, coughing up a bit of phlegm in the

process, which she dabbed away with a yellow paper towel, handy at her side.

I ducked behind a mess of books before my face slipped, revealing my disgust. I scanned the shelves, silently cursing the horrible filing and numerous disorganized books. How would I find anything here? My nose crinkled. And it smelled. Like farts. It was too late to hold my breath. Which was worse, nose or mouth? Ew.

I peeked at the woman. Her face was now sucked into the computer screen again. I could just leave...but then I'd prolong my paper. What was my topic? I couldn't think. I spied a book titled *A History of Nile* mixed in with astronomy books as I grabbed a book on the death of stars. Then I found another historical, *Important Figures of Nile*. And another, *Nile, The Beginning*. And one more: *The Most Haunted Town in America*. All of the local historicals shoved in random sections in between space and physics. God, this place was a mess. Shaking my head, I grabbed three more books on stars. Good enough for now. Clutching the books to my chest, I hurried back to the librarian.

I cleared my throat again as I placed the pile on the desk.

Clearly annoyed by the interruption, the woman scooted back in her chair and reached up to take the books, all with the speed and agility of a sedated sloth. Then she picked up the scanner. I clenched my fingers into my palms to keep from drumming them impatiently on the desk or reaching out and grabbing the scanner myself.

Beep.

She reached over to a large cabinet full of tiny drawers and pulled out a card. She inched across the desk for a stamp and took a minute to fiddle with the numbers. I watched her, wondering if I looked close enough, I might see the moss as it grew over her grizzly hair. She pressed the stamp down onto the card, one side and then the other. She stuck out her fat, gray tongue, licked her thumb and slipped the card into the pocket of the first book. There were three more. Why did I pick so many?

My eyes moved around the room as I tried to maintain my composer and quiet my unkind thoughts.

Beep.

What time did I get here? It would probably be dark before I left. Before I could stop myself, I quipped, "What time do you close?"

She paused, and her eyes crawled up my face. She pointed a sausage finger at the sign on the desk. Eleven o'clock on Fridays. Good to know. I fought the urge to roll my eyes. Instead, I checked my watch. The woman went back to the books.

I frowned as my eyes moved around the room. I read the titles on the towers of books. I had been right about my earlier assumption. Little Lord Fauntleroy right next to Fantastic Beasts? It was a giant dump of decades worth of books with complete disregard for the Dewey Decimal system. How many first editions were hidden in this mess?

I felt a nagging in my head like I did when I was missing something. My brow furrowed as I studied the books more carefully. My critical expression softened with interest as I noticed a particularly beaten-up book stuffed into the shelf.

Beep.

Desperate for something to do with my hands, other than strangle the librarian, I left the desk and pulled it out. The cover was old leather, weathered and worn. I half expected it to be a Bible, but—

"Here," she grunted.

I gave the woman a sharp look as I hugged the old book to my chest and made my way back to the desk. "This too, please."

The woman's face fell as she scrunched up her lips in a pout. "That hasn't been cataloged yet. Put it back."

I pursed my lips as I held back a nasty retort. I watched her gaze slide back to her computer screen. I was dismissed.

Silently fuming, I dumped the astronomy books into my bag. The woman was completely captivated by her computer once again. Overcome with annoyance and an impulsive immature urge, I shoved the old book into my bag along with the rest and hurried from the library, all the while ignoring my hammering heart and reassuring myself that I was just borrowing it...I'd return it. I wasn't stealing. Not really.

When I got back to our apartment, I settled onto the couch and dumped the contents of my backpack onto the coffee table. I organized my notebooks, set up my highlighters and color-coded pens, and stacked the library books neatly off to the side. My eyes drifted to the tattered book with its leather cover and gilded pages. It wasn't a Bible. I picked it up gingerly and turned it over in my hands. It was a book of fairy tales. I scanned the old beige pages and moved my fingers over the faded illustrations. They were local tales. Strange, beautiful stories I'd never heard of: some involving the lake monster, Champ, and even some about champlets and yobas. I couldn't believe it. Lacey wasn't speaking complete nonsense after all. A smile flickered on my face and, forgetting all about my research paper, I settled back into the couch, pulled the throw blanket over my legs, and snuggled up to read.

And somehow, I fell asleep.

And I dreamed about her.

THE DREAM

I was back in our room. We shared a room. We always had. They'd tried to separate us once, but we'd refused. We wanted to be close to each other and couldn't stand being apart. We were best friends as much as sisters. With only a few minutes separating us, I was the eldest and took advantage of that whenever I could—like taking the top bunk instead of the bottom. But she didn't mind. She was sweet like that. Agreeable. Kind. Polite. Along with a slight fear of heights and an incredible imagination. The better of the two of us. Everybody knew it, and I loved her for it. But really, who *couldn't* love Rebecca Green?

I was sitting on the floor with our Barbie dolls spread out all around me. It was dark in the room, the only light coming from the thin yellow beam underneath the door and our little nightlight. But even in the dark, I could tell everything was the same as it had been before...the giant doll house in the corner, the bookshelf filled with books as well as stuffed animals, the single window with the pink lace curtains, and the closet with its giant double doors facing our bunk bed.

I looked around the room for her. I had that aching in the pit of my heart, that longing for her, that needing for her to be with me. But she was gone. And I knew why.

I had to get out of there. It wasn't safe.

Still holding a doll in one hand, I ran to the door. It wouldn't open. I dropped the doll and pulled on the knob with both hands. The door wouldn't open. I wanted to scream, but I couldn't make a sound. I looked left toward the closet just as it started to open. I looked back at the door. It was covered in a large black sheet. I yanked off the cover. It wasn't a door. It was the mirror.

I stumbled back and headed for the bunk bed. I scrambled up the ladder and jumped into bed. I yanked the blankets over my head and flattened myself on the mattress, peeking through the wooden rails...just like I had before.

Then the double doors of the closet began to open.

Just like they had before.

The doors continued to open painfully slow until they were spread wide, revealing the black emptiness of the closet. And I waited for it to come for me, just as it had come for her.

But it didn't.

Instead, a short shadow stepped out of the closet into the soft light of the nightlight. A small girl of ten with long, brown hair plaited lovingly by her mother and caramel eyes that glowed golden in the dark. Her blankie was draped over her shoulders like a shawl, and her hands hung limply at her sides.

I sat up in bed and leaned over the railing, holding my hand out to her. I tried to call her, but my voice was still stuck in my throat.

She looked up at me.

Her smile curved up the sides of her face, her eyes black and beady.

And then she charged, movements twitching and spider-like, leaping at me with teeth like shards of glass.

• • •

"Hannah! Hannah, wake up!"

Lacey stood over me, her hazel eyes wide. Her hands gripped my shoulders, shaking me awake. I grabbed her arms and held onto her, panting and gasping for breath.

"It was a dream," Lacey breathed.

I nodded furiously. A dream. A dream. I sat up and tried to collect myself.

Lacey stepped back and gave me space.

"Sorry to pull you from the Dream Realm..." she murmured sagely.

I waved her words away as I tried to slow my breathing.

"...but you were shouting and..." Lacey winced, and her breath caught at the memory of whatever it was I was doing. "I just thought you should wake up."

"No, don't apologize. I needed to get out of—yeah, how did you—?"

"I could hear you from outside. You were very loud," Lacey added.

My stomach churned. "But I locked the door—"

"Oh. That." Lacey smiled shyly. "I have a key."

My head was still racing, my heart still hammering. I pressed on my chest in a vain attempt to calm it. "A key?"

Lacey slipped her hand into her pocket and pulled out an oversized antique key. "It's a skeleton key. They're magic and very rare. I found this one buried on Bird Island."

"Buried?" I blinked. None of what she was saying made sense. But did it ever? I took a shaky breath.

"You should get ready..." Lacey said thoughtfully, tucking the key into her pocket. "The champlet traps need checking."

"Right...okay. Let me just go get changed."

As I headed up the stairs, Lacey plopped down on the couch and picked up the fairy tale book that'd fallen to the floor. "Oooo, Cecily Blackwell. Is this a first edition?"

I didn't go to my room. I went straight to the bathroom. I

didn't dare glance in the mirror. Ridiculous as it was, I kept my eyes squinted almost shut and felt around for my anti-anxiety meds. The bottle was at the bottom of the travel bag. We'd been here for weeks, and I hadn't even unpacked it yet. I couldn't even remember the last time I'd taken one. But Mom was always sure to keep a current bottle on hand just in case I needed it. And I definitely needed it then.

I twisted the cap, popped the pill, and forced it down my dry throat, chasing it with a handful of water from the faucet. I tried to relax. If I didn't relax—if Mom found out about my dreams, my hallucinations...because that's what they were, weren't they? A tear burned and bled down my cheek. I'd have to tell her. But first I'd call Dr. Manning. See if she had an opening. She'd be able to tell me for sure. No need to worry Mom until I was positive there was a problem. But wasn't there? I tucked the bottle back in the bag and looked up.

There she was. At least this time she wasn't wearing my sister.

Her black eyes glittered. Her face was almost sad. I was grateful she wasn't smiling that grotesque grin.

"You're not real." I stared hard into her black eyes. "You're in my head."

She held a finger to her lips.

"Hannah..."

I jumped and looked toward the door. Lacey was gripping the doorframe and glancing nervously down the hall.

"Ms. Barbara is downstairs..."

I looked back at the mirror. The girl was gone.

I led Lacey back downstairs to meet Ms. Barbara. She was sitting on the couch, flipping through the fairy tale book. She looked up as we came down the stairs with a strange smile on her face.

She was looking a bit haggard, and for some reason she looked much older than I remembered. She placed the book back on the table and stood to greet us. "I suppose you two are off to the fair tonight?"

Lacey hung behind me a bit, as though she were trying to hide.

"Err...yes." I glanced behind me at Lacey. Her eyes stared down at her lime-green crocs.

"Well, I hate to ask, my dear, but your mother is working late again tonight, and I was hoping to get my apartment tidied. My sister's coming tomorrow, and I just can't stand the thought of giving her something else to say... Do you think you'd be able to manage it when you get back?"

I forced a smile. "Sure, Ms. Barbara."

"It isn't the end of the world if you can't. I'll understand. If my lights are out, I've gone to bed, and you'll have missed me." She gave me a coy smile and patted my cheek before heading for the door. "But, either way, do try not to stay out too late, my dear. You need to get your rest. You're looking a little haunted about the eyes."

I called Dr. Manning as soon as Ms. Barbara left. Luckily, she had time to see me before she left for the day...if I could make it in time. Courtney didn't mind taking me, especially since we were headed into town for the fair anyways. Lacey came, too, but for some reason she was quiet.

Courtney glanced at Lacey beside her in the passenger seat and then in the rearview mirror at me. "Did something happen?"

I looked at the back of Lacey's head, willing her not to say anything about my dream.

"Ms. Barbara..." Lacey whispered.

"Oh...yeah." Courtney nodded sympathetically.

"What?" I looked between the two of them, clearly missing something.

Lacey took a strand of her hair and started to thread it through her fingers like white ribbon.

"Lacey thinks there's something wrong with her," Courtney explained vaguely.

"Cassandra says her aura is wrong," Lacey murmured, twisting her hair tighter around her finger.

"Right..." Courtney shrugged. "Well, old ladies are weird. But Cassandra is even weirder. *Have you seen her snake?*" She made a face and shivered. "Changing subject. Are you guys excited for the fair? I was thinking maybe the two of you could spend the night at my house—you know, considering we're probably going to be at the fair late. Could be fun, right?"

"I have to work," I said vaguely. I wasn't about to admit that I was the Rosecrest House assistant bathroom scrubber.

Lacey didn't answer. Instead, she said, "Elijah was supposed to give me my EMF today. He left before I could get it."

Courtney turned into the ferry dock parking lot and pulled up to the ticket booth. She rolled down her window and handed her ferry pass to the pimply kid in the booth. He smiled and blushed scarlet as he swiped her card.

"Thank you, Michael," Courtney murmured as she gave him a sweet smile. "Have you seen Elijah today?"

The boy made a strangled squeaking sound. Then he cleared his throat and tried again. "Nah, he's off tonight. He's got something entered in the inventors' thing at the fair..."

"Excellent. Say 'hi' to your sister for me." Courtney rolled up the window with a polite wave and put the car back in gear. As she followed the line of cars onto the ferry, she said brightly, "Maybe he'll have it with him at the fair."

Lacey looked out the window without a word.

Courtney drove the car up the ramp and onto the boat. She put the car in park, flipped the visor down, and started to fix her make-up. "Oh! Peter's meeting us with some of his friends from school..." Her gaze flicked toward mine in the mirror. "He was hoping you'd come...said something about needing your number, so he could call you while he's away all week at school..."

I blinked. In the mirror, Courtney's cerulean eyes had darkened. I looked down quickly. Last thing I needed was to start hallucinating again.

Courtney turned in her seat to look at me. "Hey—he wasn't being creepy or anything..."

"Oh, no...it's not that. I was just thinking about—the library," I finished lamely.

"Did you meet Portia's mom? The librarian?" Courtney shuddered. "Now, *she's* creepy."

"She's a gullum," Lacey said softly, still staring out the window.

Courtney burst out laughing. "Like from *The Hobbit*?"

"No, not Gollum...a gullum. A person cursed by a flummox fairy. That's why she's so slow."

"Huh...I've never heard of that..." Courtney's face crinkled as she thought this over. Then she changed the subject back to the fair again. "Are you excited for the Sights and Seers show, Lace?"

At that, Lacey perked up a bit, and they began to discuss the show as I sank deep into my thoughts.

"Hannah?"

"What?" I flinched away from the reflection in the car window.

"I saidddd—" Courtney singsonged. "Do you want us to wait? Or drop you off? Where am I taking you, again?"

I hadn't been to Dr. Manning's office in a while. I hadn't needed to, especially since I could order my prescriptions on Mom's phone. Sitting there on her couch, after everything that had happened, was panic inducing. It brought me back to the first time I'd been there. When the dreams started.

Dr. Manning was an older woman, certainly older than my mom, with washed-out blond hair. She was tall, even taller than I was, with a long, thin, oval face, which gave her the strange appearance of being stretched. Like she was made of silly putty instead of skin.

Her face was lined as she smiled, as though her face was more skeletal than flesh. Her teeth were large in her mouth giving her the overall appearance of a horse. "I'm glad you called, Hannah. It's been a while, hmm?"

Small talk always annoyed me but even more so today. "I've been having nightmares. Trouble sleeping. And..." I hesitated on the word 'hallucinations.'

Dr. Manning nodded. "You've moved again?"

I frowned. "Yes."

Dr. Manning smiled her thin-lipped smile. "Well, Hannah, I'm glad you stopped in to talk to me. But rest assured, a major life change like a move is bound to affect you in some ways. A recurrence of your night terrors is unfortunately to be expected."

I gritted my teeth. I couldn't mention the hallucinations. I couldn't. She'd take me away just like they dragged Daddy away—

"What is it, Hannah? Is there something else?" Dr. Manning's smile had slipped.

I ran a hand through my hair. "Nothing."

Dr. Manning scribbled a note on her pad. "How about friends, are you making any this time? I know it's always a challenge for you..."

I frowned. It wasn't a *challenge*. I just preferred not to. I was going to shake my head, but found myself saying, "A few."

Dr. Manning's smile returned. "That's wonderful, Hannah. Connections are important, especially when you've lost the most important one in your life."

My hands curled into fists in my lap.

"Do your friends know about Rebecca?"

I inhaled sharply at the mention of her name. It felt like a gut punch almost every time. "One of them does...sort of. And another, but not really."

Dr. Manning arched a thin eyebrow, clearly impressed. She

scribbled something on her notepad without taking her eyes off me. "That's a wonderful step, Hannah. You know, opening up about her may increase your symptoms, but it is all part of the healing process. Are you ready to talk about your sister now—"

"No," I snapped. "I'm here because of my sleep—"

"And what are you dreaming about?" Dr. Manning asked patiently, completely unfazed by my temper.

I didn't say anything.

Dr. Manning sighed as she clicked her pen closed. "You know, Hannah, I've been seeing you since you were ten years old. We started by going over your fear of the dark and your closet. We went over your cryptomnesia and memory issues. Your disassociation. All skirting very neatly around the heart of your problem."

My jaw tightened, and I felt my own body grow rigid like an animal freezing in place to avoid detection.

"We have yet to discuss Rebecca at all."

My breathing grew labored beneath the weight of my anger. That wasn't true. She was all I had talked about when Mommy and Daddy first brought me into therapy. I'd told Dr. Manning all about the dreams, all about what happened to her in the nightmares. And then...she was taken. What more would I have to say after that?

Dr. Manning placed her notebook beside her on the side table. She crossed her legs and folded her hands over her knee. "I think you'll find that once you deal with your feelings surrounding her disappearance...and your feelings surrounding your father—"

"I've gotta go." I stood quickly and walked out the door without looking back.

The cold air hit me full in the face as I stepped out on the sidewalk. It was refreshing and cleared away some of the fog I felt beginning to cloud up my head. I hurried around the corner, squinting in the cool sunlight for Courtney's car. The two of them were just getting out when I approached, my shoulders hunched and hands in my pockets. I shivered. I should've brought a coat.

"Hey, that was fast!" Courtney smiled uncertainly. "You said a half hour at least...we were going to walk to the coffee shop. Do you want—"

"Yeah, sure," I said quickly.

"You're upset," Lacey murmured. Her brow crinkled underneath her green and yellow sequin beanie.

I bit my lip.

"Was it a bad meeting? I hate meeting with our college admissions advisor." Courtney frowned sympathetically and put a hand on my shoulder. "So judgy."

Lacey looked from Courtney to me. She opened her mouth but shut it quickly. Then she tucked her arm through mine. "Let's hurry before all the crullers are gone."

The two of them flanked me on both sides, and the three of us walked down the street, past all the little shops, until we got to the place. And with them, in the comfort of the cozy coffee shop, I started to feel a lot better, like maybe it all *was* simply delusions brought on by reminders of my trauma...or whatever Dr. Manning had said.

But then Portia walked in.

OLD NEWS

The coffee shop—Honey Bean—was packed full of teenagers and college kids, both behind the counter and in front of it. The place was noisy but not in the obnoxious cafeteria kind of way, rather in the warm Friendsgivings you see on TV kind of way. The toasty smells of hot coffee and sugary baked goods were intoxicating. The whole place was nestled and cozy, with several plush chairs angled together in multiple spots around the place. There was a giant couch pushed up in front of a low coffee table, in addition to the standard mini tables and chairs. There was a fireplace, too, and even a wall of books.

"Is your entire school here?" I asked Courtney as we took seats at one of the tiny high tables.

Courtney smiled. "Almost. It's kind of like 'the place to be' after school."

"Only for our school," Lacey pointed out. "Peter's boarding school has its own coffee shop on their campus. You never see the private school kids here."

"The owners actually just graduated. They were in Elijah's class." Courtney nodded toward the two girls behind the counter. One had a tangle of golden curls spilling from a ponytail and a bright smile as she waved to a group of girls who'd just walked in; the other girl had a short crop of brown hair and a more mischievous grin as she passed a bag of donuts to the kid in the front of the line. "Whitney and Grace. They opened this place last year. Their grandparents own a honey farm a few towns away, hence the name. Plus, it doesn't hurt that the school mascot is a hornet."

Lacey dug through her satchel and pulled out a box of teabags, her stack of cups, and the fairy tale book I'd stolen from the library. She gave me a small smile as she organized her things on the table. "I hope you don't mind? I took it while you were on the phone. My mama had a copy, but Daddy likes to keep it with her things..." Her face fell a bit as her voice gave out, and her hazel eyes glistened.

"Keep it," I said without hesitation.

Lacey blinked. "But it's—"

"Yours," I said firmly.

Lacey beamed brightly, jumped down from her seat, and gave me a tight hug.

Courtney made a little gasp. Her blue eyes widened at something behind me.

"No, Hannah, don't! Don't turn around!" Courtney hissed, her face coloring a pretty pink.

"What?" I demanded, my voice embarrassingly high with premature panic.

Lacey slipped back onto her seat and flipped open the fairy tale book. "It's just Damien Barrow. You know, Courtney, he's not a nice person."

I felt myself relax and smiled both in relief and amusement.

Courtney nibbled her lip and shrugged a little. "He sure is nice to look at though..."

"So are pufferfish," Lacey said dismissively. "He's mean to Aubrey. He makes her cry—*a lot*," Lacey added firmly, not bothering to look up from the book.

Courtney wasn't listening. "Why is he here? He goes to school with Peter..." She sat straight up in her seat, trying to see over me and the many kids between her and the front door. Her nose pointed in the air like a puppy as she watched Damien Barrow move through the shop. She scoffed in disgust. "Why is he hanging out with *Portia*?" She made a face, apparently completely cured of her infatuation, and slipped down from her seat. "Before I lose my appetite, what do you guys want?"

"Uhh...black coffee?"

"Hot water and a honey cruller," Lacey murmured, her eyes still transfixed by the pages of the fairy tales.

As Courtney headed off for the counter, Lacey looked up at me. "You didn't go to a college counselor."

"No," I admitted.

"Why did you lie to Courtney?"

Faced with Lacey's genuine perplexity, I shifted uncomfortably in my seat. "It's hard to..." The words died on my lips as I noticed Portia and a guy, presumably Damien Barrow, sitting at a table a little bit away.

Portia's beady eyes bored into me as she whispered to Damien and passed him something across the table. Then he stood and sauntered over to us, with all the annoying confidence of a guy who knew he was good looking. And if I was being honest, Courtney wasn't kidding. Damien Barrow had thick dark hair and piercing blue eyes and a bone structure seemingly chiseled from stone. He wasn't just good to look at, he was overwhelming to look at—in an oppressive, intimidating way that made me extremely uncomfortable.

"How long do you think you have?" he asked with a smile that set off his dimples.

"I'm sorry?"

"Before you get locked up like Desiree Lapierre, I mean." Damien smirked.

My eyes narrowed. "Funny."

Lacey regarded him with evident disapproval.

He tried again to get me to bite. "You pulled the sheet down, didn't you? Have you seen the ghost yet?" Damien put a hard hand on my shoulder and looked around. "Is she here now?" Damien pretended to shiver. Then he laughed darkly. "What do you think, Spacey? You see anything? I mean, other than the stuff you usually see."

Lacey didn't flinch.

My fingers clenched underneath the table.

Damien grinned. "It's a shame; I would've liked to take you out. But I don't go for cursed chicks."

I smiled. "That's okay; I don't go for jerks."

He slapped his hand to his heart and pouted. Then he rolled his eyes and gave me a nudge. "Nah, I forgot. You like nerds like Eli, don't ya?"

"Excuse me?" I raised an unimpressed eyebrow.

"I saw you at the docks the other night," Damien said with a nasty smile. "Pretty skimpy get up for a date."

My stomach twisted as the blood drained from my face. All I could think about was what I'd said on the ferry that night. What if he'd overheard somehow?

"Eli's a good buddy of mine. He tells me everything." Damien tossed an emerald-green envelope onto the table and gave an obnoxious wink before heading back to his table. Portia snorted loudly at his return, her eyes never leaving me.

I took the envelope and opened it. It was an old news clipping from the *Free Press*. I'd seen enough. My stomach soured, and I shoved the paper back into the envelope and stuffed it into my bag.

"Are you okay, Hannah?" Lacey's brow furrowed. "What was it?"

"Nothing," I lied, forcing a light smile on my face, but I couldn't make it reach my eyes.

Portia cackled in the background.

· · ·

The sight of the fairgrounds was almost enough to put a smile on my face—almost. I hadn't been to a county festival, let alone a state fair before, and the excitement and cheer of the place was infectious as soon as we walked up to the ticket master. Courtney passed up our tickets. Then she pulled out her phone.

"Peter—we're here. Did you get the ride tickets? No, we need to find Elijah first. No." Courtney smiled as her eyes flickered toward me. "Yup...yup, she's here...where's the—okay, see you there."

Courtney nodded her head toward the left, and the three of us weaved our way through the crowd past the different carnival games and food stalls. There was a large building, almost like a giant barn, at the end of the walkway. Courtney ducked inside, and we followed.

The smell of oil and gas punched us in the noses as we searched for Elijah among all the dozens of people standing by their unique creations.

"There he is!" Lacey took off at a hopping pace and threw herself at him in a desperate hug. Elijah stumbled backwards on impact.

"What are you all doing here?" Elijah patted Lacey's back awkwardly as he blinked at Courtney and me.

Lacey stepped back, still rocking back and forth on her crocs. "Do you have my EMF meter?"

Elijah furrowed his brow and straightened his spectacles as he regarded Lacey. "I have it...it's ready, but I didn't bring it—"

"Maybe Hannah can get it tonight?" Lacey smiled hopefully at me.

I didn't have time to answer. A bunch of kids, with Peter in the lead, approached. Courtney was instantly engulfed in hugs and chatter from the girls in the group. Peter sidestepped them as he gave me a small smile and pulled me aside.

"Hey—how's your week been? Court said you guys are good now..."

"Yeah...she apologized. Apparently, Lacey and I were going to spend the night at your house tonight, but I can't. Work."

Peter ran a hand through his golden hair. "Right. I've been thinking about you a lot this week—you know, 'cause of the whole..." Peter added quickly before trailing off.

Portia, who'd been smuggled into the crowd of private school kids by Damien, pushed between us. "You haven't told him about your sister, have you?"

My heart stopped. I stared down at her, this pig of a person, with her beady eyes and snotty, squashed, upturned nose pointed at me. I had been prepared for this moment. I was always prepared for this moment. But now that it was here, catching me off guard, I forgot my rehearsed response.

"Portia, what the hell?" Peter snapped.

"What, Petey? You deserve to know. Damien told me *everything*. He even found an old newspaper article about it—" Portia's smile curled nastily. "Her dad murdered her twin sister, and she protected him from the police—"

There was a loud ringing in my ears as the world began to sway. This could not be happening.

Portia's voice echoed loudly all around me. "But that's just *one* theory...most people think *she* killed her twin, and the dad covered it up. Well? Which is it, Hannah?"

12

THE FAIR

It was like all movement screeched to a halt.

Then every eye turned toward me. I could feel them moving over me like beetles.

The whispers hissed around me like snakes.

My eyes burned. My stomach heaved. I tasted the rancid bile as I forced it back down. I had to get out of there. And so, I ran. I shoved my way through the crowd of people, pushing past families and couples and strollers and backpacks. I made it out of the building and outside.

The sun was starting to sink over the top of the Ferris wheel and the lights of the fair were beginning to switch on. I needed a bathroom. I was going to get sick. I went around the side of the building and bent over, hands gripping my knees. My breath was coming fast and sharp. My thoughts streamed together as I gasped for air. How was I going to get back? I didn't want to face Courtney and her questions—I didn't even want to deal with Lacey or—

"Breathe. Just breathe."

Peter.

He pulled my hair away from my neck and rested his hand gently on my back. He rubbed as I retched.

When I was done dry heaving, he pulled a water bottle out of his backpack. I shook my head, but he pushed it on me.

"Slow, small sips."

I sipped and passed it back. "Thank you."

I refused to look at him.

I felt his eyes on me.

"Tell Courtney I have another ride home." I made to leave, but he held me back.

"What other ride? You can't call an uber—you don't have a phone. So, what—a cab? Neither of those are safe...you're angry—and you have every right to be—" he added as I began to argue. "But you're not thinking clearly."

I rolled my eyes and shook my head as hot tears began to stream.

"You need to clear your head. And I know just how to do that."

Without another word, Peter took my hand and led me through the fairgrounds to the Ferris wheel. He passed the operator two tickets and held the metal door open for me. Obediently, I climbed in.

As the ride started, our chair moved backwards sharply into the air. I let out a gasp of surprise despite myself and gripped the metal bars for support. Peter was quiet as the two of us surveyed the sun setting over the horizon. The sky was ablaze with orange and bruised purple. Far off in the distance the lake glowed, a pool of pale pink in the dying light. The black stretch in the middle of it was Nile.

The air was cold as it pushed past us, rocking the seat and making it creak. I shivered. Peter tugged off his hoodie and pushed it to me before I could protest. As I pulled it on, I noticed Peter clench his jaw to keep his teeth from chattering. His shirt billowed in the breeze, and goosebumps dotted his arms.

"Are you sure you don't want your hoodie back? You've got goosebumps..."

Peter waved me off.

Our chair made it to the highest point of the Ferris wheel and stopped.

"How's your head? Clearer?" Peter asked.

I breathed deeply through my nostrils, the cold air prickling every nose hair I had. I exhaled. "Surprisingly, yes."

Peter gave me a rueful smile. "I'm glad. And I'm sorry about Portia..."

"It's not your fault—"

Peter shook his head, his face grim. "No, it is...Damien told me Portia was chomping at the bit to throw that garbage in your face. I shouldn't have pulled you aside. It just made her come after you."

I tried to argue again, but Peter held up a hand. "Let's forget about her. She's not important."

We were quiet as the wind creaked us back and forth and the Ferris wheel began to turn once more.

Peter didn't ask. He didn't even get into any details. And yet—for the second time in one week, I felt the strong desire to open up. So, I did. "When I was ten years old, my sister was kidnapped. She was taken out of our room. My dad was the only one home with us that night. My mom was at the movies with some friends. The police never found her...or figured out who took her. Obviously, plenty of people assumed my dad had something to do with it."

I took a deep breath. "But it's my fault they never found out who did it...I was there. I saw it. But I never could give the police a proper description...so they got away.

"I knew it'd get out somehow...seven years of moving around, and it *always* manages to catch up to me. Elijah probably let it slip to Damien Barrow. Apparently, they're friends. Can you believe that?"

Peter gave my hand a hard squeeze. "I know you're not going to believe it when I say it—but it wasn't your fault. Your sister.

Your dad. Not your fault. You were what? Ten? Nothing you could've done."

I laughed through the tears. "You're right. I don't believe you. But it's nice to hear you say it, anyway."

When we climbed out of the Ferris wheel, it was dark, and the swirling bright lights of the fair were mesmerizing. And somehow, I felt a million times lighter. I gave Peter a small nudge. "Thank you."

He flashed a radiant smile. "No problem. You look good in my hoodie."

My cheeks burned. "I meant—"

Peter winked, and I gave him a shove. "You better watch it. I might keep it."

He laughed and pulled out his phone. "So, are you leaving? Because I can call my mom. She should be heading home from the hospital soon..."

I took a second to think. Did I really want to deal with Portia again? I glanced at Peter. I thought of Courtney and Lacey and how much fun we had planned to have...

"I'm staying."

Peter grinned as he tapped his phone. "Court? Yeah—Ferris wheel. See you in five."

When we met back up with them, Portia was nowhere to be seen.

Courtney looped her arm through mine and led me away from the group. Lacey bounced over to join the mini-huddle. I took a deep breath and opened my mouth, but Courtney stopped me.

"We don't need an explanation, okay?" Her blue eyes held mine. "You'll tell us whatever you want, whenever you want. And not because Portia is a little puke."

Lacey fell on me in a light airy hug. "I'm sorry you lost your sister, Hannah. But the nice thing about our lost ones—they can always be found again."

I hugged Lacey back, squeezing her tightly.

"All right, can we *enjoy* the fair now? I've been waiting for this all year! A scary ride with Cole St. Claire? Yes, pleaseee." She tilted her head into me and muttered, "Have you *seen* Cole St. Claire? Gorgeousss."

I rolled my eyes over Lacey's head, and Courtney winked cheekily.

The fair was incredible. With Courtney's and Peter's stockpile of tickets that they were more than eager to share, we were all able to ride every ride not just once, but three, sometimes even four times in a row. Lacey wasn't too keen on the thrill rides, so she hung back with a few of the girls from Peter's school who didn't seem to want to mess up their hair, along with the rest of the boys who seemed more interested in the girls than anything else. And thankfully, Portia and Damien were nowhere in sight.

So, when it was time to board the Sling Shot, it was me, Peter, and Courtney, along with Rachel, the punk cheerleader waitress, and her cousin, Cole, who looked like a young Johnny Depp, complete with the thoughtful demeanor, dark hair, and dreamy eyes. The ride sat just two on each of the three sides of the giant ball, so when I got in, Peter hurried forward to sit next to me.

"If this thing flings us into the lake—"

"Oh, come on, Peter. We'd crash into the parking lot way before we hit the lake."

Peter's laugh was strained.

I craned my neck to see him around our restraints. "Are you scared?"

"Me? No way." He glanced over at me and grinned. His face was almost as white as Lacey's blonde hair.

"You are!" I exclaimed. "You don't have to ride it—"

The operator, who looked barely older than us, came around the ball to check our restraints. He cocked an eyebrow at Peter. "You want off?"

Peter shook his head as he gripped the metal bars. "Nah, man. I'm good."

"Peter—"

"Sure..." The guy smirked as he walked away and headed down the platform to the ride controls.

"Peter...why did you get on if—"

"You were so excited for this one. I wanted to do it with you. I wasn't about to let Cole—oh, God. It's starting. How long does this—"

His scream cut his question short as the ball launched us into the air.

It wasn't really a slingshot, more like a rotating ball, turning on an axis. As we shot straight upward to the stars, the ball turned slowly, and it continued turning as we plummeted back down to Earth.

I laughed and squealed and could barely contain my delight. It was like flying. Soaring through the stars. My heart was light as I blinked out into the brilliance of the night. I let my arms fly by my sides and called to Peter, "Isn't it beautiful!"

Peter was cursing a bit but seemed to have gotten over his initial terror. "Yeah. It's—incredible," he shouted back in short gasping bursts.

Somewhere off to my left Courtney was screaming about murdering me in my sleep. Behind us, Rachel and her cousin, Cole, were shouting enough swears to make a sailor blush. And I was still laughing my butt off like we were flying through laughing gas instead of air.

When we finally stopped, Peter was a bit green, Courtney's hair looked like a beehive, and Rachel and Cole were identical white sheets.

"Never...letting you...pick...the ride...*again*," Courtney panted as she tore her fingers through her hair.

I laughed and draped an arm around her as we headed for the exit ramp.

Lacey bounded over to us as we came through the gate, all of us a little unsteady on our feet and leaning into each other a bit. "Is it time for the Sights and Seers show?" she asked brightly.

When we got to the Sights and Seers show, Lacey was the first to slip through the curtain. It was set up like a really long tent with different displays, cages, stalls, and even smaller tents positioned on each side of the interior. Several torches lined a grassy pathway cut through the middle where people walked slowly along, eying each attraction as they passed. There was a sign outside one small purple tent that read, *Tarot Readings.* Courtney pointed toward the sign as she whispered, "That's the Nile Witch tent."

Lacey slid her arm through mine. "Ooo," she cooed as she spied the sign. "The Grey sisters' tent. They're not really witches, you know."

I glanced down at her with an eyebrow raised.

"They're demons," Lacey murmured. "But I was really hoping we could stop at Cassandra's tent first. Would that be all right, Hannah?"

"Cassandra Sawyer?" I asked, bemused.

Lacey pulled me past a tent selling crystals and a stand selling candles, all the way to a small black tent set up beside a tiny paddock which housed two Shetland ponies with horns stuck on their foreheads. On a wooden stake stuck in the ground beside the tent was a sign that read, *Palm Readings, 5 tickets.* A second stake beside the ponies read, *Ask the Wizard Before You Feed the Unicorns.* Huck Sawyer stood off to the side, dressed in deep emerald robes with a tall, pointed hat, complete with a long, fake white beard.

He smiled when he saw us approach.

"Cassie's been waiting for you two." He winked at Lacey as he stroked one of the ponies' muzzles.

Lacey gave Huck a light hug before reaching for the tent

curtain. She stopped before entering. Lacey turned to Peter and glanced at him gravely. "Peter—can you wait outside? This is private..."

Peter opened his mouth to protest but seemed to think better of it and nodded begrudgingly, waving us to go on. Then he turned to Mr. Sawyer with a grin. "Hey, Huck—"

Huck cleared his throat loudly and pulled on his fake beard.

"Sorry, *Wizard*. How much is it to feed the—uhh...unicorns?"

I would've laughed, if I wasn't so uncomfortable. I eyed the black tent warily. "Just you, Lacey. Promise?" I whispered as she pushed back the flap.

"Of course," Lacey murmured. "I only have tickets for me."

The smell of burning incense engulfed us as we ducked into the tent. Inside, it was warm and cozy with the soft glow of a dozen candles. There was a low table and some plush seat cushions piled everywhere. Cassandra sat with a magazine in one hand and a mug of tea in the other. She looked up when we came in and flashed a bright smile. Her dark-red hair was piled up in a pretty mess on top of her head with burgundy tendrils falling every which way. The black snake was nestled safely in a giant aquarium tank and seemed to be sleeping.

"Lacey, Hannah, I'm so glad you found your way here..." Her smile faltered when she looked at me. "Is something wrong?"

I shook my head awkwardly.

She gestured to the cushions. "Please...sit."

Lacey pulled her tickets out of her bag as she dropped lightly onto a cushion. "Just me tonight, Cassandra."

I stayed standing off to the side, rooted to the ground.

Cassandra leaned forward over the low table between them and held out her hands on which Lacey placed hers, face up. Cassandra smoothed her thumb over Lacey's hand and traced a finger over the lines etched in her palm. Then she closed her eyes and inhaled deeply.

"Ask your question."

"What do I need to know to help Hannah?"

My cheeks burned as Lacey quickly bent over the table to stare down at her palm as though the answer might appear there in writing.

Cassandra's eyes were still closed, but I could've sworn I saw a small smile twitch in the corner of her lips.

"Lacey McGregor, strong, brave, and rare," Cassandra murmured almost theatrically, and I remembered, this was a business. She was acting. Needed to sell the customer the experience they wanted. "You are facing a great challenge. But you have the tools you need to help those you love." She closed her hands over Lacey's and kissed them lightly. "And as always, be careful not to lose your way. And don't let anyone make you doubt your ability to save the day."

She even made it rhyme. I folded my lips together to hide my smirk.

Lacey turned to smile encouragingly at me as Cassandra released her hand and opened her eyes. I tried to return Lacey's enthusiasm, but I took little comfort in any of this. It was all pretend.

Cassandra looked at me and waved me over, her rings glittering in the candlelight, her bangles lightly chiming as they clinked together. Reluctantly, I took a seat on a poof beside Lacey. "I won't be of much help to you...if you won't tell me what's wrong."

"I'm fine," I mumbled, increasingly uncomfortable not only by the attention but by the intensity with which she stared.

She held her hands out over the table. "Indulge an old girl?"

I inhaled deeply, nostrils flaring as I held out my hand for her. She closed her eyes as she cradled my hand in hers. Her hands were warm. Her thumb and fingers tickled as they traced over the creases in my palm. I was suddenly overcome with that feeling of familiarity and comfort. Her eyes flew open, and the deep green met my brown. Her hands closed over mine, and she held on in a small squeeze. "It wasn't your fault, Hannah."

"What?" I demanded.

Cassandra gave me a rueful smile. Her eyes were shining with tears. I pulled my hand free from her and stood abruptly from the poof, heading toward the door. "I'll wait for you outside, Lacey."

"Hannah...wait, please." Something in Cassandra's voice stopped me before I could pull back the tent curtain. I looked back at her.

She stood from her seat and made her way over to me. I wanted nothing more than to run, but before I could, she said, "You should go see the Nile Witch...Charlotte Grey...she can help you."

Lacey came up and slipped her arm through mine. "Thank you, Cassandra."

As soon as we exited the tent, Peter hurried over to us, wiping the pony spit onto his jeans. "Are you ready?"

"For?" I asked, still a bit irritated by the psychic ambush.

A sly smile slid onto Peter's face. "House of Horrors. It's your turn to be scared, Hannah Green."

The House of Horrors was some kind of haunted house theater. The line was insanely long. It took us almost an hour to make it through to the end. A man dressed as a werewolf sent us all through the 'house' in groups of two. Rachel and Cole. Courtney and Lacey. Peter and me.

Lacey had tried to stick with me, but Courtney had clung to her when she couldn't wiggle in between Rachel and Cole. We were the last to go through. The man waved us inside the dark entryway, and I couldn't help but press against Peter...just to make sure he was there. A girl dressed as a...murder victim? I couldn't quite tell—her face was bloodied, and she had an ax coming out of her shoulder. She smiled at us as she led us through the dim sitting area.

"Welcome...to the House of Horrors...please try not to scream...it only excites them..."

"Who?" I asked as she headed up the staircase.

She glanced over her shoulder to smile at us as we climbed the stairs, ignoring my question. "And remember—stay close and watch your step..."

As soon as we got up the stairs, we were in a dark, extremely narrow hallway. The floorboards began to bump up and down, with lights and screams emanating from below. Startled, I gasped and snatched Peter's hand. Dragging him with me, I ran down the hallway as the floorboards continued to thunder and flash and scream underneath our feet.

Peter laughed. "You okay?"

I glared at him through the dark. "Yes...I just wasn't expecting the floor to come *alive*—"

As we inched through the dark space, the only light came from tiny blue lamps way up high against the ceiling. The murder victim guide girl was moving at a quick pace, and I hurried after her as we squeezed through the walls.

Someone in a hideous dripping mask popped out from the darkness, inches away from my face. I screamed. Peter jumped.

Footsteps. Loud, pounding footsteps charged at us from behind. I peeked over my shoulder. A huge figure with a *running* chainsaw—it must've been a sound effect—was stomping after us. I scrambled to keep up with the murdered guide girl. Peter whispered in mock fear, "He's gone."

"He is?" I gasped despite myself. The murdered guide girl led us into a room, empty save for a single random couch. I had to squint to see much of anything.

"Please, wait here," she said in a low, ghoulish voice as she seemingly melted into the darkness.

"Okay...what the—?" I blinked at the spot where she'd just stood.

Peter snickered. "There's a hidden exit behind that—yeah, there. That's a curtain."

I narrowed my eyes, trying to see into the black. "How do you know?"

Peter shrugged. "I volunteer every year. Usually I'm just a ghost, but last year I was promoted to tour guide."

I smiled, relaxing a bit as I reminded myself it was all pretend. "So, what's next? Something pops out through that door?"

Peter frowned thoughtfully. "I think that girl from the TV is supposed to—"

Right on cue, a little girl with long, black hair hiding her face appeared in the doorway. She made strange twitching movements. My breath caught in my chest at the sight of her. It was all too familiar.

Before she could get too close, a guy burst through a side door. "Quick, hurry!"

Peter grinned and took my hand, pulling me through the door. I tried to smile, too. It was pretty elaborate. But then the guy shoved Peter to one side and me to another, pushing us through separate doors. "Quick, you'll find him on the other side!"

The door slammed behind me, and I blinked into the dark. It seemed like there were shadows all around the room. Then a light flashed on.

My heart stopped.

It was a mirror maze.

A DARK REFLECTION

I couldn't move.

The mirrors were black, framed in an eerie neon-purple glow, stretching out before me for who knows how long.

I tried to steady my breathing, to calm my frantic heart, to stop the stream of thoughts fogging up my brain.

To stop thinking of black eyes and a crazed, pinned-back grin.

"Peter!"

I tried to work the door handle at my back, tried to go back the way I'd come. I was sure if I screamed for help, they'd let me out. Wouldn't they? But was I really so far gone that I couldn't make it through a carnival ride?

"Peter!"

I heard him, muffled somewhere to my left. It sounded like: "Stay there."

Did he realize how terrified I was? What did that say about me, that I fell apart at the sight of a mirror? No. This was not going to be my story. I would not be just another Nile girl who was driven insane by a mirror.

I didn't need to wait for Peter to save me.

I could do this.

Something flickered in the mirror to my left. It couldn't be Peter already. I tried to think of what I knew about angles. Geometry annoyed me. Algebra was my friend. I took a step forward. The mirrors seemed to ripple.

I held out my hands and moved. I found my way left and around a corner but kept bumping into myself. Sometimes I would be so sure and then narrowly miss smashing my face into the glass.

I turned left and saw a dark figure huddled on the floor against the mirror. I braced myself for a scare. As I approached, the actor seemed to be crying. I paused as I drew closer, trying to decide if it was an actor or an actual scared little girl.

I placed a hand on her shoulder. "Hey—are you lost?"

The girl didn't look up. Instead, she nodded into her knees. "They dared me to come in here. And then they left."

I exhaled a shaky breath. "Who?"

"My friends."

My heart dipped to my stomach at the thought. Then I put a hand on her shoulder. "Well, it sounds to me like your friends are broken. You're going to need to get some new ones. But in the meantime, I'm lost, too...do you think you could help me get out of here?"

She peeked up at me then. In the purple light, her skin looked ashen and gray. "All right."

I gave her a smile and took her hand, pulling her to her feet. My eyes met the mirror above her head, and I saw it...the face of the girl who wasn't me.

I turned away quickly only to see it again.

And again.

And again.

In every mirror, all around me—the pinned-up smile, the rows of needle teeth, and the black eyes.

I felt the little girl squeeze my hand. "I don't like that face."

I stared down at her, eyes wide. She could see her. She *was* seeing her. It wasn't all in my head. I wasn't hallucinating. I hesitated, barely able to breath. "Yeah. Try not to look at her. I think it's this way," I whispered and took a step toward the sneering face.

My breath fogged up the glass.

A finger slid squeaking down the mirror.

YOU'RE NEXT

I backed up, breathing slowly. I glanced at the little girl. She smiled up at me. I looked back at the words. Could she see them?

I took a sidestep, and we walked down a different path. The face was everywhere. Black eyes watching. Smile hungry.

It wasn't all in my head.

I tried right.

Almost bumped the mirror.

It let out a low, chittering growl. I heard it. I was sure of it.

My eyes blurred with hot tears. Then I remembered. I remembered the closet. I remembered Rebecca. I looked down at the girl. At least I could keep *her* safe.

"Why don't you go on ahead?" My voice was barely audible. I cleared my throat and tried again. "Go on. It's not much farther... my friend Peter is waiting on the other side. He'll help you. He looks kinda like Prince Charming."

The little girl hesitated and then let go of my hand.

She disappeared off to the left.

My breathing was slow and shallow. I wouldn't believe it.

There was no such thing as ghosts...

Or curses...

Or monsters...

None of this was real. But deep in the back of my mind...I remembered.

And I knew it was.

I tried to turn left.

My nose touched the glass.

The black eyes glittered.

Hands with nails like knives smashed through the mirror dragging me toward the glass. I screamed and thrashed against the mirror. Nails ripped through Peter's hoodie, tore away ribbons of my skin. My hands forced it back by its cold, clammy throat, keeping it away from my face as it gnashed its teeth and hissed, "YOU'RE NEXT!"

Then its jaw unhinged, and its teeth clamped down on my face. Pain and teeth tore through me, blood gushed hot and wet, and everything went dark.

"Hannah! HANNAH!"

Hands at my armpits hoisted me up into a lap. Peter. I felt his soft hands pat my face. I gasped sharply and hugged my arms and touched my face. Nothing. No blood. No bite marks. No shredded skin. I blinked my eyes open. The lights were on in the maze. No more purple glow illuminating the mirrors.

"Drink this." Peter held his water bottle up to my lips. I sipped and stared around. The fluorescent lights illuminated all the behind-the-scenes equipment, ruining the haunted house effect. Had he stopped the whole ride for me?

"Are you okay to stand?"

I nodded shakily and allowed him to pull me to my feet. A vampire and ghoul stood awkwardly off in the corner, eying me wearily.

"What happened?" I mumbled lamely.

I knew what had happened.

"You fainted. I found you lying on the floor..."

"Did the little girl find her way out?"

"The little girl—Maddie's sister? Yeah, she's fine. Hannah...I'm so sorry." Peter was white, and his blue eyes were too wide like he had slipped into shock at the sight of me.

"It's fine." I massaged my temple. "I—I'm sorry. Let's just get out of here..."

"Exit's that way." The vampire jutted a finger toward a side door.

We left quickly, tossing muttered apologies and 'thank you's over our shoulders.

The door opened up into the night, and we took a fire escape down to the ground. We ended up behind the building in a small grassy space between the House of Horrors and a patch of trees. There was a dumpster and a lamp casting a sick waning light over us.

I stood there for a moment, holding on to the railing.

Peter placed a hand on my shoulder and looked up into my eyes. "You need a minute? I'm sorry—the mirror maze is new. I had no idea that..."

My head hurt. Everything I'd held onto, every belief I had had was exposed as a fallacy. What had just happened could not be explained by anything other than...and on top of that—*I remembered*. I remembered what had happened to my sister. But it couldn't be real. It couldn't.

"What happened to Desiree Lapierre?" I said finally. "Tell me *exactly* what happened."

"Uhh—I only know what Courtney told me." Peter took a deep breath and ran a hand through his hair. "She pulled the sheet off Ms. Barbara's mirror, and it broke."

"It *broke*?" I demanded.

Peter nodded. "She hid the empty frame underneath the sheet. Then she started to see this—this face...she said it was a girl, at first. But then it changed. She had a mouth like an alligator. Desiree saw it wherever she went. She saw it in the girls' dorm at our school. It started leaving her messages in the glass. Trying to tell her things. That it was coming for her...things like that."

"Why was she committed?"

Peter looked up at the lamp above us, squinting into the light. "The teachers found her sprawled on the grass beneath a broken window outside our dorm house. She says she didn't jump. She says the thing pulled her through the window. But no one believed her. Except for Father LaValley, the principal. He tried to convince her parents to let him counsel her instead. But I guess he got outvoted."

"Did you believe her?" I breathed.

Peter looked at me, his eyes hard. "Yes."

I took deep, meditative breaths, calming myself as best I could. I swallowed thickly, struggling to find the words. "I think I need help."

"Okay, so what can I do?" Peter asked calmly.

"I need to visit Desiree Lapierre."

BACK TO THE LIBRARY

"Desiree Lapierre?" Peter repeated incredulously.

"But first I need to work on my research project," I muttered to myself as I headed around the back alley of the House of Horrors and instantly met with the noise and lights of the fair.

"Wait, Hannah, where are you going?" Peter called after me as I pushed through the crowd.

"Hannah?" Lacey said from somewhere behind me.

"I need to see Elijah..." I shouted back.

Peter could barely keep up. "Elijah? Even after he—"

I didn't bother to answer, only rushed forward, past the carnival stalls and games with bright lights and stuffed prizes, toward the big warehouse where we'd left Elijah with his invention.

The place had all but emptied and the inventors seemed to be packing up for the night. Elijah, his back to me, hammered away at something on his machine. I wasn't going to bring it up...but as soon as I saw him, I changed my mind. If I was going to ask for his help, I needed to make sure he wasn't a jerk. I pulled the envelope out of my bag and marched over to him. I slapped it down on the table beside him. He shouted in surprise, missed the machine, and smashed his finger with the hammer.

"Son of a mother!" He hissed through gritted teeth and shook his thumb furiously. He winced in pain as he looked at me curiously. "What's the—is that Peter's hoodie?"

"Why did you give Damien Barrow an article about my father?" I demanded.

"Your father?" Elijah straightened his glasses on his nose. His eyes widened as he reached for the envelope. "What, this? It's not—"

"Oh, don't you tell me it's not what I think, Elijah Grunvald!" I snatched the envelope back and slapped it hard into his chest. "My mom told me your dad owns the freaking paper! I'm sure it was easy for you to find!" I hit him with the envelope.

"Oi! No, Hannah, listen—"

I punctuated each word with another smack of the envelope. "Do—you—realize—what I've been going through—since I moved into that—place?!" I continued to beat him with the envelope as he tried to fend off my blows with muffled yelps of protest and paper cuts. "And here you are *researching* my family, gossiping about it behind my back like I'm some kind of—some kind of *true crime case*?"

Elijah finally managed to get a hold of each of my wrists and held them down to my sides, preventing me from pummeling him anymore. I glared at him, my nostrils flaring as I fought against him. For someone so tall and gangly, he was surprisingly strong. Must be all the work on the docks. What did they *do* on the docks, anyways?

He looked deep into my eyes, his nose only inches from mine. I blinked a bit as I couldn't help but appreciate the golden swirl in his brown eyes. My breath fogged up his glasses.

"If you'd let me *finish*—" He panted a little as he recovered from our scuffle. "I was going to say: It's not mine."

I rolled my eyes and wrestled my wrists out of his grasp. "Damien gave it to me. Said you were best friends."

He shook his head. "Well, we aren't. The opposite in fact. And I didn't give him that or tell him anything. That's a computer printout. He could've easily done it at school. And why *would* I do something like that? To hurt you? You're my friend, Hannah."

I sighed, my shoulders deflating in defeat. Of course, he wouldn't. I shoved the envelope back into my bag and slung it over my shoulder. I checked my watch. It wasn't too late.

Peter came up behind me, followed by Lacey. "Did we miss something?" he asked, eying my flushed face and Elijah who was sucking on his hammered thumb. I backed up a bit, realizing how close I was to him.

"Elijah's taking me to the library."

"Err—I am? Uhh, okay, sure?" Elijah looked from me to Peter and blushed burgundy.

"I've got a paper to work on."

Elijah's truck wasn't big enough for all of us. Lacey seemed a bit disappointed when I told her to go ahead without me.

"But I can help. I'm excellent at research," she added brightly.

I glanced at Peter.

He stepped forward with a charming smile. "You know, Lace, Courtney will be pretty bummed if we all left without her. Why don't you ride with her and meet us at the library later? We'll probably still be there, right, Hannah?"

I nodded. "Definitely. It'll take a while without you there to help." But in all honesty, I felt the opposite. With Lacey helping, we'd probably be sidetracked by a hundred different things. I needed to focus, not fantasize about treegulls.

I could've sworn Lacey's hazel eyes shimmered a bit underneath the bright warehouse lights, but she smiled easily and hopped off to find Courtney. Peter called ahead to give Court the new plan, shouting after Lacey that Courtney was at the scrambler, and then Peter and Elijah loaded his machine back onto the truck and hopped in the cab, sandwiching me between them.

For some reason, the ride back to the island felt stiff and awkward. Peter was quiet, but in a surly, sour kind of way. My stomach hurt a bit, and I suspected it had to do with blowing off Lacey. And Elijah didn't say much, but when he did, he stumbled over himself more than usual. I myself preferred a quiet car ride, but this was just uncomfortable.

I cleared my throat. "You guys don't need to come in with me…I can handle it myself. If you just drop me off, Courtney can pick me up and take me home." Underneath my bag, I crossed my fingers. Please leave me alone.

Elijah shrugged. "Whatever you—"

"I'm not leaving you alone," Peter said firmly.

I groaned inwardly.

Elijah glanced sideways at Peter and then at me. "Err— Did something else happen tonight that I don't know about?"

Peter shook his head. "Nah."

I raised an eyebrow at him and frowned at his lie. "If you guys are going to help me deal with this—everyone needs to be on the same page."

Peter looked properly apologetic, and I cleared my throat, keeping my voice as nonchalant as possible. "Something attacked me in the mirror maze."

Elijah's hand slipped on the wheel as he turned to stare at me in alarm. "*Attacked* you? Some*thing*?" The car swerved a bit as he corrected his course.

I nodded, my face grim. "That's why we are heading to the library. I noticed a local historical section stuffed in all that mess earlier today, and I think it'll help me figure this out."

"How so?" Elijah adjusted his glasses and eyed me intently as he pulled the truck into the dock.

"You can't understand something if you don't know how it started."

The little library seemed even smaller in the dark. Pushed up against the woods, it looked like a tiny brick house out of a dark fairy tale. The big streetlamp illuminated the gravel driveway in an obnoxious kind of way that made me feel exposed and yet shadowed the library in darkness. The light, coming from the two windows flanking the front door, was almost completely blocked by stacks of books, and as we walked up the inclining path toward the door, I wondered how on Earth we would find room for the three of us to fit, let alone space to sit and read through the books. And once again, I'd wished they would've just left me alone.

Peter held the door open, the bell clanging loudly announcing our arrival, and the three of us all filed inside one by one.

The first thing I noticed was that the stench of the place had considerably improved, replaced by a fresh, flowery smell. I led the boys inside a handful of feet and around toward the librarian's desk. I was pleasantly surprised to see that instead of the overgrown sloth-woman, a girl about our age sat at the desk, her long, dark hair framing her oval face. Her full lips frowned slightly as she studied from a textbook propped up on the stack of books piled all over the desk. She was stroking a dove on her shoulder, which looked up, inclining its head at us as we approached.

The girl didn't notice. She was so engrossed in her reading that she was absentmindedly mouthing the words to herself.

The dove nuzzled her neck and gave her a little nip. She looked up, startled, shutting the book quickly and covering the title with her hands. "Hi; sorry. Can I help you? Oh, hi, Peter." She smiled shyly at us.

Peter squeezed between me and a bookshelf. "Hey, Maddie. We're doing a research paper on the old Rosecrest place. Do you have any books on that?"

Maddie discreetly tucked her book underneath the desk, but not before I peeked at the title: *Advanced Magic: The Psychology of Misdirection & Illusion*. She went to the card catalog and pulled out a tiny drawer and thumbed through the index cards.

She pulled out a few cards and handed them to Peter who passed them to me. "Honestly, I don't think you'll have much luck...finding them, I mean. Mrs. Molley doesn't really keep things orderly." She blushed prettily, clearly embarrassed by the mess. She hugged herself and shrugged, looking around. "I try, but I only work a few evenings a week...by the time I get back, it's all mixed up again."

I studied the cards, noting most of the titles were the same ones I had seen earlier that day, and as Maddie had warned us, they were nowhere near the section listed on their call numbers. I just hoped they were still stuck in the astronomy section and not lost somewhere else. I ducked through a few shelves. And there they were, nestled neatly in between the constellations and planets. I passed Peter *A History of Nile* and thumped *Important Figures of Nile* into Elijah's chest, keeping *Nile, The Beginning* and *The Most Haunted Town in America* for myself.

I dropped to the floor, crisscrossed my legs, and pored over the pages. The boys cracked open their books, each of them apparently too good for the floor: Peter leaned against a nearby shelf, and Elijah sat on a stool, his long legs sticking up awkwardly.

"What are we looking for exactly?" Peter asked dubiously after a few minutes.

"Anything about the house or that mirror," I muttered as I skimmed an index.

After a half hour had passed, and I'd made it through both books with no luck, I checked the index cards again and realized a book was missing. I stood quickly, the pile of books on my lap dropping to the floor, and I hurried to the proper section, praying it would be there. But of course, it wasn't.

I spent the next half hour scanning the shelves and overflowing piles for the book's call number with no luck. I went to the librarian's desk, and Maddie looked up from a Marvel comic book with a polite smile. "Need help?"

"Yes, uhm—this book? I wasn't sure if you'd seen it—"

Maddie took the card. "Oh, I'm sorry. I didn't notice before. See the black sticker at the bottom? That means it's missing."

"Missing?" I repeated. "Like, it hasn't been returned?"

Maddie shook her head. "Like, *literally* missing." She waved a hand at the place. "As you might imagine, we've a lot of books whose cards have black stickers." She pulled a pen from the cup holder and fished around for a piece of paper, finally settling on a green envelope from a nearby stack. "But I can make a note to let you know if it turns up, if you like?"

"Actually, can I just take down the book information? I'd rather try to find another copy online or something..."

"Sure." Maddie smiled and passed me back the card, handing me the pen and envelope.

"You know—if you're interested in Nile lore...you should stop by the historical society. I think it's closed on the weekends, but—"

"There's a historical society?" I quickly scribbled down the title and the author.

Maddie smiled. "Of course! We islanders *love* our legends. Rosalind Grunberg is the historian. Oh, and if it's legends you're after—we also have a book of local fairy tales by Cecily Blackwell..." She lifted up in her seat and tried to peek around the shelves. "I know I just saw it the other day—huh, well, anyway, those are rather dark, though, if you ask me. I can't even sleep after reading some of those..."

I stared down at the author name I'd copied: Rosalind Grunberg.

I passed back the pen and pad just as the bell clanged against the door. I craned my neck to see who'd arrived, expecting to see Lacey and Courtney.

"Jeez, a lot of people are studying tonight." Maddie smiled incredulously. "I never get this many people at once—"

My face fell. Portia, her pig nose squished firmly on her face, worked her way through the shelves. Maddie's dove left her shoulder in a flapping flurry of white and perched on a high shelf in the far corner of the library.

"Oh, hey, Portia." Maddie gave her a curious smile. "How was the fair?"

"Fine," Portia drawled in a dull, bored tone. "Mom forgot her purse again." Portia elbowed me out of the way and went around behind the librarian's desk, grabbing a lumpy, peeling pleather bag from under the table. She snorted. "Still practicing your little card tricks, I see...I thought you'd grown out of that stuff, Maddison."

Maddie's face burned a bright red. She opened her mouth but shut it again, tucking her dark hair behind her ears. Maddie stood from the chair, sliding it toward Portia. She scooped up her magic book, along with her comic book, and shoved them both into her Spiderman backpack. Then she slung the bag over her shoulders which hunched forward as though she longed to disappear.

Portia chuckled as she tossed her mom's purse onto the desk, knocking office supplies and spilling papers. "You can go home. Mom said I can close up."

Maddie checked her phone. "Uhh, Portia, it's only 10:30... My mom won't be here until eleven, at least—"

"Well, you better get walking then." Portia laughed loudly through her piggy nose, taking Maddie's seat and swiveling it toward the computer to turn it on.

"It's like three miles..." Maddie hesitated. "I don't mind standing, Portia. I can work on the shelves..."

Portia didn't bother to tear her eyes from the screen. "Trust me, Maddison, you don't want to be stuck here at night with Hannah Green...plus, you know I hate that stupid dove."

Maddie glanced at me and back at Portia, who gave a dismissive shoo of her hand without looking up.

"Err...okay."

With a small wave to me, Maddie made to leave, but I stopped her. "Elijah can bring you home."

"Uhh, I don't really know him that well—" Maddie whispered.

"With Peter?"

Maddie bit her lip, clearly thinking it over. "I would hate to be—"

I smiled. "It's no trouble. Really. We're just waiting for his sister to show up, anyway."

Maddie returned my smile with a shy one of her own, and I called the boys over, who were more than happy to drive her home, especially if it meant putting down the dry, old history books.

As the three of them left with Maddie's dove nestled safely in her carrying cage, I felt Portia's eyes on me, and I turned to face her.

"Well, look at you; Hannah Green, Queen of the Nile," she mocked. "You've really come into your own around here, haven't you?"

I didn't answer. My head grew foggy, and my eyes fell, resting on the stack of green envelopes piled on the desk between us. And then to the printer tucked beneath the librarian's desk.

My eyes slowly found hers.

Her smirk wavered slightly under my gaze. "That won't last once everyone finds out you're cursed. Is that what you're doing here? A little ghost research before you snuff it? Before you get chucked into a looney bin like Desiree Lapierre...or your daddy?" Portia licked her teeth and snorted.

I gave her a cool smile. "Did that make you feel better about yourself? Forcing Maddie outside in the middle of the night? And making jokes about my dad?"

Portia's smile faded.

I reached into my bag, pulled out the green envelope

concealing the news article and slapped it back onto the pile from where it came. "At least this time you're saying it to my face."

Portia's pale eyes narrowed. "I don't know what you're talking about..."

"You know, I've been in *extensive* therapy since my sister was kidnapped and my dad had his psychotic break...and one thing I've learned is that one of the main reasons that kids bully others is because they are starved for attention."

Portia bristled, her squished nose pointed high in the air.

"I can see why with a mother like yours." I nodded, shrugging sympathetically. "Plus, it's pretty obvious that you have a huge crush on Peter, and well, let's face it, he's not really giving you any attention at all, is he?"

Portia's pink face flushed.

I pulled on the pocket of the hoodie, stretching it out so she could see. "I mean—it's not like he gave *you* his hoodie to wear."

Portia's beady eyes narrowed. "Get out. Get out now," she grunted through her gritted teeth.

"And that Damien guy—isn't he dating that sweet Aubrey girl? Although, from what I've heard...he's not much of a catch...a creep, really, but I suppose you're so desperate for attention you'll take it from anybody, huh?"

Portia's face went from red to purple as the bell on the door clanged.

Lacey appeared around the overstuffed shelves. "Hannah? Courtney's waiting in the car... It really is a mess in here, isn't it?" she mused as she came up beside me. She looked at Portia curiously. "How do you ever find anything?"

Portia stood slowly from her seat and pointed a pudgy finger at me and then at Lacey, "I want you and Spacey out of here, or I'm going to call my mom and tell her you're trespassing."

"If she answers, right?" I quipped with a sympathetic tilt of my head. "She probably doesn't pick up your call very often, huh?"

Lacey furrowed her brow. "Can a person trespass in a public library?"

I smiled and wrapped an arm around Lacey. "Let's go, Lace."

Just before I shut the door, Portia shouted, "You better watch your back, Hannah, or I'll get you before the curse does!"

But she wouldn't.

I won.

And we both knew it.

MAPLE LEAF HOUSE

The library being a bust, the only thing I had left was Desiree Lapierre. Visiting hours were the next morning. At my request, Peter left Courtney out of it. The last thing I wanted was for her to feel responsible all over again. She'd spent enough time feeling guilty. I wasn't about to add to that. I didn't tell Lacey about it, either. I wanted to do this on my own. I didn't even want Peter with me, but he was the only way I'd be able to get in. I doubted Desiree would accept a visit from some girl she didn't know.

We left early. The trip to the Maple Leaf House was a slow and tedious trek through the mountains. It took us almost an hour before we pulled up into the parking lot of the facility. I got out of the car and stared at the building for a moment, imagining what it must feel like to be locked away in a place like this.

It was what they probably called 'state of the art', which was code for architecturally hip and modern. It had solar panels, cherry-red brick walls, weird slopes and angles, and lots of windows and skylights (several inches thick, of course.) There was a strange Zen garden set in the middle of the walkway and lots of giant random rocks everywhere. It all screamed 'tranquility.' But I could see beneath the surface. It was a prison dressed up like a day spa.

Peter forced a smile. Could he see it, too?

Once we made it inside, Peter was able to convince the receptionist nurse to let us see Desiree. An orderly brought us to the courtyard, which was flanked by the U bend of the building. There was a basketball court and lots of pretty sapling trees, newly planted and scattered around a small number of picnic tables. It was all very serene and pleasant. But there was a wall. A wall disguised as more modern design with pretty wood paneling and invisible fencing that revealed the brilliant forest-blanketed mountains beyond. But if you looked close enough, you noticed the wood stopped at eye level, preventing anyone from climbing the chain-link fence, and if you looked *really* hard, you could see the barbed wire at the top.

Peter and I took a seat. We didn't speak as we waited for them to bring Desiree out to us. When I saw her, I inhaled sharply. I glanced at Peter, who didn't seem to notice the fact that we looked remarkably similar. Desiree was tall with chestnut hair that framed her face in straight sheets and big brown eyes. Exactly like me.

As she drew nearer, I noticed she held a book to her chest.

Desiree smiled when she saw Peter, but her smile slipped slightly when she saw me. Taking a seat opposite us, still hugging her book, she reached for Peter's hand. "Courtney didn't come?"

"She's babysitting for the Kennedys."

"I miss her." Desiree's voice was barely above a whisper.

"She misses you, too." Peter squeezed her hand as he flashed her his most handsome smile, which, like the sun, warmed her face. He tilted his head toward me. "Desiree, I wanted you to meet a friend of mine...this is..."

"Hannah." Desiree let go of Peter's hand. "It's Hannah." She glanced in my direction but didn't meet my eyes. A tear slid down her cheek.

I looked at Peter, who stared at Desiree, his mouth slightly agape.

"That's right, Desiree," I said gently.

She ignored me and turned her head slightly toward the building. "Do you know how many windows are in this place?" she asked Peter softly. "So much glass."

"Desiree..."

She ignored me and asked Peter pointedly, "Remember when we snuck into the attic? If I'd only known. That's where it all began... You kissed me in that attic, remember?"

Peter shifted awkwardly in his seat. "Uhh, Des, I don't remember an attic—"

I tried to be patient.

I tried to sound kind.

But I didn't have time for this.

I cut him off, my eyes on Desiree. "I need to ask you about the mirror."

Desiree scowled. She glared down at the table between us. "I don't want to talk about that."

I took a deep breath. "I need your help, Desiree."

Desiree shook her head as she hugged the book tighter to her chest. "I said: *I don't want to talk about that*," she hissed through her teeth. Spit hit the table and dribbled down her chin.

"Please...I need to know—"

Desiree lifted her eyes slowly to meet mine. "You're next."

Peter glanced at me.

A shiver of fear drained the blood from my face. "What does that mean?"

Desiree's brown eyes glittered maliciously. "You're next."

"Tell me how to make it stop!"

Drawn by my shout, the orderlies, who'd been busy on their phones, looked up.

Desiree shook her head with a mocking pout, unable to hide her smirk. She licked her teeth. "You're next."

My temper rose with my fear, and I slapped my hand on the table. "Stop saying that!"

The orderlies began to make their way over to us.

She flicked her tongue like a snake. "*You're nexxxxt.*"

They pulled Desiree to her feet. She laughed, her brown hair falling into her face as they held her fast.

"You're next. You're next. YOU'RE NEXT!" Desiree flung her book at my face as they tugged her back. Peter tried to block it, but I caught it before it hit my nose.

Peter, his face pained, watched her kick and thrash as they dragged her back inside, but my eyes were on the book.

It was *A Haunting of Nile*. The missing book from the library. And scratched on the cover with a sharpie was a pair of black eyes along with a hungry, pinned-back smile.

The whole drive home, we didn't speak. I was quiet, processing everything. Things still didn't make much sense. I'd only made it halfway through the book by the time we got to the ferry and made it across the lake.

I could feel Peter's eyes on me as I flipped through the book. Every few minutes he would glance at me. It was distracting at best...annoying at worst.

"Hey—does that say Rosalind Grunberg?"

I shook my head as his question pulled me from the pages. "What?"

Peter nodded his head at the book. "The author."

I shut the book to stare at the cover. Through the sharpie marring the front, I could just make out the author. "Rosalind Grunberg. Oh, right. Maddie said she's the local historian."

Peter gave me a funny look. "Right, but she's also Elijah's grandma. I didn't realize she was an author, too."

I frowned as I turned back to the pages. How could Elijah have neglected to mention that?

Peter cleared his throat as he pulled onto Apple Shore Road. "You know, Hannah, what Desiree said back there, about kissing in the attic?"

I stared pointedly out the window, my eyes slightly wide with panic. "Oh, we don't have to talk—"

"That wasn't me—"

I forced a light laugh. "That's okay, Peter, I really don't—"

"I don't know why she would say that. She must have confused me with Elijah or something."

I snorted. "Why would she think she kissed *Elijah* in the attic?"

"Well, they went out a few times before she...you know..."

The awkwardness drained from me, replaced with inexplicable annoyance. Yet another detail Elijah had kept to himself. "Why wouldn't he have told me that?"

Peter shrugged as he turned left and drove up the long Rosecrest driveway.

The parking lot was empty except for Elijah's old pickup truck. Mom must've taken another shift.

"I feel weird about leaving you here alone," Peter said uneasily as he put the car in park. The Rosecrest House loomed above us. "Why don't you stay at my place until we figure out what to do next."

"No," I said softly, staring up at the windows of the house. "It's not the house that's the problem."

"The mirror?"

"Maybe." I nibbled thoughtfully on my lower lip. "I don't know yet."

"You know, Hannah..." Peter ran a hand through his golden hair. "I was thinking about what Lacey said...about what Cassandra told her...and I think you *should* go to the Nile Witch."

I sighed inwardly.

"I would go with you, of course." He furrowed his brow as he glanced at me apprehensively.

I shook my head. "I'll see you later, okay?"

Peter frowned, nodding begrudgingly. "I still don't like the idea of leaving you alone…"

"I'll be fine, Peter." I forced a smile.

Peter raised a dubious eyebrow. "You can't still believe it's all just a ghost story…"

My smile slipped. "I don't know what I believe anymore."

"Hannah—"

"I'll call you later, okay?" I insisted, my impatience giving my voice an unintentional edge.

"Sure."

I thanked him for the ride, and he drove away.

But just as Peter's car disappeared from view, another car came down the driveway heading toward Rosecrest. I paused, studying the vehicle. I didn't recognize it.

The car pulled up and parked beside me. An older woman, about Ms. Barbara's age, threw open the door and got out. She had on large sunglasses. Her gray hair was pulled up in a top knot. A designer purse hung off her wrist as she pressed her key fob, locking her doors with a sharp chirp. She pulled her glasses down to get a better look at me.

"Is Barbara in the garden out back? Or is she in her apartment?" the woman asked, her voice as sharp as the crease in her pants.

I regarded her coolly. "Who are you?"

The woman put a finely manicured hand on her hip. "I'm her sister, Sandra. And I'd like you to tell me where she is."

I raised an eyebrow. This woman was as unlike Ms. Barbara as I could've imagined. Ms. Barbara was eclectic and romantic as old Hollywood; this woman was as uptight and frigid as old Ivy League. My temper flared. I was potentially cursed…at the very least, dealing with—something dangerous…and this woman with her high society snobbery had hit my last nerve. I snapped. "Well,

I'd like *you* to tell me why you're trying to force her into a retirement home. She loves this place and—"

The woman smirked. "*That's* what she told you, is it?"

The front door opened, and Ms. Barbara came out onto the porch, carpet bag in hand and a large feather hat atop her thick silver braids. Her dress was willowy and light. She studied the two of us as she paused for a moment in the doorway.

"You're late, Sandra," Ms. Barbara said with a polite smile as she slowly descended the stairs and made her way to the car. She looked at me kindly. "Don't wait up, Hannah, dear. I won't be back until well after dark..."

The sister scoffed and clicked the key fob unlocking the doors, and the two of them got in the car and drove away.

As soon as they were out of sight, I slung my backpack over one shoulder and climbed the fire escape to Elijah's apartment with the book—his *grandmother's* book—tucked under my arm. This was part of the puzzle that needed filling.

I didn't bother knocking or ringing the giant bell. The stutters and whirrs of his machines drowned out the sound of the door as it shut. Elijah didn't notice me. He was completely engrossed in the pages of a giant book propped up on his workstation. He spooned dripping mouthfuls of cereal into his mouth as he mumbled the words as he read. Normally, I would've been amused, even endeared, but not now. Now, I was just plain annoyed.

I leaned over his shoulder and hissed in his ear, "*Why didn't you tell me about your grandmother?*"

Elijah flinched and choked on his cereal. I thumped him hard on the back. It took a few minutes for him to clear his airway, and I took a small bit of satisfaction at the sight of his flushed, gasping face.

He stood up and grabbed a towel to mop up his milky mess. "Jeez, Hannah...what—"

"I'll tell you what my problem is, Elijah Grunvald!" I smacked him with the book, completely losing my temper. "I told you what happened to me last night! You know how badly I wanted to figure this out! And here you are, hiding the fact that your *grandmother*—"

Elijah winced and ran a hand through his hair.

I tossed the book on the table and jabbed a finger into his chest to punctuate my point. "Yes, your *grandmother* might have vital information that could help get me out of this mess! That she literally wrote the book on this place! How could you keep that from me?"

Elijah put his hands on my arms and squeezed me gently as though he were trying to calm me with a pressure technique. "I'm sorry, Hannah. I should've mentioned it when we first started digging through the library...but my family and I—we kind of had a falling out, and I try not to think about them, definitely don't like to mention them. It's why I moved out. Moved here."

I rolled my eyes and blew my hair out of my face.

"Yes, my grandmother is the Nile historian." Elijah tilted his head, forcing me to meet his eyes. "But believe me, I didn't realize she was some kind of expert on this house—"

"Oh. Just on the town, then?" I asked, my voice sharp with sarcasm.

"Or that she wrote—you said she wrote a book on the house? Specifically?" He pushed his glasses up the bridge of his nose and blinked curiously at the table where the book sat splayed open on its pages.

"Yes. She did. And you're going to take me to her so I can get help from a sane, rational historian."

Elijah scoffed. "'Sane' might be a stretch."

"You're taking me to her, Elijah," I snapped. Then after a moment, I added softly, "Please?"

Elijah's olive skin twinged green as he stared at me. I swore I saw him gulp.

"Whatever you need, Hannah."

THE HISTORIAN

There were a lot of small private islands surrounding Nile. They dotted all over the lake between Vermont and New York, and Rosalind Grunberg lived on one of them.

"We could take my boat..." Elijah started rooting around the mess of his room for his jacket. "But it's supposed to storm...and I don't see how she could possibly help, especially if you already read the book—"

I stared at him.

He pulled on his coat without bothering to zip it, adjusted his glasses, and rubbed his neck with a grimace. "Okay, so maybe she could...*possibly*, but—"

My jaw set, and my eyes narrowed. "I know you've got some kind of family feud going on, but please, Elijah..." I put a hand on his arm. "Peter wants me to go to the Nile Witch."

Elijah ran a hand through his dark curls, apparently thinking it over.

I shook my head. "I realize I'm dealing with something that is beyond anything I ever wanted to understand, but I want to deal with it in a way that makes the most sense to *me*. And finding the author of this book...that makes sense."

Elijah looked hard into my eyes. "We'll take my boat."

When we got to the pier, it was cold and gloomy. The afternoon sun had vanished, replaced by a thick haze of cloud. The brilliant red and orange trees lining the shore were dark and slick with the damp air, and the heavy feeling of imminent rain blew in the wind. The lake was gray, churning aggressively as it knocked against the docks, threatening to spill over the sides. The boats in the harbor lurched back and forth.

Then I saw her.

My heart sank, and Elijah muttered under his breath. Lacey, dressed in a neon-pink raincoat and orange leggings, was sitting on the dock with her legs dangling over the sides. Her platinum hair was braided inexpertly beneath her cowboy hat as though she'd tried to French braid it by herself. She had the bag Cassandra had given her slung diagonally across her chest, a bucket full of live fish beside her, and a net in her hand.

Mermaids.

Elijah and I exchanged uneasy glances as we approached her. We'd both forgotten all about Lacey.

"Are you ready to spot some mermaids?" Lacey asked brightly as she got to her feet. "And I thought we could discuss our plan for saving Hannah along the way."

Elijah winced. "Lacey, I'm sorry...we forgot about the—the mermaid spotting."

"We're going to his grandmother's first."

Lacey looked curiously at Elijah, who hurried to hop into his boat.

She looked back at me. "Why are you making him do that?"

Taken aback, I hesitated.

"I'll be fine, Lace." Elijah dug in the belly of the boat for the lifejackets. "Why don't you see if Peter can take you out today?"

Elijah waved me over and held out his hand.

I eyed the boat warily. It was more like a metal rowboat with a motor strapped to the back than anything else. I found it hard to imagine the dinky little tin can would even make it to one of the islands, let alone hold the two of us without sinking.

"Peter isn't allowed to sail in the rain..." Lacey inclined her head as she watched Elijah help me into the boat. "And Cassandra said I have the tools you need." She lightly patted the beaded bag at her side as she watched me find my footing and pull on my lifejacket.

Her brow furrowed in confusion. "You don't want me to come?"

I chewed on the inside of my cheek. No, I didn't want her to come. I needed facts. I needed to focus, and Lacey was...well, she could be a distraction. I forced a smile and a lazy shrug. "You can come if you want—but I thought you wanted to catch mermaids?"

Lacey's face fell. Her whole body seemed to cave inward, and she looked even smaller than usual. She opened her mouth and then closed it. The hurt shined in her eyes.

I realized my mistake too late. "Of course, I want you to come with us—"

Lacey cut me off quickly. "You don't catch mermaids, Hannah. That would be cruel."

She picked up her bucket and ran back to the shore, sloshing water and ignoring my shouts to return.

"Great," I mumbled. Hurting Lacey's feelings felt the same as shouting at a puppy: absolutely cruel.

Elijah wrapped an arm around me in a sideways hug and squeezed. "She'll be okay."

I sank into my seat. I wasn't so sure. But all I could do was stare after Lacey as she trudged up the hill and disappeared down the road.

The boat rocked and knocked sharply against the side of the dock as Elijah untied it.

"Hold on—it's going to get a bit bumpy..."

. . .

Bumpy. Right. The whole way around the island, the boat, nose in the air, slammed into wave after wave, bouncing and banging along. The boat didn't even have real seats, only benches without back supports. I gripped the metal edges of the seat, holding on as tight as my cold white knuckles could manage. I wasn't sure which would be more mortifying: flying off into the lake or falling backward into Elijah's lap. My fingers clenched even tighter.

I squinted through the wind and the lake spray at each small island we passed, hoping it might be the one we were heading toward. But Elijah showed no sign of slowing down. The waves were growing bigger, and as the boat bounced against them, my teeth clattered together painfully.

Then the clouds split at the seams, and the rain began to pour. The wind blew icy spray into our faces and showered us in a mixture of lake water and rain, soaking Peter's hoodie through to my shirt. I glanced behind me. Elijah's glasses were useless. He'd hooked them onto the collar of his shirt, which was drenched for he still hadn't bothered to zip up his jacket, and he'd resorted to squinting through rain. I noticed, with a half-amused frown, that he was ducking slightly, using me as a shield against the worst of it.

He steered the boat all the way around the east half of Nile. When we made it to the west side, he pointed to an island far ahead, positioned in the heart of the lake.

"Bird Island," he called over the wind.

That piqued my interest, and I sat up a little straighter. For the way Lacey went on about it, I'd assumed it'd be a bit more impressive. Something more foreboding and spooky, but instead, it just looked barren and neglected. Bird Island was simply a single strip of bare rock with what looked like a large, abandoned gray barn crumbled off to one side.

Then Elijah caught my eye and nodded to the shore all the way across the lake. "That's New York," he shouted.

The rolling gray mountains in the distance looked the same as the Vermont ones on the east side, but I noticed through the gloomy haze a single string of lights shining high up in the mountain line. Now that was interesting. But before I could ask Elijah about them, he jutted his head toward the right. "That's it…"

Forgetting the lights, I leaned over in my seat. The island was on the smaller side compared to the others we'd passed. It was completely covered in trees, overgrown with them, in fact. It looked like a piece of wilderness stuck in the middle of the lake with a huge beige Victorian mansion hidden within the trees.

The house was striking. It looked like something out of *The Addams Family* with its many stories, turrets, and balconies, and I thought I could even make out the fence of a widow's walk at the top of the tallest tower. A porch wrapped around one side, and a steep set of steps led down to a path that stopped at the empty dock.

Elijah pulled the boat up to the side of it and tied it in place. Anxious to get off the boat, I tossed my lifejacket off to the side and didn't bother to wait for Elijah's help in exiting.

Bad idea.

Dizzy and sick from the ride, I staggered a bit and nearly fell backwards into the water, but Elijah was quick to pull me back. I stayed huddled up against him a bit longer than what was necessary to regain my balance, but it was freezing and somehow, despite the rain and his soaking shirt, he was warm.

He glanced at me, placing a gentle hand on my back. "You okay?"

"Sure—yup." I moved away quickly, hugging myself and pulling Peter's wet hoodie tight around me.

He hesitated before giving me a curt nod. Then he led the way up the dock and toward the house.

Though it was almost October, the trees on the island were still thick with leaves just barely beginning to change, and in the dreariness of the late afternoon and the light shower of rain, the burnt orange and deep reds were slick and shiny as they drooped down overhead.

"Your grandmother lives here?" I whispered as we climbed the steps to the house. For some reason, I felt like we were trespassing. Sailing up uninvited seemed a bit invasive now that I was at the front door.

We stopped at the doorstep, huddled together, reluctant to knock.

"Yes." Elijah's voice was low as though he didn't want to be overheard. "But my grandmother—"

The door opened before either of us had had time to knock. "'My grandmother' *what*, Elijah Grunvald?"

A tall, willowy old woman with bright golden eyes and a hooked nose appeared in the doorway. She looked like she'd come from a bohemian festival. Her dress was flowing with bright orange and red patterns and her hair, streaked gray and white, was pulled back from her face with several scarves, falling around her in gentle silver waves.

Elijah flinched. His cheeks flushed as he grinned sheepishly; the 18-year-old man, shrunk down to a child in her powerful presence.

The woman pinched his cheek and shook him. "Not a word from you in months, and now you show up in the rain? A storm's blowing in from Ottawa, haven't you heard?"

Before we could answer, she ushered us inside. "Come in, quick, before you soak the rug."

The room opened up to a grand staircase that led to giant black double doors just before splitting and curving and swirling both left and right, lifting upward and backward toward the front of the house and out of sight. Breathtaking. Incredible.

The woman regarded Elijah with a critical stare, underneath which he put his glasses back on his nose, tugged at the corners of his unzipped jacket, and tucked in his soggy shirt.

"Your sister's not here." The woman's expression softened. "She misses you very much, Elijah."

I glanced at him as he shoved his hands in his pockets.

"And who's this?" Her gaze fell on me, and she smiled encouragingly.

"This is Hannah." Elijah straightened, seemingly remembering his age as well as his manners. He waved a hand between us. "Hannah Green. Hannah, this is my bubbe, Rosalind."

"Green?" Rosalind raised a perfectly shaped eyebrow. "You've finally brought home a Jewish girl, Eli?"

"*What*?" Elijah turned purple. "Bubbe! I didn't—"

Rosalind gave him a playful slap on the arm. "Calm yourself, Elijah."

"Nice to meet you, Ms. Grunberg." I reached out my hand hastily to hide my embarrassment. Ignoring my hand, she pulled me into a hug as light and airy as one of Lacey's. Her wrists were covered in beautiful bangles and the sleeves of her gown billowed around me. "Oh, honey, call me Zan."

I blinked at the nickname.

She released me with a smile and waved her hand around the great entrance hall. "Have fun. Explore. Pick a guest room if you like—we have several. By the sound of the radio report, you'll be here a while...I only ask that you telephone your elder and let them know you are safe."

I shook my head. "We aren't staying—"

Zan flashed an indulgent smirk. "I think you'll find the weather has other plans for you."

"We're just here to ask you some questions," I finished firmly. "Elijah..." I reached for him, but he hung behind me as though he were anxious to get back to the boat. I grabbed him and pulled him forward, threading my arm through his and hugging him to my side. "Elijah said you were the author of this reference book we found...and we'd like to know more about it. The subject matter, that is."

Zan's easy smile vanished. She looked at Elijah and then back at me, her golden eyes sharp and bright. "Come with me."

She led us straight up the staircase. The stairs swirled back toward the front of the house and ended in a long, gothic hallway, lined on one side with tall knee-length windows down both stretches left and right. Despite the gray light streaming through the slated, shuttered windows, the hallway had a dark feel to it—not in a depressing way like Rosecrest, but rather dramatic and rich. The hardwood floors were a deep chocolate that met the bluish gray moldings on the wall, stopping halfway and finishing with a thick beige wallpaper. There were oil paintings hung every few feet.

Zan turned down the right corridor, wasting no time and not bothering to see if we were still behind her. The walls were high but cramped and forced us to move through in a single file. The hallway ended in yet another window, but this one was dark for it faced the woods. Occasionally, a tree branch slapped against it in the wind, and I wondered if the storm really *would* keep us here.

Zan stopped suddenly and turned sharply into a room. I skidded to a stop, rumpling the carpet runner as Elijah bumped into my back. We hurried inside after her.

Eyes wide, I moved around the room, my mouth agape.

It was a library.

A proper, grand, old-fashioned library. Books neatly lined the walls, two stories high, with a small staircase that led to the upper-level balcony that wrapped all the way around. I spun in a slow circle, taking it all in. Across from the entrance was a huge fireplace, but the thing that made me pause was what was hanging above it: an oversized mirror that looked exactly like Ms. Barbara's. The one that I'd broken. The one that was cursed.

I swayed a bit where I stood and tried to catch my breath.

"It's not the same, Hannah." Zan placed a gentle hand on my shoulder and guided me into the plush, maroon loveseat, before sinking down beside me. I blinked furiously, all the while trying to reason myself down from a panic attack.

It *was* different. Now that I looked at it properly. It wasn't the same shape and a lot smaller. A tear slid down my cheek, and I slapped it away. I didn't look at it again.

Zan wrapped an arm around me and said gently, "What did you want to ask me?"

I took a deep breath. What did I want to ask her? What is going on? How do I get the thing in the mirror to leave me alone? I opened my mouth and closed it again. After everything, I couldn't figure out what to say.

Elijah, who had positioned himself a bit away from us, was lighting a fire in the fireplace just below the mirror. He picked up a poker and stoked the flames to life. "Why don't you start at the beginning, Bubbe... You seem to know more about this than anybody."

Zan stiffened at the edge in her grandson's voice, but her voice was patient and gentle. "I wrote that book after my best friend had an...encounter...with the thing in the Rosecrest mirror. She was never the same afterwards. And so, I decided to research the mirror and the house and do my part to warn people away from that place...but I see it hasn't worked. Not even my own grandson listened to me..."

Elijah pulled off his jacket and draped it over a wooden chair at the table. He held out his hand for the hoodie. I peeled it off, and he hung it by the fire to dry.

"I read your book...most of it." I hesitated. "You mention the possibility of a witch—"

"Jemima Blackwell," Zan murmured, nodding.

"—cursing the mirror in the late 1890s. But you also say that the theory doesn't hold because there've been rumors of the house dating as far back as—"

"1860, when the mirror was first purchased by Harriet Vantine and hung in the Rosecrest House."

"You also say there are written accounts of travelers who stayed at the Rosecrest seeing a girl with long brown hair and dark eyes in the mirror. Four cases in which the mirror supposedly broke as someone looked at it. And of those cases, all reported to a friend or family member that they had begun to see the girl elsewhere."

"Yes..." Zan nodded. "But, interestingly, the sightings of a girl only began *after* Jemima Blackwell inherited the property... Prior to her ownership, there were only rumors of the house itself."

I frowned. "I don't understand..."

Zan's kind smile crinkled her golden eyes. "The Rosecrest House was built by the Vantine family in the early 1800s. In 1860, the family decided to turn it into an Inn. And back then, there was a constant follow of visitors in and out of the house. Many of those guests reported differences in their family members and travel companions. People seemed to change overnight. Dark, twisted versions of who they were before their stay. People used to whisper that the Rosecrest House had sucked out their souls."

Elijah and I exchanged uneasy glances as Zan continued, "It wasn't until *after* Jemima Blackwell took over the Rosecrest that people began to claim they saw a ghost in the mirror and everywhere else..."

"But—" I paused, struggling with the part that didn't fit. "I don't just see a girl...I see a monster."

Zan inhaled sharply and looked at Elijah for confirmation.

He nodded. "It attacked her last night."

Zan took my hand and gave it a squeeze. "When did the mirror break?"

I swallowed, my stomach sick. "Monday."

"You need to see Charlotte Grey." Zan stood and headed over to the desk in the far corner, her gown and scarves flowing behind her. She pulled out the desk drawer and started scribbling out a note. "She has a place above the pub—"

Elijah scoffed angrily. "And there it is, your answer for everything. 'Go see the Nile Witch...she can fix everything from bad break-ups to dying girls with cancer.'"

Zan lifted her head and stared at him coolly. "I'm far from an expert in this—"

Elijah snorted. "Says the person who literally wrote the book on—"

"Speculation and guesswork!" Zan snapped. "On the history of the house and that wretched mirror! I never claimed to have any idea as to what is truly lurking in the depths of the foul thing. Who knows what it is! A ghost, a demon—all I know is what I put into the book. I don't know the first thing about getting rid of it. So, unless you want Hannah to become warped and forever changed, reduced to a dark reflection of herself, then—"

I stood abruptly from the couch. "I need a minute. Just—give me a minute." I left the library as they both continued to bicker in barely restrained tones.

In the hall, I leaned against the wall trying to block out their voices. The rain was tapping gently against the windows across from me. The rhythm was relaxing, soothing, and drew me closer. My hands lightly pressed against the cold glass as I stared out over the water.

The clouds had darkened from soft white to dark gray, and the rain poured hard over the lake, which was almost black save for the white caps that curled with each wave. The thick mass of trees on the island leaned hard in the wind as it sheltered the old house from most of the storm, the leaves blocking most of the rain. There was barely a soft sprinkle streaming down the windows.

The light glow coming from the library shined on the glass, reflecting back at me. But of course, it wasn't my face I saw in the mirror.

I inhaled sharply and flinched away. But before I could move, hands like claws shoved through the window, snatched my arms, and pulled me into the glass.

THE TRUTH ABOUT REBECCA GREEN

It was dark. As though I'd dropped into a starless sky. And yet light seemed to be surrounding me...no, *coming* from me.

I was glowing like the moon in the night.

And I wasn't alone.

A girl, shining softly in the darkness, stood a few feet from me. She was draped in a black dress that seemed to shimmer and drift like smoke off her white skin. Her brown hair was long and loose, blowing slightly in an intangible breeze.

I had seen her before.

Before her dark reflection had changed to a monster.

I had to get out of there.

I turned around—back toward what should've been the hallway. Should've been Zan's house...but it was only more darkness. Emptiness. Nothingness.

"You're next," the girl said softly from behind me. Her voice was strange and muffled as though she were speaking from far away.

I turned back to face her. "Let me out of here...please," I added curtly.

"I can't." The right corner of her mouth twitched.

My eyes narrowed. "What do you want with me?"

She held her finger to her lips. Then her muffled voice deepened as she snapped, "*I'm trying to tell you. You're not listening.*"

The left corner of her mouth twitched.

"I'm listening, okay? What!" I backed up a step.

"You don't have long..."

Her distorted voice trailed off.

"Long before what!"

"You're...not...listening."

Her black eyes glittered.

"I don't have time for this." I turned my back on her and stretched my arms out in front of me. The window should be there. If I could just smash through it somehow...I swiped my arms in front of me, but there was nothing. Only emptiness. Then I remembered. Desiree. She'd fallen *through* the window. From inside of her dormitory. They'd found her outside. Hope filled me, and I squared my shoulders. I had to go forward.

I whirled around, ready to jump, but I couldn't.

I was nose to nose with the pinned-up smile and the razorblade teeth.

Not razorblades...shards of glass.

Like a broken mirror.

A low, muffled growl was vibrating from the smile. That strange chittering burr. I could feel the thing preparing to strike. But this time, I acted first. I ducked my head down and lunged at its torso, shoving it backward into the dark.

"You should call her parents, Elijah..."

"No, I don't want to worry her mom." A warm, damp cloth touched my face. I winced and squinted my eyes open. I was lying on a bed in a small room that seemed to emanate a cozy glow.

"But she may need to see a doctor…"

I could hear a soft crackle of wood in a fireplace and the whistle of the storm outside.

The cloth dabbed at my face.

I didn't want to wake up. I didn't want to deal with mirrors and ghosts and the nightmare that I was living. I'd just keep my eyes shut and let Elijah pat at my forehead for the rest of my life.

"She doesn't need a doctor." Elijah's voice was hard and firm.

I peeked through my eyelashes at him. His face was lined with concern, but his dark eyes burned like hard coals. Was he thinking of Desiree and what the doctors had done to her? He didn't want me locked up with her. My heart swelled at the sight of him and forgetting my plan to stay asleep forever, I reached out and put my hand over his.

Startled, he looked down at me and squeezed my hand. "Are you okay, Hannah? Do you want a doctor?"

My eyes fluttered as I took stock of my condition. My body was sore. No pretending it wasn't. I definitely didn't feel like getting up just yet. But nothing seemed broken—or eaten.

I nibbled on my tongue trying to decide what to ask first. "What happened?"

"We heard a crash…I found you face down on the porch roof, covered in glass." Elijah looked a bit green, and his hand crushed my fingers together.

Zan moved closer to the bed and smoothed my hair from my face. "Do you want to tell us your side of things? From where I'm sitting—you smashed face-first through a window, yet you haven't got a single scratch on you…"

I winced. "I'm sorry about the window, Zan."

She scoffed, waving away my apology. "My gentleman, Charles, is boarding it as we speak."

I took a deep breath and explained everything.

Elijah's face was hard as he listened.

Zan frowned. "I don't understand—"

"That makes two of us," I muttered. "But I don't want to understand anymore. I just need to get rid of her." I glanced at Zan. "Can the woman—Charlotte Grey—can she help me do that? Like, what would it be?" I looked at Elijah with a grim resignation. "An exorcism on a mirror or something?"

Zan shrugged her shoulders, looking utterly lost. "I have no idea, honey. I just know: you need to see her. You're running out of time..."

I rolled my eyes. "That seems to be the message."

Zan lightly touched my shoulder. "No, sweetie, I mean—my best girlfriend. She had seven days, and then...it was like all the others said: she changed overnight." Zan's voice broke a bit, and she cleared her throat, dabbing her eyes with the end of one of her scarves. "She became a completely different person by the end of it. And I would hate to see that happen to someone Elijah cares about. It wasn't fun for me...I can't imagine—well, anyways." She straightened herself and went for the door. She lingered in the doorway as she gripped the frame. She pointed at Elijah. "Be a gentleman. I'm sending Charles up with some coffee...and *your* room is upstairs. Don't forget that."

There was a plush reading chair in the corner of the room by the fireplace. Elijah pulled it up against the bedside and settled into it with a weighted sigh.

He dug his cellphone out of his pocket and passed it to me. "Nile reception is usually spotty at the best of times. But you seem to be in luck—full bars."

I checked the time before I called. Mom was still working, so I left a message and gave the phone back.

"So...you have a butler?"

Elijah smirked. "No. He's more like...Bubbe's boyfriend..."

I blinked in surprise. Amusement tickled the corners of my lips.

Zan's 'gentleman' came in just as Elijah tucked his phone away. He paused in the doorway and nodded respectfully.

I sat up in the bed and smiled curiously. Charles was handsome in his crisp, tailored jacket. He was fairly tall, with neatly combed curls, and a tidy, trimmed black and silver beard that covered most of his face. He had a thin-lipped smile that curved with mischief and crinkled his dark eyes, which glittered behind his small spectacles. He looked like a school professor or a museum curator... something smart and studious.

"Elijah and Hannah, I take it? I'm Charles...where would you like all this?" He spoke in a soft, gentle voice with a slight hint of a woodchuck accent buried underneath. He held out the tray as he entered the room with a little bow of his head.

"Err—thanks... Uh. You can put it on the dresser..." Elijah said awkwardly.

"Very well. Please let me know if you need anything else." He placed the tray down and left the room with another small bow.

I smirked and glanced sideways at Elijah. "Zan has good taste."

He shrugged and leaned back in the chair. He pushed his glasses up the bridge of his nose. "She met him at a senior speed dating, fundraiser thing."

A comfortable silence settled around us before I said, "You don't have to keep me company..."

Elijah raised an eyebrow.

I felt my cheeks burn. "Okay," I admitted. "Honestly, I'd appreciate the company."

Elijah smiled. "We've got books in the nightstand...standard Grunberg practice."

He leaned down and pulled open the drawer and passed me a book. *Jane Eyre.*

I smiled and propped up my pillows. "A personal favorite."

Elijah cracked a weak grin. "I had a feeling." And he settled into read *A Haunting of Nile.*

I tried to get into the story, but I couldn't. I ended up reading the same sentence over multiple times, causing poor Janc to be bullied repeatedly before I gave up. I shut *Jane Eyre* and leaned back against the headboard.

Elijah peered at me over the top of his book.

I looked at him. "Do you know about my dad? I mean...the stuff I *didn't* tell you."

Slowly, Elijah put the book down on the nightstand. He met my eyes with an even gaze. "Yes."

"You heard Portia?"

Elijah shook his head. "I remembered your name. My dad was the crime beat reporter at the time...something happens like that in Vermont...people talk about it. And they remember."

"Right." I nodded. Unable to look at him, I stared at the bedspread. I nibbled my lip as I struggled with what to say. "It wasn't like they said...but I *did* see it. And it wasn't my daddy. It wasn't even a person."

Elijah didn't speak, and he didn't move to comfort me. He simply stayed perfectly still as though he thought a movement might spook me, and he let me let go.

"I'd been seeing it in my dreams for weeks. I didn't tell Rebecca. I didn't want to scare her. She was special. Tender-hearted. Good. So unlike me—stubborn with a cruel, nasty temper. Rebecca was the better twin. Everyone knew it, but I didn't mind... I was proud to call her my twin. I could never do anything to hurt her. And telling her about the monster that lived in our closet...that it was going to—"

My voice broke on the words, and I took a shaky breath.

I tried again. "To g-get her... Well, I couldn't scare her like that. So, I told my parents instead. I told them over and over and over. I warned them it would happen. They told me it was just a dream. They kept telling me to forget about it...it wasn't real. Then after the first week, they started getting mad...they didn't show it, of course. They tried to be patient with me, but I could tell... They thought I was acting out, doing it for attention, making things up because I was jealous of my sister."

I sniffed as a few tears leaked from my eyes, nodding understandably. "I could see that. Why they thought that, I mean. I was always the jealous type. But never of Rebecca." I shook my head as it all came flooding back in vivid detail. "I was *never* jealous of Rebecca," I repeated softly before taking another shuddering breath.

"And then one night, Mom went out with her friends to the movies. Daddy tucked us in...and I remember feeling really anxious, you know? Like that feeling you get in the pit of your stomach that something bad is going to happen, something that is going to change everything in a really *bad* way? Something that you can't take back..." I swallowed. "I didn't want Daddy to leave us. I asked him if we could sleep in their room...but he said no; he was going to stay up and watch the basketball game. He said it was past our bedtime. We had school in the morning. Didn't want to be late for the bus. He said goodnight. He shut the door."

I licked the saline from my lips. "I told Becca to sleep in my bed. I *begged* her, but she was afraid of heights... She said I could sleep in her bed if I wanted..." Tears swelled in my eyes, blurring my vision. My lip quivered. "And I said no," I moaned, my voice watery with emotion. "I said no because I knew what was going to happen."

Elijah made a move as though to take my hand but instead pushed his glasses farther up his nose and adjusted the frames.

I took a deep, raspy breath and kept going. "I stayed flat down on my mattress, my covers up over my head, peeking out through the slates in the railing. I just stared at the light coming from underneath our door. I felt like as long as Daddy was awake, nothing would happen. And I kept telling myself it wasn't real. It was a dream. All the things my parents had had me repeat back to them for the past few weeks. Then I fell asleep." I bit my lip as it trembled. I dropped my gaze to the blankets tucked around me and stared hard at one paisley printed on the fabric. Disassociating, my therapist called it.

"I woke up. The murmur of the basketball commentators, the glow of the TV underneath the door, were all gone. It was dark and silent. I remember the moonlight. It pooled in the center, bathing everything in blue, illuminating the middle of the carpet, and casting black shadows around the edges of the room. I'd turned my head to stare at the closet. I was so scared I could barely breathe. And it was so slow, so patient, I could barely tell the closet doors were moving. And when they were finally opened wide, this *thing* crawled out of the closet.

"It was long and thin. It was dark. It blended in so well with the shadows, I could only see its eyes—reflective and glowing like an animal's in the night..and its teeth—white, as its mouth hung open in this evil, hungry smile. It crawled on its hands and knees, with its back arched and shoulders hunched low, its head skimming the floor.

"I wanted to scream. I wanted to yell for Daddy. But I didn't. I just watched as it crawled across the carpet, up onto Becca's bed, disappearing underneath my bunk.

"There was a moment, just a few seconds of silence, and I scrunched my eyes tight and repeated in my head over and over that it was a dream. It wasn't real. I willed myself to wake up. But then, Becca's scream ripped through the quiet and the *thing*, its teeth tearing through Becca's arm, dragged her kicking and sobbing, backwards into the closet."

My face was wet. I couldn't look at Elijah. The shame kept my eyes focused on that one paisley print in front of me. "She'd screamed for me...to help her. But I'd stayed tucked up in bed, watching in silence as she'd been ripped away by the meat of her small arm.

"I was a coward," I breathed bitterly. "I should've at least run for Daddy the second they'd disappeared. But I was too scared. Too afraid it'd come back for me next."

I inhaled deeply, nostrils flaring as I finished. "But in the end, I didn't need to. Her scream had woken him, and he'd come running. Of course, he was too late. He'd slapped on the lights. The blood trail was bright on the floor. A long ruby ribbon smeared across the cream carpet toward the closet. He'd looked at me. His eyes were so big...just *horrified*, because it was just like I had said. Just like I'd warned them." I licked my lips, the salty tears sharp on my tongue. "He ran to the closet, throwing the door back as far as it could go, slamming it against the wall. There was a small pool of red in the middle of the closet. And her blankie. Nothing else. Daddy went berserk...absolutely insane. He let out this—this *bellow*. He pounded all the walls inside the closet and then ran from the room, tearing the place apart, searching for his baby girl.

"He'd called the police at some point. Mom came home to a house full of cops. They'd wanted to question me. My dad argued with them. He knew what I would say. They insisted. I told them the truth at first...but that made Mom cry harder. So I changed my story to whatever made the most sense to them. Told them what they wanted to hear. Yes, sir. No, sir." I took another gulp of air.

"Anyway...then Daddy went off his meds. And with his bipolar disorder, well, he went into a manic depression, quit his job and his practice... He had been a highly respected psychologist at the university. But he just spiraled from there. And I think he wanted to...spiral, I mean. Because nothing mattered after Becca. He was committed a few times... The last time he got out of the hospital, he seemed better, like he'd found hope somehow. But then he spent all our savings on private investigators, and then psychics, and when he brought the monster hunters from the Internet home, Mom had had enough. We'd lost the house by then and were couch surfing at that point. Anyways..."

A strange, sad silence settled between us as I took steady, deep breaths.

"You tell a story so often you start to believe it," I said finally. "That's why I fought so hard against what I was seeing in the mirror. I'd rather have a psychotic break...than remember what really happened to my sister. But now I remember. And I won't forget again."

I looked at Elijah. His sad smile crinkled the corners of his eyes, the warm, golden swirl in the brown setting off a flutter in my stomach.

Quickly, I broke the moment before he could lie and say it wasn't my fault. I was so tired of hearing that. "So, why haven't you seen your grandmother in months?"

Elijah's smile slipped, and my cheeks burned.

"I'm sorry. I know it's rude, and it's personal, but—"

"My little sister, Noa, got sick. Terminally sick. She went through the medical treatments to give her more time, but they just made her miserable. She started to give up. My grandmother was convinced the Nile Witch could help. My parents agreed. I disagreed. I thought they were giving her false hope...and taking her off her medical treatments would only kill her faster. We all argued. And I moved out."

I studied his face. "Your baby sister is dying, and you haven't seen her in *months*?"

Elijah's eyes shone with shame just before he squinted and looked up at the ceiling. "I tried to visit a few times, but I, uhh..." He cleared his throat. "I just can't bring myself to make it all the way."

"Why?" I demanded.

Elijah shook his hand through his hair like he had an itch he couldn't scratch. "The doctors gave her until last June... It's almost October. She's now considered a miracle case...cured. How?" Elijah shrugged. "I couldn't wrap my head around the whole witch thing...but mostly I've stayed away because...well..."

"You were wrong?" I suggested.

Elijah nodded with a watery laugh. "Yeah. I'm ashamed that I was wrong... If they'd all listened to me, with the doctor's timetable...even with her treatments, she'd be dead right now."

I stared at him trying to process his confession.

"That's why I keep that damn cat. Noa wouldn't let me leave without it."

I blinked. "So, you're overwhelmed with guilt because your sister's alive...?"

Elijah shrugged. "I guess it sounds insane when you say it out loud."

"Just a bit." I pursed my lips to stifle my smile. "But since when is anything around this island 'sane?'"

"'We're all mad here,' huh?" Elijah smiled, the slow bob of his head conceding my point.

I made a face. "Not that. Don't ever quote that..."

Elijah laughed. "Too lame?"

"Cliché!"

Elijah chuckled, but then his face grew serious, and he cleared his throat. "I'd like to go with you to see Charlotte Grey. Is that all right?"

Nibbling the inside of my cheek, I studied him for a moment. Normally, I'd have said 'no.' But taking in the serious shine in his eyes and the hard line of his mouth, I knew he wanted to go for his own reasons as much as my own. Somehow, that made me welcome the idea. I nodded slowly.

And we settled into that calm silence once more.

He reached for his book.

I reached for mine, watching him as he began to read. His hair fell a bit into his eyes, so dark and focused they were as he pored over the page. His forehead creased in pensive reflection; I watched his mouth as he began to mutter the words softly as he read. "Can you promise me something, Elijah?"

Elijah's eyes found mine. "Anything."

"When we figure out how to get rid of the ghost or whatever it is, you'll go see your sister?"

A smile tugged at the side of his lips, setting off a dimple in his cheek. "Deal."

I bit my lip, holding back the one question I still needed answered. The one I felt ridiculous asking. Elijah's warm brown eyes melted my defenses, and I said in a voice barely audible, "And if I turn into a different person by the end of this...you'll still be my friend?"

"Always."

GHOSTS, DEMONS, AND DOPPELGANGERS

The storm was over by morning. When I woke up, feeling rested for the first time all week, warm sunlight streamed in through the door, pouring in from the windows in the hall. I glanced at the chair beside the bed and could barely contain the smile that tickled the corner of my mouth. Elijah had fallen asleep in the chair; his glasses on top of his head and his arms folded across the book. His mouth was hanging open, and he was snoring pretty impressively. There was a light shadow of stubble across his face. I pursed my lips together to hide my smirk as I shook him awake.

We found Zan and Charles in the kitchen having breakfast in a little nook tucked into a bay window. As soon as we walked in the room, Zan jumped up, twisted the blinds on the windows, and flicked on the light switch. Clearly, she wasn't risking me witnessing any more ghostly reflections. I was torn between insult and gratitude, unable to decide how I felt about it.

We had planned to make a quick exit, but, despite our protests, Zan insisted we have a decent meal before we set out. So, our plates piled high with sausage links and pancakes, we settled down beside the couple.

Zan and Charles each had a piece of the newspaper in one hand and a mug of coffee in the other. They both exchanged a glance over their papers. Then Charles cleared his throat. "What are your plans for the day?"

Elijah looked at Zan over his coffee. "Don't worry, Bubbe; we're going to see Charlotte Grey today."

Zan held up her hand and pointed at Charles, feigning innocence. She picked her mug back up, pausing at her lips. "You'll have to visit her place above the pub. Opens up around five. She doesn't like people stopping by the cottage... She's got a house full of girls. I think they might be your age? Homeschooled, of course."

I raised an eyebrow at Elijah as though that was impressive. He snorted into his coffee.

Zan continued, without catching the joke, "You know, I don't blame Charlotte, really. Nile children can be downright nasty to the Greys. Always been that way since the founding. You know—" And Zan went into a long tale of the Nile witch trials back in the 1700s.

When we were done eating, the couple walked us to the front door. Charles gave me a small bow. "Here is your sweater." He passed me Peter's hoodie with a crinkled smile. He turned to Elijah. "And here is your coat."

Zan wrapped her arms around Elijah in a tight hug. Before he could pull away, she put her hands on his cheeks. "Don't be a stranger, my sweet boy."

Elijah nodded stiffly, and she released him. Then, in a flutter of fabric and scarves, she wrapped around me. I squeezed her back. She stroked my hair and gave my cheek a gentle pinch. "You listen to Charlotte, do as she says, and you will be fine."

Instead of being encouraged by her words, I began to feel sick. I forced a smile as my stomach churned uncomfortably.

We thanked them and left for the dock.

Elijah helped me in the boat and started the engine.

"What will we do until five?" I tossed loudly over my shoulder as we rolled through the gentle waves.

"Figure out what we're dealing with," Elijah shouted back.

"This is it." Elijah passed it to me.

I raised a skeptical eyebrow. I turned the small radio over in my hands. "Lacey's EMF detector?"

He sat back on his stool. "Yup. I was thinking about it last night while I was reading Bubbe's book. She goes over the history of the house and the mirror...but it's all rumors, like she said. So, I figure, before we go to Charlotte Grey, we'd better be able to tell her what it is we're up against. How could she help us otherwise?"

I nodded slowly. "Okay...so we take this down to the mirror? Or—what? I mean...we don't know anything about paranormal activity. Or what types of things might be out there...nothing."

"That's why I called for help."

I scoffed. "Who do you know that could possibly help—"

An impatient rap at the door answered my question. Impressed despite myself, I flashed a smirk at Elijah as he waved for me to go answer the door.

Peter and Courtney both ducked inside the apartment without waiting for an invitation.

They were both dressed identically with matching black back-packs to complement their black cargo pants and black hoodies. Courtney had even painted her nails black, and her thick honey-blonde hair was pulled back in a smart ponytail complete with black scrunchie.

But they each carried something different: Peter had a huge encyclopedia which he lugged inside with both hands, and Courtney had a pink notebook tucked carefully underneath her arm.

Peter headed toward Elijah, who still sat at the stool at his workstation, and dropped his book onto the worktable like an offering.

Elijah immediately started thumbing through it.

Courtney moved to the couch, pulling the cat into her lap as she took a seat and surveyed the room with her nose crinkled. "I forgot how cramped it was in here. Eli, you're a slob. How can you even *think* in this mess?"

Elijah didn't hear her. He was too busy muttering over the pages.

Peter gave me an encouraging smile. "So, I was up all night with this thing…"

I moved over to watch Elijah turn the pages. It was an encyclopedia of…monsters by the look of it. Just a week ago, I would've written it off as a gimmick, but now I was harkened by the contents.

"Where did you get it?"

With each turn of the page, another grisly illustration appeared. The paper was old and stained.

"Same day delivery," Courtney said softly as she scratched the cat behind the ears. "He ordered it as soon as he dropped you off yesterday. I wish you would've told me you were seeing her, Hannah," she added, clearly hurt.

Thankfully, Peter cut in, saving me from an awkward explanation and apology. "Based on this book…it's either a ghost or a demon. Which narrows it down just enough to give us a starting point."

"A starting point for what?"

Elijah glanced over his shoulder at me. "Process of elimination."

"Right." Peter pulled the book toward him and flipped between two earmarked pages. "So, the difference: a demon would leave behind a rotten smell, and a ghost would lower the temperature."

I shook my head, trying to remember a bad smell or unexplained cold. This was all so ridiculous. "How do we know this book is even reliable...I mean, who's to say this is even true?"

Elijah turned in the stool to face me. "This is all we have to go off of..."

"Well, I never smelled anything..."

"Desiree said she felt cold," Courtney said from the couch. "So, it could be a ghost."

"And of course, there's the other thing..."

I frowned. "What other thing?"

"Ms. Barbara's the tricky part..." Peter ran a hand through his golden hair as he flipped to another page.

"Ms. Barbara?" I gave him a funny look.

Peter nodded slowly. "Last night, Elijah mentioned there's been a strange hand off of the property over the years."

My brow furrowed as I looked between the two of them. "'Last night?'— Did you call Peter while I was sleeping?"

Elijah adjusted his glasses, and Peter looked sharply at me. "You spent the night here?"

My cheeks burned. "No, we went to visit his grandmother... and the storm—" I shook my head, cutting off my rambling, and got to the point, "Why were you making calls behind my back?"

"No, not—it wasn't..." Elijah cleared his throat and tried again. "I was up reading through the book, and I wanted to ask Courtney a question about—"

"You called *Courtney*?" I asked as a tight knot of inexplicable jealousy twisted in my stomach.

"He wanted to ask about Desiree...if she'd ever felt weird around Ms. Barbara." Courtney shrugged. "I told him about Peter's book..."

I frowned, massaging my temple as I tried to keep everything straight. "Ms. Barbara? Elijah—explain."

He pulled Zan's book out from his bag and handed it to me. "The house was built by Merritt Vantine in the early 1800s. His granddaughter, Harriet Vantine, was the last Vantine to own the

Rosecrest House. After that, the house didn't pass through the generations like most of the old houses in Nile. But it hasn't ever been *sold*, either. The Rosecrest House has been passed to different people—inherited almost randomly."

"Right...I read it all yesterday. So?" I muttered as I flipped back through the book.

"Right. Ms. Barbara—Barbara Blake inherited it from a 'Kathleen Murphy,' and before that, Harriet Vantine left it to Jemima Blackwell."

"The witch?" Courtney asked sharply.

"Blake and Murphy aren't local names..." Peter pointed out. "Maybe they were both new to Nile...like Desiree and..."

Me.

As I skimmed the pages, I came to the same conclusion. The house had been passed to three different people outside the original Vantine owners throughout the centuries...all young women...all recently moved to town. Then I felt that nagging, scratching in the back of my head. I'd forgotten something. "What about Jemima Blackwell's sister? Ms. Barbara said Jemima killed her in the house..." I looked up from the book to meet Elijah's eyes.

"There is no record of Jemima's sister dying—or *any* girl dying in the house...at least—my grandmother didn't find one. The ghost story Ms. Barbara's been telling is made up."

I chuckled darkly; the irony of being surprised that a ghost story wasn't true. "So, what does this have to do with anything? I mean, so what?" I closed *A Haunting of Nile* and passed it back to Elijah.

"Okay." Elijah took a breath and eyed me anxiously as he tucked the book back into his bag. "*Listen* before you roll your eyes, okay?"

I snorted and nodded impatiently.

"All right." Elijah slid the encyclopedia toward himself and started slapping through the pages. "Some Rosecrest accounts say they see a ghost, and some don't—but! The thing they all have in common is the change in their loved ones' personalities, right? So, Peter found that there are (supposedly) monster doppelgangers." Elijah tapped the back of his hand on a page. "There are species of monsters that can take on a human's form. So—say there's a monster in the house, one that takes the form of a person until they get too old, and then they change into another one?"

Peter nodded. "Right, but the problem is—we don't know any specifics because the book barely mentions doppelganger creatures for more than a few paragraphs." Peter cut in front of Elijah and gestured to the page with a sheepish shrug. "They say there's a lot of different kinds and yet don't bother to give a single example. Which is ridiculous considering they go on for a whole *chapter* about the different types of vampires."

I pulled the book close to read. The illustrations showed something that looked like a ghost, but then another that looked like an old lady. I cleared my throat and read, "'Doppelganger creatures vary in species. Methods in which they take the form of their victim, as well as the reasoning behind such metamorphoses, are as numerous as the beasts themselves. Habitats also range all across the spectrum, e.g., some lurk in dark, damp places, some prefer hot and dry, etc., etc. The diets of these doppelganger monsters differ dramatically, as well; for example, some feed on the brain fluid of sleeping children, some feed on human flesh (living and/or dead), some have more parasitic tendencies—'"

Courtney came up behind me. "'Take the form?'" She scrunched her nose up. "What does that mean? Like, shapeshift?"

Peter shook his head. "It's not very clear. Like I said, it's all general and really vague...and remember, I got this book off the Internet. It's not like it's some reputable paranormal reference." Peter scratched his chin as he studied the page. "Unless it is...no idea."

"So, now in addition to a ghost or demon or whatever—you think Ms. Barbara's a *doppelganger*...who has been—" I checked the book and read, "'feeding off' me?" I threw up my hands in exasperation. "Wouldn't I *know* if I'd been getting nibbled on in the night by the old lady that lives next door?"

Courtney made a face. "Ick."

I sighed, my shoulders rolling forward in frustration. "Are you telling me that we could be dealing with two different spirits, or monsters, or whatever?" I stared at Elijah, studying his face.

He didn't flinch underneath the weight of my gaze. "It could be one. Some doppelgangers make you hallucinate." Elijah pointed at the page. "And right here, it says some of them don't like cats... Ms. Barbara is allergic...except all the times she's stopped by—she's never once sneezed."

"'Some of them.'" I rolled my eyes, and I moved back to look at the encyclopedia. I stared at the illustration of the creature as an old woman and slapped the page with the back of my hand. "But it doesn't say anything about mirrors. The thing that keeps attacking me is always in a reflection. So, that doesn't fit with any of this. And in Zan's description of the mirror of Rosecrest, it says a witch might've cursed it."

"Jemima Blackwell," Elijah said.

"Right," I said, exasperated.

"But, Hannah, that rumor doesn't fit, remember? The accounts of the mirror go further back than Jemima," Elijah pointed out, pushing his glasses farther up his nose.

"You really think Ms. Barbara's a monster, Elijah?" Courtney murmured.

"Well—that or there's a ghost in the mirror...either one," Elijah said quickly.

"*Well, which is it?*" I demanded.

"There's only one way to find out..." Peter said grimly.

We decided to check for signs of ghost activity first. Because, as Peter said, and we all agreed: it was the quickest...but the real reason was no one wanted to go throw Elijah's cat at Ms. Barbara.

Courtney wanted to test Elijah's bathroom mirror. ("It's right there.") But even *I* knew it didn't work that way. If we were going to check for signs of a ghost, it would have to be somewhere the ghost had been before. I suggested we check out the mirror in my bedroom. Afterall, it was where I first saw it. Therefore, if it *was* a ghost, we'd be able to pick up something with the EMF detector.

Except we never made it to my apartment.

As we descended the fire escape, Ms. Barbara's sister pulled up. She exited the vehicle, as did a man I'd never seen before. He carried a briefcase in one hand and a tablet in the other.

Sandra Blake looked at us, eying Peter and Courtney up and down. "A little early in the year for Cabbage Night, isn't it? Or are you little hoodlums heading for old Grey Lane?"

"We're just heading in for lunch, actually..." I led everyone to the porch, but Sandra rushed past us and put a hand on the front door.

I raised an eyebrow.

She pursed her lips and forced a smile. "I hope you don't mean in your apartment?"

"Actually—"

"Because," she interrupted forcefully, one hand splayed across the door as she waved her partner over with the other. "I'm afraid you'll have to wait. I'm showing the apartment to Mr. Baker. And we will be a while."

"Wait, you can't—"

"Actually, Mr. Grunvald, I can. Barbara gave a—" She checked her phone, looking down her nose and reading, "A '*Ms. Elizabeth Green*' 24 hours' notice...is that your mother, dear? It's a shame she didn't think to tell you...can't imagine why. Anyhoo...if you'd all —" She waved her hands as though to shoo us off the porch. "It'll only be an hour at most."

We all backed up down the stairs. I watched, the corner of my mouth twitching with irritation, as the two of them slipped inside the house.

"That's another thing—I doubt very much that monsters have sisters...even rotten ones like that."

"What do we do now?" Courtney scowled after them.

It was obvious to me. Though I had wanted to avoid it at all costs, now it was our only option.

"She said *my* apartment...we can still check the mirror in the entrance hallway..."

"The one with the sheet?" Courtney went white.

"You said you broke it," Peter reminded me.

"Yeah, well...so did everybody else."

LOSING LACEY

We waited a minute to make sure the two of them were inside my apartment before we entered the house. We all squinted into the dim entryway and stopped, clumped together at the front door, staring at the black sheeting hanging on the back wall. Courtney's breath was coming in soft, halting gasps. Peter stood rigid in front of me. Elijah's hand found mine only for a second. He gave my fingers a squeeze before he pulled out the EMF meter.

Elijah moved down the narrow hallway toward the sheet. We followed, closely knit around him. I glanced up the stairs at Ms. Barbara's door, silently praying she wouldn't come out and find us. He flicked the switch on the meter. The tiny lights came on, giving off a faint, greenish glow.

"How will we know if—"

The meter began to beep. The closer we got to the mirror, the faster the beeping became.

Courtney stopped halfway, pulling at Elijah, trying to get him to stop. "Okay—now we know...*let's get out of here*," she hissed.

Peter hesitated beside his sister. Elijah kept going, and I followed.

"Elijah...we've got our answer. Time to go," I murmured, my feet still moving slowly beside his.

Elijah was inches from the sheet. He held the meter up to the blanketed mirror. The beeps were now so fast they blurred together into one long, constant sound. He looked at me and then back at the sheet. He was going to pull it down...and could I blame him? He was like me. He wanted to see it with his own eyes. To see that it really wasn't broken anymore. He wanted to understand.

He switched the meter off.

Silence rang in my ears.

I felt the nagging feeling of something coming. I inhaled sharply. Before he could make up his mind, before he could even begin to lift the sheet, I snatched his hand and dragged him away from the mirror.

Ms. Barbara's door creaked open overhead as the four of us rushed for the door. Her voice froze us in the doorway. "Hannah? What was that noise? I thought...oh, hello, Mr. Grunvald. Peter. Courtney. What are you all doing down there?"

They all mumbled 'hello's, while Elijah discreetly tucked the meter in his back pocket. Ms. Barbara had on a flowing night-gown, and her silver hair was long and loose at her shoulders. It was past noon. Why was she still in her nightgown?

"Sorry, Ms. Barbara," I called up to her. "Phone malfunction. Did we...wake you?" I asked uncertainly.

Ms. Barbara lightly touched her hair and smiled. "I had some trouble sleeping last night." She studied us all for a moment. "I thought I'd see you when I got home from the *facility*..." her voice lowered with disdain, but she quickly recovered with an easy smile. "But your mother said you were caught out in the storm..."

"Err...yeah. We were marooned on Zan Grunberg's island."

I could've sworn I saw her smile slip. "Where are you all off to now?"

"We're heading to Peter's house," I lied quickly, suddenly becoming increasingly uncomfortable beneath the weight of her stare and the penetration of her questions. I opened the door, nudged Peter and Courtney through, and shoved Elijah out onto the porch after them.

"See you later, Ms. Barbara!" I called before shutting the door quickly behind me and joining everyone outside.

I raised an eyebrow as I looked at them—all hunched together looking awkward and uncomfortable. Then I noticed Lacey, standing beside her bike in the driveway, looking hurt.

"Hi, Lacey!" I smiled and headed down the steps to meet her.

"I came to visit Miss Cassandra..." Lacey said softly as she kicked the stand on her bike. She ducked her head down and started for the back of the house without another word or backward glance.

I hurried after her and put a hand on her arm. "Wait. Lacey, what's wrong?"

Lacey stopped and looked up at me. Her big hazel eyes shined, but her face was calm beneath the brim of her patchwork tulip hat. Carefully, she tucked a long, platinum strand of hair behind her ears, one of the many that had been forgotten in her poor attempt at pigtails. Then she said gently, "It's all right, Hannah. I understand. You don't have to make a big deal about it..."

"What are you talking about?" I tried to smile, laugh it off, but for once, Lacey didn't seem to think there was anything to smile about.

"It's all right. I'm used to being left out. I get it." She bobbed her head up and down as though just remembering something and pulled the beaded bag off her shoulder. She held it out to me. "Before I forget—here. The tools you need."

Obediently, I took the bag as my thoughts raced, trying to find something to say.

She bounced a bit on the balls of her feet, her eyes downcast and sad. "There were pages missing...in the Nile fairy tales...I thought you should know...she ripped them out."

I wasn't listening, I was too busy trying to think of something to make her stay. Nothing. I had nothing. I could only stare as I watched her walk away. "Wait, Lacey—"

Her pace quickened, and she disappeared around the corner, toward the Sawyers'. My shoulders slumped as I stared down at the beaded bag. When I turned back to the porch, everyone was looking at me.

"What happened?" Courtney asked, eyes wide.

Elijah frowned and shifted where he stood. "She wanted to help...yesterday. But we told her we didn't need her."

"I did," I corrected him dully as I approached. "And now we're all hanging out without her..."

Courtney made a low whistle.

Peter gave me a sympathetic pat on the back. "She'll come around."

"Right." I sighed heavily and slipped the bag over my head, diagonally across my chest. Running a hand through my hair, I tried to focus on the bigger problem at hand. "Okay...so, we know it's a ghost. What now?"

Elijah, clearly still troubled by the run-in with Lacey, waved us toward the fire escape and led us up to his apartment.

As we all assembled into the room, Peter went to the kitchenette and pulled out a can of salt. "According to the book—and I have to stress this because who knows how accurate the thing is— salt repels them." He tossed me the salt can. I turned it over in my hands as he continued, "And iron...but it doesn't kill them. I don't even know if they *can* be killed...being already dead and all..."

"So, how can I stop it from haunting me?" I tucked the salt can into my backpack and moved back to the book that was still open on Elijah's worktable.

"That's why we're going to Charlotte Grey," Elijah said. "We just have to wait a few more hours until she opens."

"You're going to the Nile Witch?" Courtney asked in surprise.

I didn't bother explaining, let alone looking up from the book. Instead, I scanned the page detailing ghosts as I went over the history of the house and the mirror in my head. Something nagged at the back of my mind. I was forgetting something.

I jumped as Elijah put a hand on my shoulder. "I'm going to head down and give Lacey her EMF meter. She's been waiting for this for a while."

I blinked. "Okay..." I had half a mind to ask if we could hold onto it for a bit longer, but I didn't. It didn't feel right to keep her meter on top of excluding her from everything. Besides, I already knew the ghost was out there...I didn't need an alarm to alert me.

I watched Elijah head out the door and then turned my attention back to the book. After a few minutes, I could feel eyes on me. Peter and Courtney were looking at me expectantly.

"What?"

Peter and Courtney exchanged a glance, and then Peter said, "We're going with you...when you see the witch, I mean."

I sighed. "I appreciate the offer, really, I do. But I think all four of us would be a bit much."

"So, Elijah is going with you, then?" Peter asked stiffly.

"Yes."

"Honestly, I'm good with sitting the witch out." Courtney laughed lightly. "Peter and I can just wait here for you to get back."

I nodded. "Sounds like a plan."

Before Peter could argue otherwise, Elijah threw open the door and ducked inside. His face was a bit pale as he straightened up and pushed his glasses far up his nose. "Lacey never showed up at Cassandra's."

We assumed she just took a detour and decided to go for a walk in the woods. Peter and Courtney spent the rest of the time looking for her while Elijah and I loaded up in his truck and drove to the pub. I tried to keep my mind focused, but it was hard when I kept picturing Lacey getting dragged into a window by a ghost...which sounded ridiculous even then. Plus, I didn't really want to think too much about where we were going. Whenever I stopped to consider the fact that we were on our way to a witch, panic quickly began to set in, complete with heart palpitations and labored breathing. Better to not think, just act...at least in this instance.

Elijah held the door open for me, and we went inside the pub. The whole place was a clash of noise and rowdy chaos. Country music blared from the stereo, and people everywhere were shouting over each other and sloshing their mugs of frothy beer. Occasionally, a loud crack of pool balls smacking together punctuated the din. Elijah took my hand and pulled me around the outskirts of the place, narrowly avoiding all the patrons. A few men eyed me hungrily, and I made a point to shoot them rude looks.

Elijah pushed me toward a staircase that led up to a loft-type area, overlooking the whole place. Golden Christmas lights were strung along the banister, giving off a happy glow. But before we made it to the stairs, a tall man staggered in front of us.

He had a gaunt, haunted look about him. His skin was loose and ashen gray. His pale blue eyes were bloodshot and sunken into his skull. He reeked of alcohol. He grinned a leering, nasty smile as Elijah stopped short, grabbed me, and pulled me into him.

Staring at the repulsive, pathetic man before us, I imagined this is what my daddy might look like now, and the whole thing made my blood burn.

"Mr. Barrow." Elijah nodded stiffly, his hands still holding me fast.

"Eliiiijjah Grunvaaaald..." the man slurred, his voice sounding like one prolonged burp. "Haven't seen you around in a while. You and my boy get in ter it er sumthin'?"

"Something," Elijah said shortly. Barrow. So, this was Damien's dad. Ew.

Mr. Barrow glanced at the stairs behind him and then gave Elijah a sly smirk. "What choo need the Nile Witch for, boy? Got in ter some trouble?"

Elijah didn't answer.

The drunkard didn't take the hint. "And I'm guessin' this pretty little Amazon is the trouble?" His eyes flashed, and he gave a husky chuckle.

Elijah's hold on me tightened.

"She's a tall one, ain't she?" He eyed me up and down, sliding his tongue across his yellow teeth. "Why, I haven't seen a girlie with legs that long since—"

That was it. I scowled at him, elbowed Elijah off me, and then shooed the drunk away. "Move, please. Before I tell the bartender you're harassing underaged girls."

Mr. Barrow rolled his eyes and held up his hands, moving just enough to let us squeeze by him. I slipped past, rubbing against the wall to avoid brushing against him. He grumbled something nasty under his breath. My brown eyes blazed, and I whirled around to flash a finger at him, but Elijah grabbed my hand and shoved me up the stairs.

Mr. Barrow slinked away into the crowd.

"He's even more charming than his son," I muttered.

Elijah nodded grimly. "What was it you said? 'You have to start at the beginning to understand?' I guess it can also be said for people, too, huh?"

I slowed my step as I glanced at him, a small smile playing at my lips. My heart did a little flutter in my chest as he continued up the steps. He'd not only remembered, but he'd quoted me. "Elijah—"

He stopped short at the top of the stairs, pulling me up to stand beside him, eye to eye. "Yes?"

I blinked, once again marveling at the golden swirls in his dark eyes. My face burned, and I pushed past him. "Let's go."

The loft opened up to a little sitting area, almost like a cozy living room, complete with books and a TV. There was a door positioned in the middle of the back wall with a sign that said in narrow, loopy letters:

Speak Friend and Enter.
(and please, silence all devices)

I exchanged a glance with Elijah as he hastily turned off his phone. All right, maybe I could appreciate the *Lord of the Rings* reference.

I hesitated only for a moment, pausing at the rug thrown over the hardwood floor. I was crossing a line. I could feel it. I was going to a so-called witch for help. This was something from which I couldn't come back. Everything would be different from that point forward. I gritted my teeth and led the way, marching across the carpet, and I knocked pointedly on the door.

THE NILE WITCH

I expected a throaty 'come in' to murmur from inside, but instead the door flew open revealing a woman—a young woman—with long, golden hair twisted up into a knot on top of her head, with little golden tendrils framing her face. Her large blue eyes were bright and kind as she gave me a small smile. She was as tall as me which was odd. I wasn't used to meeting other women eye to eye. But it wasn't just her height that made me stare, it was her youth that I found most jarring. Even more so than her gentle, kind demeanor. She couldn't have been much more than thirty-five. Yet the way people spoke of her, I assumed the infamous Witch of Nile would be a crooked old crone.

She peeked past me to see Elijah, and her smile warmed her face like sunshine in the morning. "Hello...you must be Elijah Grunvald. You look just like your grandmother. She told me you were coming...and you must be Hannah Green."

She held the door open for us, and we walked in.

Just as the Nile Witch herself was surprising...her...I don't know—office? Her office was surprising. I expected more of what Cassandra had had at the fair: scarves and poofs and jewel tones, all medieval/Renaissance inspired. But though there was a happy string of lights boarding the ceiling, everything else about the room screamed 'Dr. Manning.'

Centered in the room, on top of a large round rug, was a small cream couch and two soft-blue plush chairs with a white antique coffee table in between them. There were a few lush green plants here and there with a large bundle of blue hydrangeas nestled sweetly in the middle of the coffee table. There was no window, but the room was so bright and cozy, it didn't seem to need one. There was a white hutch that perfectly matched the coffee table pushed up against the left wall and a small coffee bar in the opposite corner. But what really caught my attention was the built-in bookcase that lined the length of the far wall, complete with a sliding ladder that would make a Disney princess proud.

"My name is Charlotte...please, have a seat. Would anyone like coffee?" Her voice was soft and soothing, the kind of voice that put you instantly at ease. I felt myself relax despite every better instinct.

Elijah glanced at me as we both sat down on the couch. I shrugged, and he said, "Two coffees. Black, please, ma'am."

Charlotte busied herself off in the back corner of the room brewing the coffee, humming lightly to herself.

I took my time to scan the room, noticing for the first time the thick candles and various herbs and bottles organized neatly on top of the hutch. I glanced at the bookshelf, squinting to read the titles, and noticed that most of them were old with peeling spines, making distinguishing the words nearly impossible.

As I studied her room, Charlotte made polite small talk until she finally approached the obvious, "So, how can I help you two this evening?" She passed us each a mug and took a seat in one of the plush chairs opposite us.

Elijah put the mug down on the table and dug into his pocket for his wallet, pulling out several crumpled bills. "How much is it for a spell?"

I looked at him sharply. "A spell?" I thought we'd come here for advice. I didn't realize he had something specific in mind.

Charlotte smiled. "Why don't you tell me what's troubling you...and then we can go from there."

Elijah blushed, folding his cash and stashing it back into his wallet.

I rolled my eyes.

"Hannah, why don't you start?"

I took a deep breath. "Have you heard of the mirror in the Rosecrest House?"

Charlotte frowned thoughtfully. "I've heard the rumors about the house being haunted...You'll have to forgive me. There are so many legends in Nile, I'm not completely familiar with the story of the mirror..."

"There's a mirror in the entryway. The landlady keeps a black sheet over it. I pulled the sheet down, and it broke...the mirror broke. And ever since then, I've been seeing this girl...only she's not a girl all the time—she's like a monster. Everywhere I go, in any reflection I see. Like I'm cursed."

Charlotte nodded. "When the Lapierre girl had her accident last spring, I called immediately and offered my services to the Rosecrest owner." Charlotte winced. "Suffice it to say, she didn't seem too thrilled with the idea. I feel she may have certain prejudices that are commonplace in Nile. The women of my family are something of a Nile legend ourselves. Not always welcome in certain circles. And I'm afraid, I can't be too helpful unless I've investigated the mirror myself..."

I exchanged a glance with Elijah over my mug. "We're pretty sure it's a ghost. And I just want it to leave me alone."

"Do you think we need a spell for that?" Elijah asked a bit too nonchalantly, leaning forward, his elbows on his knees, tossing his hair like a James Dean impersonator. I pursed my lips to hide the smirk that threatened to spread and put my mug to my mouth to stifle the snicker. Apparently, I wasn't the only one who thought Charlotte Grey looked young.

Charlotte didn't seem to notice. She sipped her coffee, quiet for a moment. "I feel reluctant to give you a spell without seeing the mirror for myself..."

My shoulders slumped a bit.

"Do you think you could convince the owner to allow me to..."

I shook my head.

Charlotte placed her mug down on the table and nibbled on her lip. Elijah blinked. I elbowed him. He adjusted his glasses and cleared his throat.

"You say you see the ghost—how do you see it? What triggers that?"

I swallowed as I remembered the river...the bathroom...the mirror maze...the window... "Any reflective surface."

Charlotte stood quickly and went to her hutch behind the chairs. "Would you be willing to call the ghost...so that I could see it for myself? At least that way I'd be more comfortable providing a—"

"You can't see it. No one else has seen it...well, aside from a little girl at the fair."

Charlotte took a vanity tray from the hutch, hugged it to her chest, and walked over to me. "Witches can see things ordinary humans can't. Young children also can be more sensitive to the supernatural. And if it *is* a ghost, well, ghosts can be seen by anyone they want to see them. Ordinary or...other." She smiled. "I'm sure it won't be a problem."

I eyed the tray in her arms. My heart began to pulse violently as my throat began to close. I moistened my lips as my mouth dried. I couldn't answer.

"I promise you will be completely safe," Charlotte added gently.

I tried to laugh, but all I could manage was a choking sound. I cleared my throat. "Fine."

"Uh, I don't—Hannah are you sure, I mean…this seems…" Elijah lost his words and rubbed his neck as he tried to come up with more.

Charlotte held the tray out for me, and I took it in both hands. Slowly, I held it up to my face so that I was staring deep into my brown eyes. Charlotte moved behind the couch, resting her hands gingerly on my shoulders. Elijah squeezed my knee, but then hastily pulled his hand away as though he'd done something wrong.

A smile tickled the corner of my mouth. He was such a blundering goofball. Charlotte's grip on my shoulders tightened, and I saw my reflection change. The girl stared back at me, but instead of smiling evilly or morphing into a monster, she simply looked at me. Waiting. I furrowed my brow and inclined my head.

Charlotte's breath tickled my ear. "Ask her what she wants."

"What do you want?"

The girl shook her head. Then she held up a finger to her lips and disappeared.

Charlotte came around and took the tray from me. She placed it back on the hutch and took her seat again. She cupped her mug in both hands and drank deeply.

"Did you see it?" Elijah asked, impatience high in his voice.

Charlotte nodded, placing her mug back on the coffee table.

"No," I said firmly.

Surprised, Elijah looked between the two of us, confused.

My cheeks grew hot. "No, I mean…the girl *was* there…but she wasn't. She was different. She usually changes into a monster and tries to bite off my face."

Elijah tried to scoff, but it came out like a strangled cough.

Charlotte studied me closely.

I shifted uncomfortably underneath the weight of her stare.

"Well?" I demanded.

Charlotte took a deep breath and answered evenly, "It is not a demon which is quite a relief. But I'm not so sure you should exorcise this ghost just yet."

"What?" Elijah and I demanded in unison.

"Ghosts are an interesting kind of creature...you see, ghosts are simply human souls left behind on Earth. Usually due to unfinished business, but, for one reason or another, they have held on instead of returning to the Creator—which is where they truly belong. And the longer they are here, the more angry and violent they can become..."

"Why is that?" Elijah asked, leaning forward.

Charlotte smiled sadly over her mug. "It can be extremely difficult for them to communicate with us. Especially in the beginning. And coupled with the fact that they are no longer meant to be here—well, imagine feeling so strongly that you have a purpose, a reason for staying on Earth, but being unable to fulfill it. In the end, most ghosts end up consumed by their most violent emotions, losing any kind of rational thought in the process."

"Then why do you feel like I should keep it around?" I asked dryly.

Charlotte smiled slightly. "The ghost that I saw in that mirror didn't seem to be trying to threaten you."

My mouth gaped. I could only stare, torn between offense and disbelief.

Elijah adjusted his glasses. "Ms. Grey, this thing has ripped Hannah through a second story window. The only reason she didn't end up on the ground was due to an awning roof. I'd say that's threatening behavior."

I nodded, unable to speak. What if she refused to help me? What if it was just like my parents, and she didn't believe me?

Charlotte gave a sympathetic nod which only made me want to shove *her* through a second story window.

"Has she given you any messages before this one, verbal or written?" Charlotte asked.

I swallowed thickly and cleared my throat. "'You're next' and 'you don't have time.' Things like that. Wait, 'before this one?' What message did you see?"

Charlotte's blue eyes were sharp as she fired another question, ignoring mine. "Desiree Lapierre was taken to the Maple Leaf House immediately following her fall through the window?"

Elijah hesitated. "Yeah— How did you—?"

"And she is still alive?" Charlotte prompted.

I snorted into my mug. Coffee bubbled and popped in my face like chocolate milk. "Alive? Maybe. Tormented? Absolutely."

"And Zan mentioned in all the accounts there isn't a single mention of a death following an encounter..."

At that I looked at Elijah. This was true.

"And when you asked the ghost what she wanted, she shook her head. What does that tell you?"

"That she doesn't want anything?" I answered tentatively. It was then I remembered Charlotte Grey was a homeschool mom. This felt like a lecture day, and she was playing with the Socratic method—supernatural edition.

Charlotte nodded encouragingly, a small indulgent smile playing at her lips. "Right. She doesn't want anything or perhaps —she *can't* say anything. And with the last message, her finger to her lips...that is pretty clear in and of itself."

"Enlighten me." I said unimpressed.

"She can't speak. Or she doesn't want you to speak. And coupled with the 'you're next' and 'running out of time'—"

"'You don't have time,'" Elijah corrected, clearly much more captivated by her lecture than me.

Charlotte's smile warmed her eyes. "Indeed. I strongly feel like this ghost is warning you."

I stared at her. "Right. It's warning me that it's going to kill me."

Charlotte took a sip from her mug. "That is also a very real possibility...but—"

"Then tell me how to get rid of it...or make it leave me alone... or whatever," I snapped.

Charlotte nodded. "I can give you an exorcism spell for a ghost."

"We can use a spell...without...err—" Elijah fiddled with his thumbs.

"Being a witch? Well...no, not really. It's a bit complicated to explain, but in its simplest terms: I can give you a spell that you can then...activate at your leisure." Charlotte sipped her coffee and then licked her lips. "Think of it like a bomb...I create it, you detonate it. Make sense?"

I considered this as Elijah made an impressed 'ahhhh!' sound with his throat.

"So, would you like a spell to exorcise the ghost?"

"What happens to the ghost when it's exorcised?" Elijah asked, leaning forward again, this time *literally* on the edge of his seat.

"I appreciate that question, Mr. Grunvald." Charlotte smiled. "Quite responsible of you."

Elijah's cheeks turned a brilliant shade of scarlet.

I mumbled under my breath.

"When a ghost is exorcised, either from a person or an object, it is sent on. That is to say—on to either Heaven or Hell. Ghosts, after all, are really just lost souls."

Charlotte laughed lightly as the silence fell. She waved her words away. "But enough theology. Would you like a spell to exorcise this ghost?"

"Yes," I said firmly.

Charlotte's blue eyes bored into me. "Are you absolutely certain?"

"Yes," I repeated impatiently.

Charlotte stood then and collected our mugs. "If you'll excuse me for just a moment, I'll be right back with your spell."

Then Charlotte left the room through the black door by the hutch.

As soon as she shut the door behind her, I muttered, "'Back with my spell.' Of all the most ridiculous—"

I blinked.

She had just left through the black door by the hutch.

The black door that hadn't been there before...had it been there?

I ran a hand through my hair. My head felt foggy and confounded. I glanced at Elijah who was staring blankly at the door.

He straightened his glasses. "Was that—I mean, did you see—?"

I shook my head.

Elijah let out an uneasy chuckle, and we settled into silence.

After a moment, Elijah nudged me. "Well, what do you think?"

I took a deep breath. "I feel...better. Like I can deal with this now."

Elijah nodded thoughtfully. He bit his lip as his brows furrowed.

"What?"

"Oh, nothing..." he said quickly. Too quickly. My eyes narrowed. He shrugged. "It's just...what if Charlotte—"

"Charlotte?"

"*Ms. Grey*...what if she's right? What if the ghost is trying to warn you about..."

I crooked an eyebrow. "Ms. Barbara?"

Elijah's tan skin blushed a deep red, and he shrugged again.

I rolled my eyes. "Well, then why don't you ask her about doppelgangers when she gets back?"

Elijah pointed at his chest. "*Me*?"

"Why not? She likes you best."

Elijah made a choking noise from deep in his throat as his face blushed purple. "You think?"

I rolled my eyes. "Oh, my God," I muttered as I smacked him

on the shoulder. "Get over yourself. She's a freaking *mom*...easily twice your age. *Or more*," I added harshly. "It would make more sense for you to date *me*."

"*What*?" Elijah gulped, pushing his glasses up the bridge of his nose so hard he winced.

"Oh, you know what I meant!" Now it was my turn to blush. "As in: both situations are equally *insane*." Angry and thoroughly embarrassed, I crossed my arms over my chest and hunched down in the couch. "Never mind. Can we get back to the life and death issue at hand, please?"

Elijah nodded. "Yeah. Let's do that." He slapped his knees and stood up with a 'whelp.'

Eyes narrowed, I watched him side-eyed as he walked around the couch and stood by the books.

Elijah ran his fingers over the book spines. "You know, I'm surprised she didn't have a secret doorway hidden behind the bookcase." I nodded begrudgingly as Elijah touched the top of a book and began to slide it out. "Like pull a book and—"

The black door opened.

Elijah released the book, and it fell to the floor. He dropped quickly to scoop it back up, but before he could replace it, Charlotte said kindly, "Oh, please. Keep it. Things like that don't happen by accident."

"Except...they *do*," I muttered.

Charlotte held a cloth bag in her hands as she took a seat in the soft-blue chair. She leaned over the coffee table and held the bag out to me. "This is an exorcism spell."

I half expected something to happen or to feel something 'magical' as I took it in my hands, but it was just an ordinary pouch.

"You need to go to what you believe to be the source of the ghost, in this case a reflective surface like the mirror. It's best if you go to a place in which the ghost has already been, make the ghost show itself, and then light the bag, releasing the spell. The spell will do the rest."

"'Light the bag?'" I made a face. "You mean burn it?"

"Yes. And do not, under any circumstances, try to open it before then. Magic is like science, dangerous if not respected."

Elijah pulled out his wallet. He counted out his twenties and passed her the bills. He'd handed her well over a hundred dollars. My face grew hot. I hadn't thought about how we'd pay.

Charlotte smiled and closed her eyes as she cupped his hands in hers. I pursed my lips, expression souring, as I watched Elijah's eyes flutter, his cheeks redden, and his throat gulp. Then Charlotte's eyes flashed open, and she released him abruptly with a nod of thanks. I stared at Elijah with a cocked eyebrow, but he, clearly flustered, only shrugged and shoved his hands roughly in his pockets.

She went to the hutch and tucked the money in a drawer before slowly turning around to face us. I felt her eyes move over me as Charlotte studied me closely.

Cradling the spell carefully in my hands, as though it might explode at any moment, I tucked it away in the front pocket of Peter's hoodie.

"Once you've exorcised the ghost...it might be a good idea to take it one step further and destroy the mirror."

My confusion must have shown clearly on my face for Charlotte added, "In the event that there is something...dark...about this mirror. You'll want to take this holy water." She passed me what looked like an old glass soda bottle. "Soak the mirror, pinch of salt, and burn it. Don't worry. It will catch. Holy fire is a powerful element. Then collect the ashes and bury them."

"Under the full moon?" I muttered.

Charlotte grinned. "If you'd prefer..."

Just as we got to the door, Charlotte stopped us with a final warning. "I say this only because I strongly caution you to wait: if for any reason you decide you do not want to exorcise the ghost, you'll need to destroy the spell. Spells kept for too long…let's just say they have an expiration date. To destroy this spell safely, just as with the mirror, you'll need to soak it in holy water and then burn it. Do you understand?"

"Yes."

"And trust your *instincts*, Hannah. That's most important. Trust in your instincts…"

"Right. Sure. Thanks." I gave a little impatient wave, and we left.

Elijah was quiet on the drive back through the island.

"So, I've been thinking…our best bet would be the mirror itself—the one underneath the sheet." I looked at him. He nodded distractedly. I frowned and tried again. "Based on everything we read, all the accounts of the mirror, it won't be broken anymore. It'll be back together again…so, we should be able to make the ghost appear…"

Elijah nodded again, clearly disturbed by something.

I glanced over at him. "What?"

Elijah flinched a bit and forced a smile. "Uh, nothing."

I frowned. "There's something you aren't saying…"

Elijah shook his head, stretching his arms out in an odd shrug, as his hands gripped the steering wheel. "Nah, just—"

"What is it, Elijah?"

He winced and looked at me sideways. "You know when I gave her the money? And she—"

"Held your hand for forever?"

Elijah's cheeks burned a deep red again. "Right. Well, she—I heard…I mean I *think* I heard her voice…like, in my head." He tapped his skull for reference.

I blinked. "You heard her voice in your head?"

"Yeah, like she was talking…but she wasn't."

I was quiet for a moment. If I could believe a spell might save me from a haunted mirror, I suppose I could believe in a telepathic witch…maybe. "What did she say?"

"Err...well, she said—she suggested that you might be some kind of psychic."

"What?" I snapped angrily.

Elijah fumbled a bit underneath the heat of my anger and spoke in a rapid rush as though all the words were connected in one long breath. "She said that there are a lot of different kinds of 'seers,' and you are the most unusual she's seen. She said that you wouldn't want to hear it from her and hearing it from me would be best."

"She thinks I'm a psychic?" I exclaimed incredulously. "And not just a psychic, an *unusual* psychic? As opposed to a *normal* psychic?"

Elijah gave me a sheepish smile before he shrugged and turned back to the road. "I mean—you said you were having dreams about your sister for a while before it happened...and—"

"*A psychic*!" I snapped. "Of all the ludicrous, ridiculous—"

"I'm only relaying a message." Elijah's voice was firm as it had been when he was arguing with his grandmother. "But if we're gonna believe in ghosts and evil mirrors and monsters and witches and spells...why can't we believe in the very real possibility that you might be a psychic? Maybe those dreams about your sister didn't come from the creature that took her...maybe they came from you. And you said the dreams stopped shortly after you started your sleep meds? Maybe they've been sedating your—your powers or something."

I scoffed and glared angrily out the window at the trees and the dying rays of sunlight streaming over the horizon.

I refused to believe that.

I would not believe it.

I couldn't believe it.

Because if I was psychic that meant that not only did I let it happen...I was *responsible* for what happened in more ways than I'd ever realized. For if I was psychic, I didn't just dream about it, I *knew* about it. I was complicit.

I didn't speak the rest of the way home, despite Elijah trying his best to make a case for psychics. ("Lacey says Cassandra's a psychic...we could talk to her when this is all over." "You know, I read a strong case in a scientific journal for the déjà vu phenomenon.")

When we got home, my anger vanished as soon as we pulled up to the house, replaced by an annoyed curiosity. Someone was sitting in the rocker on the porch. And it wasn't Ms. Barbara.

2 1

MISSING

It was her sister.

The sun was sinking into the trees behind Rosecrest, casting shadows along the house and darkness over the porch. The two of us made our way up the stone path that cut through the bare bushes, branches nettling our clothes, and we headed toward the fire escape. The plan was to wait in Elijah's apartment until Ms. Barbara was asleep. Then I would slip into the house and light the spell and be done with it. My heart was light with nerves. Instead of feeling hope, my stomach was sick with dread.

Sandra Blake, seated still in the rocker, stared at us shamelessly as we passed. Just before I could touch the wood of the staircase, she called out to me.

"Hannah? Is that your name?"

I stuffed both my hands in the pocket of the hoodie to keep the spell secure. With an inward groan, I made my way to the porch. "Yes?"

Sandra stood from the chair, heading down the steps to meet me. She glanced pointedly at Elijah. "I was wondering if I could speak with you...alone."

Frowning, I nodded to Elijah, who reluctantly headed up to his apartment.

The woman smiled a strange, pained smile. "I wanted to apologize. I'm sorry...if I've come off rudely. It's just that my sister has always made things difficult when all I've ever done is try to help her. And it doesn't help that you look so much like her." She reached out to touch my hair. I flinched away from her.

"I'm sorry. I guess I'm getting sentimental. It's hard to let go of the place. Rosecrest." She glanced back at the house. "I grew up here, too, you know."

I didn't respond. I glanced over at the fire escape.

"Right. You probably want to get back to your friend...Barbara and I used to be friends...we'd play hide and seek all throughout the house. With Elijah's grandmother, actually. Little Peter's grandpa, Peter, too." Sandra laughed lightly. Her brown eyes shimmered as a tear slipped down her cheek.

That got my attention. "Wait—did you say Elijah's grandmother? You mean, Zan?" I massaged my temple as I tried to make sense of my thoughts.

Sandra pressed a light fingertip to the tear. She sniffed as she forced a weak smile. "Yes. I was a bit younger, but they always included me in their games. That is, until they had their falling out. Barbara never wanted to play with anyone after that..."

She sighed with a rueful smile. "The old woman who owned the place, Ms. Kathleen, she absolutely *adored* us; she even left Barbara the house and a modest fortune when she died...but not even that made Barbara happy. She was never the same again."

Sandra was still talking, something about a time in the attic with Peter Blanchard, but I wasn't listening. My mind was going too fast. Zan said her friend broke the mirror.

It was Barbara. Barbara broke the mirror. Then Barbara changed. She wasn't a doppelganger. She was a victim of the ghost, too. She'd known the whole time.

Something else...I was missing something.

Sandra sighed again. "Well...I have to go. Perhaps I'll see you in the morning?" Sandra walked briskly to her car as though she didn't want to linger near Rosecrest after dark.

I watched her as she opened the car door. "You're coming back tomorrow?"

Sandra looked back at me, her hand on the car door frame. "Yes...Barbara hasn't said—?" She rolled her eyes, the frostiness of her disposition returned. Sandra bristled, and her foot quivered a bit as though she longed to stamp it. "The house is as good as sold. I'm taking Barbara to the Cedar Grove retirement facility tomorrow."

"Why would she—?"

"She didn't want to. She has to. That's what happens when you don't have money to pay your property tax." Sandra sighed again and gave me a polite, patient smile. "You have nothing to worry about, Hannah. I've already spoken to your mother and the other tenets...well, not Mr. Grunvald...he's been impossibly hard to get a hold of. Perhaps you could let him know? The new owner is content to honor the prior leasing agreements."

And with that, she got into her car and sped away down the long stretch of driveway, and her headlights slowly faded out of sight.

"Oi!" Elijah called down, leaning over the railing.

On edge, his shout had made me jump. High.

I looked up at him, annoyance crinkling my forehead.

"Lacey's still missing."

They'd left us a note scribbled on a coffee-stained sticky note.

H & E,

We can't find her. It's been hours. Getting dark. We're going to tell her dad.

Peter
P.S. Elijah—turn on your phone!!

As I read, Elijah called Courtney.

They had gone to every place they could think of: her yoba traps in the stream, her gippypuck houses she put underneath trees, and the entire Apple Shore Road and back to the docks. They had even tried Edwin Martin's machine shop and his wife, Catherine's, souvenir stall.

Then when the sun had started to sink, they drove to the Charlebois Inn and told her daddy she was missing, who then told the sheriff, who had had half the island combing the woods for her. But now it was too dark. They were sending everyone back home until morning. Mrs. Blanchard had called just before Elijah had to make sure Peter and Courtney were on their way. Apparently, if one Nile kid went missing, more tended to follow, and she wanted them home immediately. But Courtney said Peter had a UV drone, and they were going to use it from her bedroom window to search the woods by their house.

When Elijah finally hung up, we sat in silence for a moment. Elijah and I didn't bring up the ghost...or the Nile Witch...it just felt in bad taste when Lacey...I suddenly felt hot and cold all over. Then Elijah went to the monster encyclopedia and poured himself over it. I sat lifeless on the couch, my brain foggy with worry and guilt. Elijah was muttering to himself about ghosts and monsters. My brain was barely processing anything. All I could do was stare unseeing at the cat sitting on top of the bookshelf, its tail twitching impatiently.

At midnight, the alarm on Elijah's phone went off and sent us jumping out of our skin, the cat included. Hissing furiously, she leapt down from the bookshelf and darted out of sight.

Elijah quickly tapped off the alarm. "Are you ready?"

I blinked stupidly in a haze from sleepiness as well as heartsickness. "Lacey's missing."

Elijah nodded. "Yes, she is."

I shrugged my shoulders, my arms limp at my sides. "Well, how can I begin to worry about something as ridiculous as ghosts when my best friend is missing, and—like, *everything else*—it's all my fault?"

"It's not your fault—"

"It is."

"—and I think..." He trailed off and scratched his head.

"What? That the ghost took her?" I said dully.

Elijah grimaced and shook his head. "No. I think it has something to do with all of this, though. Down at the docks, Lacey said she had the tools to help you. Maybe someone or something wanted whatever it was she had." Now it was his turn to shrug. He shoved a hand through his hair as he continued to think aloud. "Was it the EMF meter? No, she wanted that for her dad—but that's a tool that could help..."

My eyes widened. The air rushed out of my lungs, and I couldn't seem to call it back. I slapped at my side for the beaded bag.

"What is it?"

I didn't speak. I couldn't. I pulled at the snap and slowly slipped my hand inside. My fingers curled around something hard and heavy. It was her skeleton key. I held it up for Elijah to see.

Elijah's face was blank with bewilderment. He put a hand on his head and waved the other. "Why would she want to give you a key?"

My heart sank like a deflated balloon. I put the key back into the bag and snapped it shut. "No idea. It's her skeleton key. She said it's magic."

Elijah shook his head looking remarkably like a brown Golden Retriever. "Forget the bag. Yes, Lacey is missing. But we can't do anything to find her in the dark. What we *can* do is deal with the ghost. And Lacey would want us to deal with it, yes?"

"Yes."

We headed down the fire escape as quiet as we could manage. The cold wind rushing up from the lake pushed us back and sent the old wooden staircase swaying with soft creaks. I didn't realize until my feet hit the grass below that I'd been holding my breath. I took a deep gulp of air, hoping to steady my heart. Elijah came behind me. As we turned around the corner of the house, I stopped dead in my tracks. Elijah slammed into me.

Ms. Barbara was out on the porch.

The moonlight pooled lightly at her feet and the ember of her cigarette burned red in the breeze. She rocked lightly.

"You haven't been sleeping much lately, Miss Hannah..."

My blood went cold, congealing in my veins. There's no way she could see us, not from where she was and with the dark...how did she know it was me? But she was wrong. It wasn't only me. I slapped behind my back at Elijah. He got the message and slipped back around the house, hidden in the darkness.

"Come, my dear. Out of the shadows. It isn't polite."

I gritted my teeth and gently placed my hands into each side of the hoodie pocket, protecting the spell.

She took a drag from her cigarette. The ember burned orange, illuminating her face. Her eyes looked black and cold.

"What are you doing out so late?"

"Lacey's missing." I approached her slowly. I came to the bottom of the porch steps and stopped.

"Yes. I was just thinking about our little Lacey." Ms. Barbara paused for a moment as she took another drag, blowing out a curl of smoke. "Where do you think she is?"

There was something in the glint of her dark eyes, then, and the twitch of a smirk at her lips that made a shudder move down my spine.

"I'm sorry, Ms. Barbara, but it's pretty late," I said slowly. "I should be getting back inside."

Ms. Barbara stopped rocking. "That's a good idea, dear. Your poor mother's been waiting all evening to see you, I'm sure."

I gripped the porch railing but didn't move. "Can I ask you something, Ms. Barbara?"

She smiled, her teeth blue in the moonlight. "Anything."

I spoke in a voice hard and cold. "Why didn't you tell me you had pulled the curtain down and broken the mirror?"

"I think the better question is..." Ms. Barbara lifted her cigarette slowly to her lips and inhaled, allowing the smoke to pour from her nostrils like a dragon. "Why didn't *you*?"

Frozen in place at the bottom of the staircase, I couldn't move. I couldn't speak. She'd known the whole time.

"Curiosity killed the cat, you know." Ms. Barbara chuckled darkly, flicking the butt of her cigarette into the bushes. "Don't pretend you're any better, Hannah."

She pushed up from the rocker and went to the door. "You're next, after all. And there's nothing you can do to stop it." Her hand rested on the handle; she looked back at me, her smile like a crescent moon in the dark night of her face. "And don't worry about Lacey. I'm sure she'll turn up."

She slipped into the house and shut the door lightly behind her. Someone came up behind me and rested a hand on my shoulder. I jumped and slapped at the hand as I whirled around and shoved them backward.

"Oi, Hannah! It's me," Elijah hissed, grabbing my wrists and forcing them to my sides. I went limp, and he pulled me into a tight hug.

"Elijah..." I breathed, pressing my cheek in between his neck and the soft flannel of his shirt. "She knew. Ms. Barbara knew it was after me the whole time. And I think she knows something else...I think she knows how to save me, but she won't. The ghost came for her all those years ago, and now I'm next..."

Elijah's head lifted off my shoulder, and he pulled back from me to search my eyes. In the darkness, he looked much older, much stronger, than his goofy, inventor vibe usually allowed. His jaw was hard, and his forehead furrowed with concern. "What did she say?"

My eyes prickled, and I stepped away from him. Hiding my face, I rubbed my eyes with the heel of my hand and combed my fingers through my hair. "Nothing, really...it was just like she was...*glad*," I finished lamely. "Almost excited."

Elijah gestured to the house. "You sure it's safe to use the spell now—even though she's still awake?"

I looked up at her window. She probably was watching us as we stood there.

"It doesn't matter now. She's known all along. Let's go."

We ascended the porch steps at a cautious pace. I couldn't stop the harried beat of my heart, and I had to work to keep my breathing steady. I opened the door, and we entered the house. Ms. Barbara had left the old lamp lights on in the entryway. I glanced up at her door, looming ominously above the stairs. It was shut. At least she wasn't waiting at the top of the stairs for me. Now *that* would've been freaky. My eyes moved to the black sheet at the end of the hall. My hands went into the hoodie pocket to rest on the spell. Elijah and I moved forward one slow step at a time, careful not to creak the floorboards.

The sheet was still—a huge monster towering before us. We were inches from it. I pulled the spell out of my pocket, holding it out by the bundled top. Elijah passed me his lighter, and I palmed it tightly, my thumb ready.

Then I pulled the sheet.

It billowed as it fell to the ground at our feet.

I dropped the lighter.

Elijah stepped back.

The mirror was still broken.

THE TOOLS

We flinched away from the empty frame. I snatched the lighter from the ground and pushed Elijah toward my apartment, fumbling for my key as I shoved the spell bag back into the pocket of the hoodie.

"Wait—shouldn't we—?"

Ignoring his protests, I kicked the door open and forced him inside, slamming the door behind us.

My chest heaving, desperate for breath, I leaned against the door. Then I reached behind my back and locked it.

"Shouldn't we cover it back up? What if—"

"It was broken... It shouldn't *still* be broken..." I stared wide-eyed at Elijah in the glow of the TV light as each scene flashed in his glasses. I was panicking. I needed to calm down. "It was *broken*. It shouldn't be broken." I grabbed Elijah by the jacket and shook him. "*Why was it broken?*"

But he didn't have time to answer. A figure lifted itself off the couch. The two of us grabbed each other. My nails dug into Elijah's arm, ready to fling him behind me and torch the spell in one motion. I fumbled for the bag.

"Hannah?" It was just Mom. "What are you—who is that with

you?" Mom mumbled, her voice thick with sleep. She leaned over and turned on the table lamp.

Elijah and I released each other, and he stumbled a few steps back from me. I slipped the lighter back in my pocket. He gave a little wave and awkward jerking bow as he said, "Elijah Grunvald, Ms. Green. From upstairs. Sorry, we were just—"

Mom rubbed the sleep from her eyes as she squinted at us. I saw the untouched popcorn on the side table and *A New Hope* on the screen. Great. I'd forgotten about movie night, on top of everything else. "I'm sorry, Mom...my friend, Lacey, went missing today, and I forgot all about—"

"Lacey's missing?" Mom murmured sleepily as she switched off the TV and brought the popcorn into the kitchen. "She was here earlier."

"She was?" My voice was thin and breathless. Weak.

Mom nodded as she moved to the coffee machine. "She left something for you."

"Did she say where she was going when she left?" I hurried forward into the kitchen, Elijah following close behind me. My legs were wobbly. I grabbed the back of a chair, and I squeezed it hard, willing myself not to faint.

Mom shook her head as she gathered three mugs. "Sandra came back because she couldn't find Ms. Barbara. Lacey left quickly after that."

Elijah and I exchanged glances. Elijah straightened his glasses and took the mug of coffee from Mom with a polite smile. "Err— what did Lacey leave for Hannah, Ms. Green?"

Mom passed me a mug and gave Elijah a weary smile. "'Elizabeth' is fine, Elijah. And please, have a seat."

I stayed standing, but Elijah dropped obediently into a chair.

Mom went to the kitchen counter and passed me the small iron compass Lacey had gotten from Edwin Martin's wife. I turned it over in my hands. It was just a scrap of metal. Nothing helpful at all. I tucked the compass into the beaded bag still hanging across my chest.

"Well, I have work in the morning." She cupped my face in her hands. "I'm sorry she's missing." Then she gave me a quick peck on the forehead and let go. I bit my lip. I wanted to tell her everything. About every weird, crazy thing that had happened to me that week. But as I looked into her dark, tired eyes, I couldn't bring myself to deepen the worry lines already etched into her face.

"I hope the two of you don't stay up all night worrying. You can't do anything until the sun comes up." Then she headed up the stairs.

We waited in silence, listening for the creaks of the steps and groans of the floorboards as Mom made her way to her room. My ears prickled at the sound of the door shutting. I looked at Elijah.

He pushed his glasses up farther on his nose and drank deeply from his mug. My mind was a mess of too many things—Lacey, ghosts, Ms. Barbara. I needed to take it one step at a time. Step one: get rid of the ghost. But how when the mirror was still broken? The mirror in my bathroom? My bedroom? Absent-mindedly, with one hand still on my coffee, I reached into the beaded bag and fingered the key and the compass, pressing them hard into my palm as I thought. I took a sip of coffee. There was warmth in my head and a sudden clarity in my thoughts.

Then I remembered.

I slammed my mug down. Coffee sloshed onto the table. Elijah flinched, spilling some coffee down his front.

"How do we get into the attic?" I demanded.

Elijah blinked. "I don't know...uhh, Ms. Barbara's apartment, I guess? Why...?"

Ignoring his question, I considered his answer for a moment and a slow smile spread across my face. I slapped him hard on the back. "That's not the only way."

. . .

I grabbed a hammer off his worktable. Elijah held up a hand and passed me a crowbar instead. I rolled my eyes, dropped the hammer into his hand, and took the crowbar. He pulled off his coat and rolled up his sleeves, then went for the books. Quickly, he pulled them from the shelf and tossed them out of the way. The cat watched everything from a spot on the couch, her eyes narrowed disapprovingly.

I wedged the bar in between the shelf and the wall—or rather the door—and pulled. Hard. It took a while, but I managed to tear the bookshelf apart. Bit by bit, pieces of wood broke away, though some of the more stubborn pieces remained, jagged and held fast by the nails. One final heave, and I shoved the shelf away, and the door was finally revealed.

I looked at Elijah. He finished clearing away the books and bookshelf debris and stepped back to survey my handywork. He ran a hand through his hair and stared dubiously at the door. It was small, just like his front door, with an old-fashioned doorknob with a gaping hole for a key.

"You really think there's another mirror in there?" he asked softly, as though worried someone might hear us.

I tossed the crowbar aside. It clanged as it hit the ground. I flinched. "I know there is. Ms. Barbara told me herself. She said that Kathleen Murphy told her to never touch the mirror—'especially not the one in the attic.'"

"And you don't think we should just use another mirror?" He waved toward his bathroom. "Like that one, for example?"

"No." I fixed my eyes on the little door in front of us. I rested my hand on the beaded bag. "I can't explain it, but I just know we need to get in there. I can feel it. The attic is where we need to go. And Charlotte said it needed to be the *source* of the ghost, right? Well, if we can find another mirror identical to the one downstairs...I think we need to use it. She said magic is like science, and science has rules, logical rules that make sense. And this makes sense to me."

Elijah nodded, his face grim and set. "Sure, if we can find one... but what are the chances of finding an *identical* mirror?"

I fought the urge to stomp my foot. Instead, I tossed my backpack roughly at his chest. "I told you, I can't explain it, Elijah, okay? I just know we need to try the attic. Now stop arguing and put on the backpack. It has the salt can and holy water."

He raised an eyebrow, clearly intrigued. "Is this like a psychic thing?"

I shot him a murderous look, and he held up his hands in surrender. "All right. Fine. But when we get in there, we need to be extremely quiet. Ms. Barbara will be able to hear everything through the floorboards."

My stomach twisted and cramped. Great. No pressure.

He reached for the crowbar and adjusted his grip like a baseball player. I raised an eyebrow. He blushed as he shrugged. "Just in case..."

I rolled my eyes. What was his idea for Plan B, smash the ghost to pieces? I swallowed, my tongue thick in my mouth, and approached the door. I tried not to think too much about anything other than this next right step: open the door. Anything after seemed too overwhelming, too debilitating. I checked the spell and the lighter. Both were secure. I turned the knob. It was locked. My heart sank.

I looked at Elijah. He scrunched his mouth up to the side and scratched his chin. "Well, that should be an easy pick. I mean, I don't have lock-picking tools, but I should have a paper clip somewhere—"

I shook my head. Tools. How obvious. But how could she have...but then, did it matter at this point? I dug into the bag and pulled out the skeleton key. Elijah made a little gulping, gasping noise and straightened his glasses. I slid the key carefully in the lock. It clicked as I turned.

And I opened the door.

I slipped the key back into the beaded bag. Cautiously, and

barely breathing for fear of making a sound, Elijah and I ducked underneath the short doorway.

It was like we were in a small tunnel, or rather an extremely cramped hallway, consisting of a handful of stairs that led upward. Quiet as we could manage, we took the steps one at a time, each squeaking slightly under our weight, and entered the attic of the Rosecrest House.

It was pitch-black and impossible to see. Light from Elijah's apartment leaked in behind us, barely spilling onto the floor at our feet. Elijah stood close to me, and we kind of leaned into each other so as not to get lost. We didn't move farther than the landing.

"There must be a light switch somewhere..." I whispered.

Elijah grabbed me hard and squeezed. "Did you hear that?"

"*No*," I hissed sharply. "Help me find the switch."

Elijah didn't loosen his hold, instead he pulled me into him with the crowbar extended. "Seriously, Hannah, something moved out there."

"Oh, please," I snapped angrily. "How could you possibly have seen *anything*?"

I squinted blindly into the darkness and felt the wall for a switch. My hand was covered in cobwebs by the time I found one. I wiped my palm on my jeans before slapping it up. An overhanging light, suspended in the center of the attic, turned on with a small pop, casting shadows instead of illuminating the place. It was as anyone might expect an attic to be: full of old junk.

Rows and rows of it. There was no clear path anywhere. But unlike any ordinary attic, it wasn't cramped or claustrophobic. It was massive, stretching the entire length of the house. Not only that: it was high—at least 20 feet or more to reach the ceiling. And even more than that, in the center of the attic, in the middle of the hoard beneath the single lightbulb, there was a rickety unfinished staircase that led straight up to a trapdoor in the roof. I stood, mesmerized, staring up at the thing, as though it led straight up to the sky.

Elijah gave me a gentle prod with his elbow. "Come on...we've got a mirror to find."

I nodded, my eyes sliding down from the ceiling and resting on a giant black armoire sitting all alone at the base of the staircase.

"Elijah..." I breathed. It couldn't be so simple...but I was sure.

I ran for it as fast as I could manage, weaving through all the piles of forgotten things, until I came to the clearing at the base of the staircase and stopped short at the foot of the armoire. It was old, dusty, and painted black. It had the same sinister effect that the sheet had downstairs. Elijah came up behind me, panting and clutching his side, the crowbar limp in his hand. "What—is—you —don't think it's—do you?"

I raised an eyebrow at him, allowing him a moment to catch his breath. "I do."

I pulled the spell bag out from my pocket and gripped the lighter in my hand.

"You want me to open it?" Elijah whispered.

I shook my head. It had to be me.

"Get behind me, Elijah," I murmured.

He frowned, opened his mouth to argue, but then shut it quickly. Reluctantly, he slipped behind my back, placing a reassuring hand on my shoulder, holding the crowbar out at the ready.

I hesitated as I stared hard at the black armoire. My breathing grew labored as I realized: it reminded me so much of our bedroom closet. Elijah squeezed my shoulder, bringing me back. I gritted my teeth and inhaled deeply through my nose.

"You can do this," Elijah murmured.

Palming the lighter, I pulled open the first door and then the second. And there it was, a second mirror of Rosecrest.

Slowly, my shadowy reflection faded, replaced by the ghost girl I'd come to know so well, her long hair framing her pale face and her eyes so dark they looked black. Her eyes bored into me, and I was drowning in them like black pools. Her smile began to stretch like there were hooks in her cheeks. Her glass shard teeth gnashed, splintering in places. I held the spell bag out in front of me like a grenade with the lighter ready in my right hand.

But then, she changed.

Her lips slipped back into place. Her teeth were human again. Her dark eyes widened in horror as they slid from me to the spell bag in my hand. She began to shake her head furiously, shouting a message I couldn't hear. She slapped against the mirror. The vibrations rumbled against the glass as she pounded harder and harder.

But I didn't stop.

I flicked the lighter.

The flame licked the bag.

It burst into flames and then exploded in a burst of sapphire stardust. The little fragments of blue glitter shimmered all over the mirror, the inside of the armoire, and even me. And then there was a scream—a tortured, moaning scream, and the ghost was ripped from the mirror, her arms still outstretched.

The ghost stood before me, as real and ordinary as myself. She looked at me, her dark eyes sad, and she reached for my face. I couldn't move. She touched my cheek, but I only felt cold. Her dark eyes shimmered, and she whispered, "You're next."

Then her whole being glowed with warmth and light, and she was gone.

I blinked, slowly processing what had just happened.

Elijah's hand was still clamped on my shoulder, his fingers digging in as he held me back, firmly against him. I hadn't felt it before...but it hurt.

I turned my head, looking back at him as he leaned over my shoulder. "Elijah, did you—?"

"See?" His eyes were wide as he licked his lips and nodded. "Yeah—as soon as you lit the—and she came out of the—yeah." The crowbar shook slightly as his arm wobbled. Elijah's hand tightened even more. I winced, and he let go with an awkward apology.

He stepped back from me and waved a hand at the mirror in

the armoire. "So, it's over? The curse and the ghost and...now we just have to burn the mirrors?"

I ran a hand through my hair. I felt shaky. Maybe my nerves were shot from the whole ordeal, but something didn't feel right. I didn't feel like I had conquered evil. I didn't feel safe. I felt... vulnerable and scared.

And Lacey was still missing...

My hand slid into the beaded bag, and I fingered the key and compass. I stared down at my boots trying to collect my thoughts. The wooden baseboards were coated with inches of dust. Our shoes had kicked up a lot of it as we'd run up to the—

I inclined my head. A third set of footprints headed to the right side of the attic and disappeared around a mound of junk. I elbowed Elijah and pointed to the prints. His mouth fell. He looked at me. Was he thinking what I was? I held a finger to my lips and jutted my thumb out.

We split up. Elijah went left, and I went right. Eyes on the dusty floor, we weeded through the piles and rows and shelves. Occasionally, we'd peek across the room to check on the other, just to be safe. Halfway through the attic, I didn't find anything. It was hard to see the footprints the farther away from the light I got. Plus, some of them seemed to mix with my own.

My eyes lingered on a large couch pushed against the wall covered in a mound of old clothes.

I froze mid-step.

The mound of clothes was moving...no. *Breathing.*

My heart quickened as hope tickled the corner of my mouth. I hastened to the couch and touched the top of the pile. It flinched away from my touch and then grew deathly still. Before I could pull the clothes away, she burst out of the fabric with a fire poker and stabbed at my chest.

"HEY!" I cried out in alarm, dodging away from her as the poker ripped a tear in Peter's hoodie.

Elijah shouted back to me in alarmed confusion, but I had no time to respond. Lacey, eyes closed tight, had pulled back the poker for another swipe. "Lacey, stop! It's me!"

Lacey's eyes were bloodshot and cloudy from sleep. She dropped the poker and jumped at me, clinging to me in a desperate hug. I held her, smoothing her white-blonde hair back from her wet face. "*Where have you been?*"

Elijah came up behind us and grabbed us both tight. "What are you doing here?" he grunted as he crushed us both in his lean arms.

We released her, and she sniffed. Her soft voice was thick with emotion as she breathed, "I wanted to help." She looked up at me, her wide hazel eyes hard on mine. "I knew I could help. I gave you the skeleton key...you have it, don't you? You need it. But I forgot to give you the compass...so I left it with your mother. And then when Sandra came and couldn't find Ms. Barbara in her room, I thought I'd be able to sneak into her apartment and find some kind of proof." She shook her head sullenly as she murmured, "Everyone always wants proof."

"Proof of what?" I asked bewildered.

Lacey shook her head again. She took a deep breath, and her gentle, patient tone returned. "But Ms. Barbara came back, and I had to hide. So, I climbed her staircase to the attic."

"Proof of what?" I repeated.

Lacey blinked, tilting her head as though it were obvious. "Ms. Barbara isn't Barbara Blake."

"What?" I demanded.

Lacey passed me a locket. I cracked it open. Inside were two portraits, clearly sisters.

"That's Sandra." Lacey pointed to the littlest girl on the left, but my eyes were on the other portrait. "And that's—"

I tried to swallow. My mouth had gone dry.

"—Barbara Blake."

I looked at Elijah, my eyes shining. "It's the girl in the mirror."

Elijah grabbed the locket. "Wait. How can the girl in the mirror be Barbara Blake? Then who is—"

"*What* is," I breathed.

Lacey nodded serenely. "Cassandra said her aura is wrong."

I shook my head. Tears spilled unchecked from my eyes as I stared at Lacey in bewilderment.

"Cassandra's a psychic like you, Hannah," Lacey explained matter-of-factly.

"Me?" I repeated, numb from the feral fear fogging my thoughts.

Lacey was still talking...I could barely hear her. My knees wobbled a bit, and I felt like I might fall.

"But Cassandra's sight was messed up when Desiree moved in. And again when you moved in. She doesn't know what Ms. Barbara is but—"

"She's a monster," I whispered.

The light overhead began to flicker as a strong, musty stench filled the air.

Then a voice hissed, "*And you're next, Hannah...*"

23

THE END

A high cackle pierced the air, sending a wave of terror through my body, all the way down to the soles of my feet.

Lacey's hazel eyes widened, and she held the poker like a sword. Elijah choked up on the crowbar as the two of them scanned the room for her, peeking over piles of junk and craning their necks around stacks of stuff. But I saw her first. My heart pounded. My thoughts blurred. Fear paralyzed every rational thought.

She was hunched over at the far end of the aisle like an overgrown rodent sitting on its hindlegs. Her hands, strangely long like claws, were held out in front of her with her elbows tucked into her body. She didn't look...right. She didn't look human. Her flesh was swollen and squishy and pink. Her back curved up far too high, as though her spine was shaped like a hook. Her head was bent low, level with where her chest should have been. Her eyes were like tiny black holes. But it was her smile—her smile that made my heart stumble in my chest. It was stretched too wide, curving sharply up her face revealing glass shard teeth. She was covered in black rags that seemed to be smoking and disintegrating off her right there as she stood—so still, watching and smiling.

Suddenly, she scurried behind another pile of junk and disappeared.

The way she'd moved was unnatural and way too fast.

There was a rustling off in the distance like the sound of an enormous rat as she scurried somewhere out of sight.

"Elijah..." My voice was barely audible, a low breath on my lips. "How do we kill it?"

Elijah shook his head. The knot in his throat bobbed up and down as he swallowed. He sputtered over his words. "Er—Charlotte—Charlotte said...uhmm."

"Iron repels evil," Lacey whispered, holding her poker steady in front of her like a fairy princess with her sword. "Your crowbar isn't iron, Elijah, is it?"

Elijah made a strangled noise as he shook his head, still gripping his crowbar like a bat.

There was another scurrying sound toward the left.

We all twisted around.

She—*it* was standing at the other end of the aisle now, no longer resembling a woman at all, let alone a human. It stood just as before: hunched over, head low, beady black eyes staring unblinkingly with a grotesque smile baring its sharp teeth.

"Elijah..." I moaned. He needed to snap out of it. I needed him to snap out of it.

He squeezed his forehead as he tried to think. "The book—the book said..."

"ELIJAH!"

The thing moved fast. Impossibly fast. Its whole body wiggled side to side as it rushed forward, stopping halfway to us. Taunting us and tilting its head from one side to the next. Its glass teeth glittered in its insane hooked smile.

Elijah and Lacey pushed in front of me, shielding me from her. I tried to think. "*Elijah what did the book say!*"

Elijah's voice was strong and sharp as he struggled to remember. "Nothing! There was nothing in the book about a giant, wormy, rat thing! What did Charlotte say to purify evil?"

"I don't remember! You were the one hanging on her every word!" I snapped.

"Now's not the time to be jealous, Hannah!" he snapped back.

"Well, what do we do?!"

Elijah groaned in frustration as he tried to recall the witch's instructions. "She said salt, holy water, holy fire."

The thing let out a low, chittering growl. Tears streamed down my face as I remembered the mirror maze. The creepy growl that sent my skin crawling. My heart sank. She'd tried to warn me. The ghost girl. Barbara Blake. She'd warned me, but I hadn't listened. Then I remembered Rebecca, and the closet monster, and Daddy. Always ignoring what's right in front of me. But not anymore.

"I'm next," I whispered.

The thing scrambled around a pile and disappeared.

Then it was at my ankles. It ripped my legs out from under me. My hands smacked the floorboards just before my face hit the dust—hard, sending black spots bursting in my vision. And it dragged me away.

Elijah shouted.

Lacey screamed.

They ran after me. But they couldn't keep up. The thing was too fast.

The wood scratched and splintered into my stomach as it yanked me through the attic. I tried to think, but I couldn't. All I could do was kick and thrash, but it was too strong.

It pulled me in front of the black armoire. In front of the mirror. It seized me by the back of the hoodie, its claws ripping and tearing through the fabric, and flipped me over onto my back so it could leer into my face. Saliva oozed from glass shard teeth, dripping down onto my face.

I knew what would happen next.

Barbara Blake had shown me.

Tears streamed down my face, blurring my vision as much as my thoughts.

"HANNAH!"

Lacey charged forward and stabbed the monster in the shoulder with the poker and wrenched it back again.

The thing fell backward with a screech.

Elijah reached down to me, and I grabbed his hand. He yanked me upward as I clambered to my feet. The thing was gnashing its teeth, its tiny beady eyes rolling wildly in its head. Elijah swung the crowbar like an ax, cracking it down on its skull. It didn't even flinch. With its attention on Elijah, I grabbed the thing, and I shoved with all my might, forcing it through the armoire and its face into the mirror. There was a sickening smack as its head cracked against the glass.

Lacey came up beside me and stabbed again, this time sticking it in the back with the poker. It howled in pain, whipping around to face us. Both arms tucked into its sides, it snatched Lacey and threw her into the door of the armoire with a dull thud. She crumpled into a pile.

Elijah flew past, crowbar swinging, as he aimed at its head again. The thing moved to the side, grabbed him by the arm, and tossed Elijah across the room with impossible strength. He hit the wall and dropped out of sight.

Then something black came flying through the air, hissing and spitting.

The cat.

Her back arched and hair on end, she latched onto the thing, her claws digging into the raw flesh. The monster howled a piercing squeaking sound as the cat's growl vibrated through her body. I watched, eyes wide in horror, as the cat tore at the creature. My heart quickened with hope. Maybe it would be okay.

But it wasn't.

The thing ripped the cat off its back, its shard-like teeth barred.

It gripped the cat in both hands and bit down hard, ripping fur and flesh. Blood drenched the black fur as the monster munched. Its teeth crunched like broken glass as it devoured the cat.

Hot tears poured down my face as I blinked in shock.

The creature, breathing heavily, closed its black eyes as though savoring the taste. Then it looked at me.

It smiled and spoke in a low raspy growl. "I've been waiting for you, Hannah. *For so long...*"

I backed up slowly.

Lacey wasn't moving. She hadn't moved.

"To eat me?"

The thing laughed, a low, groaning chitter. "In a way. Just like Barbara Blake. And all the others before her."

"I don't get it. The book said—"

"A book written by humans? You think *humans* could even begin to comprehend a creature like me?"

"So, what are you?"

"A mawkit...an ancient creature of the mirror realm...I can only exist outside the mirror for a little while...unless I can find a suitable host...within which I can burrow..."

Burrow. This monster would force its way inside me. Living in my corpse. My stomach heaved. I swallowed the bile with a grimace. It made a chittering sound as it inched closer.

"First, I'll sink my teeth into that beautiful face, then I'll burrow inside your meatsuit and store away your precious little soul into the depths of my mirror to feed upon at my leisure...*for years and years...*"

It moved closer.

I had to keep it talking. I had to think. "But you already had Barbara Blake, why did you need me?"

The thing hissed in disgust. "Souls expire...they rot well before they're all used up...her meat is downstairs right now...a festering corpse shell...I like fresh flesh...as well as fresh souls..."

The thing was inches from me. My head was too foggy. I

couldn't think of anything to do. All I could manage was a small whimper. "But you left Desiree alone...why do you want me?"

"I had to leave her alone—there wasn't room for Desiree yet... Barbara Blake's ghost was still rotting away in the mirror...if the soul hadn't been spent, it must be exorcised by the host to make room for the next to take its place. The wretched little witch Jemima Blackwell saw to that...magic has *rules*, you see. Before Jemima, I was taking dozens of souls at a time, hoarding them all safely away in my mirror...but Jemima was smarter than I gave her credit for...she tricked me—putting a curse on my mirror...limiting my storage space, if you will...to protect her sister. After that, I could only have one host—one soul—at a time. And the soul must be exorcised by the next host. And Desiree didn't finish. She didn't exorcise the ghost. The wretched Barbara Blake scared her off. Kept her away. So, I needed another. But you were tricky Hannah, I'll admit that; the hardest yet."

"How's that?"

"Of all my girls, you were the only one whom I couldn't *tell* to exorcise the ghost out right. You refused to believe...could not be manipulated...and yet...in the end...I always can manage it. After all, I needed another."

"I'm next," I breathed.

"Yes, Hannah. You're next."

The mawkit's jaw unhinged, its teeth protruding at all angles.

Then her teeth crunched on my skull.

A BIG BREAKFAST

"Hannah...are you all right?"

My breath was coming hard and fast. I blinked rapidly trying to figure out what was happening. My hands flew to my face, checking for teeth. For blood.

"Hannah—take a deep breath. You fainted."

"I fainted?" I gasped. My heart was racing. My hands cradled my face. "It was a dream?"

"Here, come on..." Elijah gripped underneath my armpits and lifted me to my feet. He kept an arm around me, holding me up. My knees trembled, and I wobbled where we stood.

Lacey took my hand and gave it a squeeze. "I didn't mean to frighten you, Hannah. But Cassandra's sight was messed up when Desiree moved in. And again when you moved in. She doesn't know what Ms. Barbara is, but—"

My eyes widened, and I whispered the words I'd already said: "She's a monster."

The light overhead flickered. The musty stench filled the air.

The voice hissed, *"And you're next, Hannah..."*

A high cackle pierced the air.

But I knew where it would be.

I grabbed Elijah and tore my backpack off his back and tossed it over my shoulder. I yanked the poker out of Lacey's hands and charged up the aisle to meet it, ignoring Lacey's calls and Elijah's shouts to come back.

It appeared right in front of me just where it had before. I swung the poker with all my strength. It scurried out of the way and grabbed my ankles from behind, dragging me toward the mirror just as before. I felt the wood splinter into my skin as the hoodie pulled up and my stomach slid against the floor. It was so fast. I struggled to hold onto the poker. The mawkit flipped me over, claws ripping and tearing the hoodie. Its saliva dripped. It opened its jaws.

But this time, I was ready.

I wrenched the poker up. I stabbed the iron point down the back of its throat. The mawkit fell back, away from me, screaming in a high screech. Elijah and Lacey hauled me up to my feet. I tore off the backpack and unzipped the pocket, seizing the salt and the bottle. I tossed the salt to Elijah who rushed up and shook the can furiously all over the creature.

As the salt touched its flesh, it singed and burned like the embers off the sparklers at Peter's lake house. The mawkit gagged violently on the poker, black beady eyes glittering viciously as it struggled to yank the iron rod out of its throat. It couldn't seem to touch the poker without burning its hands, too. I dumped the bottle on top of its head, drenching it in holy water, and flicked the lighter, setting it ablaze as I jumped back.

Before I could blink, the mawkit burst into flames and disintegrated completely, falling to the floor in a pile of ash and dust.

The iron poker clunked to the floor with a clang.

Elijah grabbed me, pulling me into him in a furious hug. Lacey fell on us, too, and the three of us held each other until light poured into the attic through the cracks in the boards.

• • •

We salted, soaked, and burned both mirrors right there in the attic. Then we swept up all three ash piles into a trash bag and buried them deep in the garden as the sun came up over the lake.

Elijah called Courtney. He told her it was over. Lacey was safe. The ghost was gone. No more specifics. They were too horrific to share.

Then just after he walked me to my door and saw me into my apartment, Elijah left to drive Lacey home, even though it was only a few miles up the road. I think he was scared she'd disappear again.

Mom was downing the last of her coffee as I walked through the front door. She set her mug in the kitchen sink, and I grabbed her around the middle and didn't let go.

"Have you been up all night?" Lightly she stroked my hair and murmured, "I'm so sorry Lacey's missing, sweetheart. I'll ask around at the docks and maybe—"

I shook my head furiously into her shoulder. "We found her."

Her hold on me tightened, and then she pushed me back to look at me from arm's length, to search my eyes. "Is she okay?"

Tears leaked down my face, and I gave her a watery smile. "She's safe."

And I was safe.

Mom smoothed my tears from my cheeks, cupping my face in her hands. "I'm so proud of you." She pulled me into another strong hug and squeezed tight.

I wanted to tell her. I wanted to tell her everything, but before I could, she said brightly, "Oh, did you hear? Rosecrest House is being sold!" Her face fell a bit. "Poor Ms. Barbara is getting taken to an old folks' home this morning." She released me and went to grab her purse. "But the great thing is the new owner will honor the rental agreements! No moving. And the thing you'll get a kick out of...she said the upstairs cleaning service won't be necessary after today! One final clean. So, you don't have that added to your plate anymore. Isn't that wonderful?"

I nodded slowly, still processing...everything.

"Well, I'm off." She studied me with a glint of amusement in her dark eyes. "Maybe take a shower? You look like you've been to Hell and back. I'll see you tonight? Try to be home. I miss you these days." She kissed my head, and then she was gone.

I stared after her, frozen in my thoughts.

A shower. A shower and a fresh change of clothes sounded amazing.

I went to my room. Standing at the dresser, I looked deep into the mirror as I pulled out my clothes. No ghost. No nosebleed. Just an ordinary mirror. My clothes bundled under my arm, I tried to lift the mirror from the wall. It came away easily. A small giggle escaped me. Then I hurried to the bathroom.

Stripping off my clothes, I smiled into my reflection. No ghost. No nosebleed. Nothing. Just me. I fluffed my hair a bit, turning right and left to check the different angles of my face. Then I spent an hour in the shower. When I got out, the mirror was fogged. I watched it closely as I dried off and dressed. No words. No warning. Just a mirror. I laughed out loud and skipped my way downstairs.

Warm, delicious smells of syrup and buttery baked things wafted up to meet me from the kitchen. My heart fluttered, and I took the last few steps two at a time.

Elijah was in the kitchen. Making breakfast. A *real* breakfast. I laughed, soaking in all the goodness of the day. He flinched a bit before turning his head. I went over to stand beside him at the stove. My eyes widened in delighted surprise.

"What'd you do—go grocery shopping?" I scoffed at the spread. Pancakes. French toast. Waffles. Eggs. Sausages, both link and patty. There was no way we had more than a box of cereal in this kitchen.

"Yes," Elijah said simply, a small smirk twitched in the corner of his mouth.

I raised an eyebrow. I still couldn't believe he took the time to do all this. "How can I help?"

Elijah pointed an eggy spatula at the table. "Sit."

Warmth filled me, spreading from my heart outward. Taking a seat, I smiled so big it hurt. Elijah started dropping plate after plate of food in front of me, arranging it smartly all around the table. He poured me a steaming mug of coffee, then one for himself. I held the mug to my nose and breathed in deeply, the rich smell flooding me with comfort and cozy feelings.

I was safe.

I was home.

And Elijah had just made me a big breakfast.

Life was pretty close to perfect.

And then he had to ruin the mood.

"What happened up there?" he asked around a mouthful of pancake.

I slid a piece of French toast around the edge of my plate, sopping up the syrup as I thought over his question. As far as I was concerned, the nightmare was over. I didn't want to deal with anything like that ever again. I popped the drippy bite into my mouth and shrugged.

Elijah raised an eyebrow at my silence. "It seemed like you knew it was going to show up..."

I made a 'hhmmm' noise around my toast.

"And you knew Lacey was in the attic, didn't you?"

I scoffed and stabbed at a sausage link.

"Hannah..."

I scowled and bit off another sausage link. "Why—why can't we just enjoy this delicious breakfast?" I pointed my fork at him. "Why do we have to spoil it by bringing up—"

"The fact that you're psychic?" Elijah said dryly.

"So says the Nile Witch and the Rosecrest Psychic, but if they were so sure, why didn't they just tell me themselves?"

Elijah's mouth twitched as though he were fighting a smile. "Hannah...you can't say you're not a bit contrarian when it comes to all this..."

I shook my head, muttering to myself, as I stabbed another sausage link. "Right, because I'm just so hard-headed and unreasonable. Everyone has to go behind my back and manipulate me into thinking and doing things, instead of just coming out and saying it like a person."

I glanced up at Elijah who was drinking deeply from his coffee mug. My eyes narrowed. "I can see you smiling over there. Don't even bother to hide it."

Elijah snorted, sending coffee spraying. He choked a bit as he laughed.

I rolled my eyes and snapped at another sausage. "I don't know why you had to ruin a perfect breakfast. You realize I've been living off stale cereal for the past, I don't know, *decade*?" I shoveled more pancakes into my mouth.

Elijah, still smiling, took a bite of eggs. "You are hard-headed. But it's one of your most admirable qualities."

My cheeks burned.

"Okay," I said coolly. "Fine."

He raised an eyebrow and sipped his coffee.

I took a deep breath. "I saw everything before it happened. Just like I saw that monster crawl out of the closet..." My voice broke. "And drag my sister away."

Elijah slowly put down his mug, as I dissolved under the truth with a defeated shrug. "So, I'm psychic. And I let my sister die."

Elijah frowned as I stabbed a sausage and muttered, "Me being psychic just means I'm even more responsible for what happened to her than I thought."

Elijah raised a dubious eyebrow. "How?"

I scowled at the sausage impaled on my fork. "I didn't just have the power to know the future—I had the power to *change* the future—and I did nothing to save her. It's my fault. I'm responsible."

Elijah shook his head. "No, you aren't, Hannah. I'll say it again. And again. As many times as I have to: you saw it happen, and you told your parents. You warned them over and over and over. They told you it was a dream. Over and over and over. You were a little kid, Hannah. And you need to forgive yourself."

A tear slid down my nose and landed in my coffee. "How?" I breathed.

Elijah hesitated, then gave me a rueful smile. "I'll think of something." He pointed his fork at me. "While I'm thinking, finish your food."

Elijah took another gulp of coffee.

"Fine. But this afternoon, we're going to see *your* sister."

He choked on his coffee again.

This time, it was my turn to smile.

We were almost done breakfast when there was a sharp, crisp knock on the door. Elijah held out a hand. "I'll get it. You keep eating. But leave me at least one more link, would you?"

I gave him a sly smile as I stabbed another sausage. "We'll see."

Elijah waved me away and opened the door. It was Sandra. She walked inside without waiting for an invitation. She looked extremely disturbed.

"Uhh...hello, Ms. Blake..." I started to stand from the table, but she held out an impatient hand.

"No, please. Sit. I was hoping your mother would be in—?" She craned her neck toward the stairs as though she might see her.

"Err, no, sorry. She works at the west dock until dark..."

Sandra winced a bit and shuffled her feet as though she longed to stamp her designer heel into the old wood floor. Instead, she threw up her hands and began to pace. "Well, that's just the cherry on top, isn't it?"

"What's wrong?" Elijah asked.

"'What's wrong?' What's *wrong*, Mr. Grunvald, is that my sister has—again—had the last laugh!"

The fork slipped from my hand and clattered on the plate. My smile vanished, the warmth left me, and I only felt cold.

Elijah and I exchanged panicked glances. She was gone. *She was gone*; she couldn't possibly—

Sandra continued to pace as she dug her phone out of her purse and began scrolling furiously. "I'm going to have to call Mr. Baker, and then make arrangements, and then—"

"Ms. Blake, what—"

"I'll tell you what, Mr. Grunvald!" Sandra cried dramatically as she flopped down onto his empty chair. "My sister passed away last night."

There was silence. My mouth fell open a bit. Realizing, I quickly shut it and cleared my throat. "Uh, are you sure she—?"

"Yes, Miss Green, of course, I'm sure. I saw her myself. Dead in bed. I've been on the phone with the lawyers all morning!"

Elijah put a hand on his head and blinked. "You—saw her... uhh..in bed?"

Sandra scrunched up her face and stared at Elijah as though he were stupid. "Yes, I saw her!" Sandra rolled her eyes and stared down at the remaining food on Elijah's plate, her mouth in a small pout. She picked up his fork and poked at a bit of egg. "But that's not even the worst of it," she whined.

I open my mouth to ask but shut it again. I blinked rapidly as Sandra poked a sausage and took a large bite. "She *told* me...she said last week," Sandra mumbled around a mouthful of sausage, waving the fork around and pointing it at me. "Absurdly, if you'll believe it, she wanted to leave Rosecrest to *you*. She wouldn't hear of it any other way. 'Over my dead body,' she said." Sandra chuckled darkly. "That nasty old hag."

"Uhh..."

"*Now*, I'll have the extremely unpleasant business of telling

Mr. Baker the deal's off." Sandra rolled her eyes and finished Elijah's sausage in one huge bite. "There will be an autopsy, of course, to make sure there was no foul play…but barring that…" Sandra shrugged and leaned over to stab the last sausage link. "This house is yours, Hannah."

I coughed, choking on my coffee. I sputtered, sloshing more coffee down my front. Elijah hurried over and smacked me smartly on the back. Sandra raised an eyebrow at the two of us and stood smoothly from the table.

"Well, anyways, no need to do a final cleaning. Unless you want to…your house. And I'll be back tonight to speak with your mother…" She eyed me uncertainly as I continued to cough.

Then she left.

I gasped for air and cleared my throat.

I couldn't speak.

I glanced at Elijah, who was staring moodily down at the table.

"What?" I asked, my throat still burning.

"She ate the last link!"

I'd planned on napping. After all, we'd been up all night. But I couldn't sleep. And somehow, I found myself at the bottom of the cellar stairs, standing in front of Cassandra Sawyer's door.

I knocked lightly on the door. Cassandra opened it a moment later, her dark-red hair in a wild tangle and a warm smile on her face.

"Hannah! It's so good to see you—"

I didn't speak. I couldn't find the right words, so, silently, I allowed her to guide me into her living room, overflowing with plants.

"Please, have a seat…"

I sat on the edge of the cushion, careful to keep my back straight for the black snake was curled up inside a giant aquarium just behind the couch.

Cassandra poured two cups of tea and set them out on the coffee table before sitting gingerly down beside me. We sipped in silence for a few moments, until I finally managed to speak. "I don't understand..."

Cassandra nodded with a sympathetic frown. "It's hard...especially for Seers who come from Unseeing families." She placed a gentle hand on my knee and gave me a little squeeze. "Would you like me to explain it to you?"

I nodded, struggling to maintain my composure. I hated crying, especially in front of people.

"Have you seen *Star Wars*?"

I blinked and glanced at her sideways. "Yes..."

Cassandra smiled. "Okay, well, God...Higher Power, Yahweh, Allah, whatever you want to call them...the *Creator* is connected to all of us through magic—which is kind of like the Force in *Star Wars*. Anyone can tap into the magic through prayer and meditation, but some humans are born a bit differently—think like the Jedi or even the X-Men; they are a different evolution of human... These people have magic flowing through their veins. It's actually in their genetic code, specific magic genes which allow them supernatural skills that ordinary humans cannot duplicate, no matter their prayer or study...that's witches like Charlotte Grey...and Seers like me...and you."

I took a deep gulp of tea. "Charlotte Grey told—well, she gave Elijah the impression that I'm 'the most unusual psychic she's ever seen.'"

Cassandra nodded, her face warmed.

I didn't smile. "What does that mean?"

"Well, Charlotte is a unique case herself. Witches are powerful beings, but not many of them also possess psychic abilities. Charlotte Grey is one of those few. For her to identify you as unusual, well, it simply means you have incredible powers."

"Yeah, okay." I scoffed into my cup, sending tea up my nose.

Cassandra gave me an indulgent smile. "I suspect you've been suppressing them for a while...many magical children, not just Seeing children, and, again, particularly those in unmagical homes, subconsciously suppress their abilities, sometimes for years, as a defense mechanism, shielding them from a potentially hostile environment."

"So, one day I'll just start bending spoons and—"

Cassandra laughed incandescently. Her emerald eyes sparkled. "Maybe. Once you let down your defenses and allow yourself to blossom."

I was quiet for a moment, and Cassandra continued, "There are many kinds of Seers...all with different abilities. There's no telling what you might be capable of; for example, I am a clairsentient. This means I am extremely sensitive to others and objects around me. I don't have premonitory visions or audio experiences, but I am highly *aware* of things...like I can sense the power of another paranormal being close to me. Take when I moved in last spring— as soon as we pulled up the driveway, I knew there was something wrong with Ms. Barbara. I almost told Huck I wanted out, yet I also had a strong sense that I needed to stay here, that *I* was needed here." She placed a gentle hand on my knee. "And I knew just by looking at you that you had the Sight, as we say; and right now? Just by touching you, I can feel the weight of the guilt you carry."

Instinctively, I shoved her hand off me and crossed my arms over my chest.

"It wasn't your fault, Hannah."

I looked at her sharply.

Cassandra's eyes shined and a tear spilled down her pretty face. "Your pain is so sharp in your heart, your thoughts are so loud in your head, your memories so vivid in your mind. I can tell you, Hannah, there was nothing you could've done against an evil like that, whatever your abilities."

I scoffed, shaking my head angrily. That wasn't what—

"*And Becca doesn't blame you, either,*" Cassandra added firmly.

"Psychic or not…" My voice broke. I closed my eyes. Tears leaked unchecked down my cheeks. "How could you possibly be sure that she didn't?"

"She *doesn't*," Cassandra repeated, smiling as she tucked a strand of brown hair behind my ear. "You can ask her yourself, if you like."

TOGETHER

It didn't take long to drive to the Nile school. It was a small building squished between two farms. It stunk badly of cow manure despite the cold. Elijah parked, and we got out to wait for dismissal. I hadn't told him about Cassandra. I didn't want him to worry about me when he needed to focus on his sister.

"How many grades?" I asked, studying the size of the building.

A bell rang from deep within the school.

"It's K through 8, but barely more than five kids in each grade... Noa is in 8th..."

He straightened suddenly as the kids began to pour out of the building. He didn't even need to point her out. The resemblance was uncanny. The willowy girl, so like her brother, towered over all the other kids. She turned her head as if sensing him, her mess of brown curls bouncing prettily. She adjusted her red horn-rimmed glasses and froze on the sidewalk at the sight of him. My heart stalled in my chest. Time seemed too slow. What if she walked away from him? Then her face split into an enormous smile as she pushed her glasses up the bridge of her nose and ran across the street to meet him. She threw her arms around him with breathless laughter.

He stroked her hair and said, his voice cracking, "It's good to see you, Noa."

"Good to see *you*." She pulled back from him, her smile wide and still laughing. She tousled his hair and gave his head a playful shove. "Took you long enough. I hope you kept that cat alive..."

Noa stepped back from him and raised an eyebrow at me. She jutted her thumb in my direction. "Who's this, your girlfriend?"

My face burned, and I hastily shook my head. "I'm his neighbor. Hannah."

Noa smiled coyly. "Ahh, the girl next door." She gave Elijah a wink and a punch in the arm as he blushed up to the roots of his hair. "A bit of a cliché, eh, Eli?"

"Just get in." He pushed her toward the passenger door, and she hopped happily into the truck. I slid in beside her.

"Glad to see you're still as charming as ever," he muttered, fighting the smile tugging at his mouth.

"Charming? Hey—you're the one with the girlfriend, not me." She snickered as he slammed the door. I stared straight ahead, face burning and completely mortified.

I had Elijah drop me off at home. He needed time with his sister, and I didn't say so, but I needed time with mine.

Cassandra had said all I needed was something of Becca's that she'd touched. It would be that easy. She wanted to do it with me, but I felt I needed to do it alone. So, Cassandra packed me a cloth bag with a few things, and I went up to my room, shutting the door behind me.

I went to the dresser. The box had already collected a thick layer of dust on top. Slowly, I turned the lock and opened it. I tried to breathe, but my breath caught somewhere between my heart and my ribs. Inside the box was everything I had left of her: notes, drawings, friendship bracelets, but underneath all the knickknacks —Becca's blankie.

She'd called it—him—Bop.

He used to be a bright lime with white polka-dots, but his color had faded to a soft pale-green. I frowned at the brown stain in the corner. Becca's blood. I'd hidden him before the police could take him away as evidence. Not even Mom knew I had him.

Gingerly, I pulled him out, sliding him carefully out from underneath all the other treasures, and held him up to my face for a moment, inhaling the scent of him...of her. Then I sat down in the middle of the old wood floor and unpacked Cassandra's bag.

There was a thick white taper candle, a lighter, and a black cloth with some strange symbols etched around it in a circle. I spread out the cloth, placed the candle in the center, lit it, and hugged Bop to my chest.

Then I closed my eyes and whispered her name, "Rebecca... Becca...can you hear me?"

Nothing happened.

My eyes blurred, and I let go. "Cassandra said it'd be hard to reach you...since you've—you know, moved on...but she said you would be able to hear me. Like leaving a message on a machine..." I sniffed loudly, and continued, my voice thick with emotion and lower lip trembling, "I just wanted to tell you that I love you so much. And I'm so freaking sorry about what happened. I didn't— I should've helped you. I should've tried...done more. I just—I need you to know that. I'm so sorry."

And alone in the unbearable silence of my room, I buried my face into Bop and cried until I had nothing left.

Mom found me quiet in front of the half-burnt candle, cradling Becca's blanket in my limp arms. She didn't process the scene at first. "Hannah, sweetheart, Elijah's downstairs...he said he's been knocking for a while. Sandra Blake called. I came home as soon as I could—"

She stopped mid-step.

I looked back at her, eyes red and face crusty. Her eyes went to the blanket...and then the candle and the cloth. "Hannah, what—"

I didn't answer right away. Instead, I snuffed out the candle, and, holding Bop tightly against my chest, I stood to face her. Her eyes were panicked and her face pale.

I took a deep breath. "I'm going to tell you something that's going to be hard for you to hear...but I need you to listen and believe me."

"Hannah—" Mom took a step back, shaking her head.

Again, I wanted to tell her everything. About what happened to Becca, about my dreams, but I couldn't do that to her. "I'm not going to be taking my sleep meds anymore because I don't need them."

Mom blinked and swallowed, licking her lips as though tasting her words. "Hannah—"

"But I'm going to start seeing Dr. Manning again. Regularly."

Mom hesitated, as though torn between fear and relief. "Well, that's—"

"I also want to visit Daddy."

Mom winced, inhaling sharply as though I'd slapped her.

"I think I can help him."

"Hannah—"

"And I'm going to start working at the docks, so you don't have to pull two shifts," I added in a rush.

Mom bit her lip to stop it from trembling. Her dark eyes shined, and she rushed forward to pull me into a rough hug, crushing Becca's blanket between us. She stroked my hair and rocked me as we stood. "Sweetheart, you will *not* be working at the docks."

"But—"

"No. Didn't Sandra tell you? Ms. Barbara—that sweet, wonderful woman, didn't just leave you this house...she apparently had an enormous stash of cash stored away in her closet...and incredibly, *you* are her sole beneficiary. That means—no more double shifts for me, and...sweetheart, that means college for you."

My heart flipped as it leaped into my throat.

Mom smiled, her eyes bright. "And I think that visiting your dad..." She leaned back to look at me, smoothing her thumb across my cheek. "That's a *beautiful* thing to do." Tears glistened in her eyes as she smiled. "And I appreciate you talking to me about your meds, and if you feel like you don't need them, I trust you to know your body...but I also appreciate you being self-aware enough to know that Dr. Manning would be a good idea."

I blinked, my dry eyes itching. "You aren't disappointed?"

Mom shook her head, still smiling, as she blinked back tears. "No, sweetheart, I'm *proud* of you."

Before I could speak, there was a tiny tapping at one of the windows. We both turned, and my heart made another leap.

It was an owl. Perched on the old balcony railing. Staring at us through the grimy window.

"Oh, my God," Mom whispered.

I went to the window and pulled it open. A gust of cold lake air flooded past me into the room, whipping my hair back and pressing against me. The owl blinked slowly at me and then bowed its head before it turned and took off with strong beats of its wings into the sky. Mom came up behind me as I watched it fly off toward the forest and placed her hand on my shoulder. "If I didn't know better, I'd say that was..."

"Becca."

But it wasn't.

And deep down I knew it, too.

Mom went to shower, and I headed downstairs.

Elijah was waiting for me in the sitting room with a book tucked neatly under his arm as he stood over by the fireplace with a hand rested on the mantelpiece. If it wasn't for his flannel shirt and jeans, he would've looked like a gentleman caller in that show about the duke. He straightened as he saw me come down the steps, adjusting his glasses and pushing a hand through his hair.

"I didn't expect you back so soon. Now's not really a good time..." I eyed him warily. "What is it? Is Noa okay?"

"Yeah, she's, uh, she's fine." Elijah smiled awkwardly. "I just dropped her off at my mom's house. We got coffee at, uh, well—*I* got coffee; she got a hot chocolate. At the diner." He rubbed the back of his neck and held out his hand. "And thank you—for pushing me to...you know, show up there." Elijah swung his arm and shoved it in his jean pocket. "But, on the way home, I realized something, and I felt like...I needed to...well—"

"Elijah..."

He scrunched up his face in a strained wince and passed me the book he'd been holding. "This is the book that jumped out at me at Charlotte Grey's place...I thought maybe..."

Seances, Summonings, and the Ways of the Wayward Souls, by Winifred Blackwell. I looked up at him, meeting his eyes with a heavy stare. "You think I should try to summon my sister?"

Elijah flinched and shrugged. "I mean—"

"I think that's a great idea, Elijah."

He blinked and stumbled over a few words before he managed, "Uh, good. Glad I could help."

I ran my thumb over the cover. "This is exactly what we'll need."

Elijah inclined his head, his brow furrowed and a bit confused.

I took a deep breath. "Cassandra gave me the tools to connect to Heaven...but Becca's not there." I took the book to the kitchen table and began to flip through it.

Elijah came up behind me almost hesitantly. "She's not—well, then, where...?"

"I don't know," I murmured as I pored over the pages. "But we've got to find her, and help her get there—just like we helped Barbara Blake, the *real* Barbara Blake..." I muttered rolling my eyes.

"How—"

I smiled at him. "We'll have to start at the beginning, won't we?"

Elijah pulled out a chair and dropped into it looking stricken.

"How do you feel about a road trip into the mountains?"

Elijah straightened his glasses and gave a sheepish, lopsided grin. "If that's what you need. I'm here for you, Hannah."

We planned to leave early in the morning, but I had one more thing to do first.

Lacey.

I headed down Apple Shore Road to wait at the bus stop for her. The wind coming off the lake was cold and biting, and I shivered a bit as I walked. The sun was barely up over the mountains across the water, and its weak yellow light gave no warmth. As I hiked up the hill and the stop sign came into view, I smiled at the sight of her.

There she was, sitting at the end of the road, cross-legged, her back against the rail of the stop sign with a small, brown paper lunch bag beside her. The Nile fairy tales were open on her lap. She had on a bright-green beanie with googly eyes protruding from the top. Her hot-pink puffy coat engulfed her, making her appear extra small. And her legs, in their yellow polka-dotted leggings, bounced a bit as she read.

"Hey, Lace."

She turned slightly as I came up beside her. I dropped the beaded bag next to her lunch. "Thank you for these. You were right. They were just what I needed."

Lacey picked up the bag and ran her finger over the beading. "You don't have to say that. I know they didn't help."

I dropped down beside her in the cold, damp grass. "They did. I realized it last night."

Lacey inclined her head and stared at me quizzically with her big hazel eyes.

"They helped me find you," I said earnestly.

"They did?" Lacey scrunched up her face trying to make sense of it.

"It's a kind of psychic thing." I smiled. "You were right about that, too. I was holding them, both the compass and the key, and *immediately* I thought of the attic. I didn't put it together then, but now it makes so much sense, don't you think?" I took her hand and gave it a squeeze. "Without you, Lacey, we never would've beaten that thing. And I would've been trapped in the mirror—just like Barbara Blake had been—my soul getting sucked on while that thing walked around wearing my skin." I made a face.

Lacey smiled slightly and passed me the book. "Mawkit. It was a mawkit. See?"

I stared down at the page and saw a drawing of a black shadow in the depths of a mirror with a hunched back and sharp, curved smile. I looked up at Lacey, torn between disbelief and annoyance. "It was here all the time?"

Lacey shook her head. "Well—yes and no. No, it wasn't because Ms. Barbara had ripped out the pages. Remember when she came into your apartment right before the fair?"

"She was looking at the book..."

Lacey nodded sagely. "And she'd ripped out the story of the mawkit... I swapped your copy for my mom's after I noticed the pages were ripped."

I stared at her in disbelief. "Lacey...you're incredible."

Lacey shrugged as she smiled shyly. "I keep trying to tell people...but everyone always wants proof..."

Suddenly overcome with love, I reached out and pulled her into a tight hug. "I'm sorry I hurt your feelings, Lacey."

"It's okay, Hannah," she murmured into my arm as I crushed her to me.

I shook my head, my eyes hot. "It isn't. You were right about everything, and I just...wasn't listening." I pulled back from her to meet her wide eyes. "But I am now. And I hope you're listening when I say: I'm so lucky to have a best friend as special as you."

Lacey's eyes fluttered, and her cheeks colored a soft pink. "Me, too."

The bus pulled up then...well, it was more like a tiny purple van. The kind of thing that takes skiers up to the mountains, stuffed full of kids. It came to a stop beside us with a creak, followed by a bang and a shudder, right before it released a big black cloud of smoke.

Lacey and I stood up, brushing the wet grass and dirt off ourselves as she collected her things. I glanced at the van and saw Portia's piggy nose nearly pressed against the window.

Lacey gave me a small wave.

"Maybe you can convince your daddy to let you homeschool," I called to her as she climbed up the steps. "And we can hunt for yobas all day."

Lacey's smile shined like sunshine. "I'll see you later, Hannah."

I watched the van head down the road to the docks and load onto the ferry before I turned back down the road to Rosecrest... back home.

Elijah was loading his truck with a duffel and a cooler as I made it up the long stretch of road.

He looked up at me as he tossed in a few more things. "How is she?"

"She's Lacey...better than the rest of us."

Elijah smiled at that and nodded in agreement.

I surveyed the inside of the truck and raised a dubious eyebrow at Elijah. "How long do you think we'll be? A month?"

Elijah blushed and rubbed the back of his neck. "I know it's just there and back...but better to be over prepared than under. Also, I got a couple more books from Charlotte, so—"

"*Charlotte*, huh?"

Elijah's olive skin blushed burgundy, and he straightened his glasses as he continued sharply, "*So*, the books will be accurate...as far as the paranormal...more accurate than anything Peter could've found on the Internet."

I could barely hide my smirk. "Right."

Elijah shoved his hands in the pockets of his Carhartt jacket. "Plus, she gave me a contact number...some guy named DeVarney who might be able to help if we get into trouble..."

I nodded in mock sympathy.

Elijah scoffed and gave me a gentle push. "Never mind. Oh. And I got you this..."

He passed me something wrapped in a brown paper bag. I raised an eyebrow as I opened it. "A hoodie?"

Elijah nodded.

"This is *your* hoodie..." I stifled a snicker.

Elijah shrugged and mumbled, "I know you liked Peter's...but it was all shredded by the end of—you know, after...and I thought you'd like a new—uh, well, it's not *new*, but a different one."

I grinned.

Before I could say anything, Elijah cleared his throat. "Are you ready? I packed bagel sandwiches for the road..."

"With sausage?"

Elijah grinned as he shoved me toward the door. "Get in."

"Hang on...there's one thing you forgot..."

Elijah stared after me as I ran up the staircase into his apartment and returned to the truck with the cat in my arms. He cocked an eyebrow, looking down his glasses at me.

I grinned and shrugged, nuzzling my burning cheek into the cat's soft black fur. "She's grown on me, I guess. And I'd hate to leave her alone in that stuffy mess of yours all day. Plus, you never know if she might come in handy..."

Elijah shook his head with an indulgent smirk, and we both hopped inside.

Elijah started the truck. The radio blasted Rob Zombie before he hastily turned it down. I glanced at him sideways as he pulled out of the parking lot and down the driveway. He drove us toward the docks, his face focused and hard with determination. I smiled slightly as I studied the sharp edge of his jaw, his hooked nose, and prominent forehead. The face of a scholar and yet when broken in a grin, surprisingly masculine. The dark eyes so serious behind the tortoiseshell glasses, and yet so quick to crinkle in a smile. And for all his awkward stuttering, he was an incredibly strong guy when he needed to be. I realized then, with pleasant surprise, that not only was I grateful to have him with me...I was happy.

Sure, I could face the insanity of a supernatural world on my own...but why when I could drag the long and lanky Elijah Grunvald along with me?

Elijah glanced at me sideways, catching my eye. "Are you okay?"

"Sorry." My cheeks burned, and I quickly looked away. I stared out the window and watched the lake as it churned beyond the docks and the white caps as they crashed into the rocks on the shore, struggling to find words to explain—without coming off... awkward. The cat purred in my lap as I stroked her back. "Just thinking."

"About?"

"You look just like your grandma, did anyone ever tell you that?" I quipped with a sly smile.

Elijah chuckled, his lopsided grin setting off his dimple. "All the time."

I shook my head and lifted the cat off my lap and placed her onto the dashboard. The cat curled up in the window, glaring at me with half-closed yellow eyes.

I dug the bagel sandwiches out of Elijah's backpack, passing him one and opening my own. "No, really what I was thinking was that—" I took a big bite and closed my eyes. *"Dis ish sho good,"* I moaned around a bit of bagel.

Elijah snorted. "Good."

"I was thinking..." I swallowed and cleared my throat. "I'm glad you're coming with me, Elijah Grunvald."

Elijah arched an eyebrow and smiled curiously.

"Well, I mean," I added, around another bit of bagel. "Not that I couldn't do it myself, but...you know." I shrugged as I chewed.

Elijah's smile broadened to a cocky grin. "I know."

I pointed my bagel at him. "Don't get all bigheaded on me... there won't be room left in this truck with all the other junk you packed."

Elijah laughed and turned up the radio.

I rolled my eyes and pulled out one of Charlotte's books.

Then Elijah shifted the truck into gear and drove off the ferry ramp, turned onto the highway, and headed for the mountains.

As the trees passed by in a blur of green, the words on the page also began to blur, and I felt myself nodding off. Slowly, I drifted to sleep, warm and confident that we could handle whatever came our way.

Together.

But as my head lulled back against the seat, and my mouth opened just enough to be embarrassing, I dreamed about her on the car ride there...

Thank you so much for reading.

This story will always hold a special place in my heart because it was the first story I ever finished all the way through to the final draft.
Yes. That's correct. The first story ever.
Surprisingly, I wrote *Dark Reflections* before *Seraphina Grey Summons a Demon*. Without Hannah's story, I never would've gotten the courage to finish Seraphina's.
And that is why *Dark Reflections* will always be a quiet favorite of mine.

Before the story came to be, it began with the cover. I saw it and fell in love with it and wrote a story about it—with little nods to a few of my favorite spooky movies sprinkled throughout.

I had so much fun with this story, and I hope you enjoyed reading it!

WELCOME TO THE NILE UNIVERSE

Sign up for the Courcy Camp newsletter for exclusive (free) early release access to *The First Hunt of Phoenix Grey* at

cristinecourcy.com/newsletter

But if newsletters (or eBooks) aren't your thing, pre-order *The First Hunt of Phoenix Grey* at **www.cristinecourcy.com/exclusive-releases** or your preferred book seller!

Seraphina Grey Summons a Demon

Book One of the Grey Sisters Saga

Available Now

A witch without magic. A demon out for blood. A dark family secret. How can teenage witch, Seraphina, solve the mystery and hunt down the demon when she can't even do magic?

Phoenix Grey and the Blood Farm

Book Two of the Grey Sisters Saga

Available Now

Kidnapped kids...butchered babysitters...and a trace of dark magic. Is this a case even Logan can't solve? Phoenix sure thinks so...

CRISTINE COURCY

SERAPHINA GREY & THE CARNIVAL OF NIGHTMARES

GREY SISTERS SAGA, BOOK THREE

ABOUT THE AUTHOR

Hi, I'm Cristine!
I love old sitcoms and slasher films.
When I'm not writing, I'm playing Animal Crossing or Harvest Moon 64.
When I am writing, I like to write dark fantasy with a light heart.
This means I want to disturb you without leaving you feeling yucky at the end of the story. In short, I'm inventing a new genre I like to call 'cozy dark fantasy.'
My books are heavily influenced by my experiences growing up wild on an island in the middle of the lake.
Almost all the things I write about are inspired by real life...but for legal purposes— that's a lie.
To read more lies and see photos of the things that *did not* inspire my writing, sign up for my newsletter at cristinecourcy.com/newsletter.

Connect with me online:
WWW.CRISTINECOURCY.COM

goodreads.com/cristinecourcy

facebook.com/cristinecourcy

instagram.com/cristinecourcy

threads.net/@cristinecourcy

youtube.com/@cristinecourcy

x.com/cristinecourcy

tiktok.com/@cristinecourcy

amazon.com/author/cristinecourcy

reamstories.com/cristinecourcy

www.ingramcontent.com/pod-product-compliance
Lightning Source LLC
Chambersburg PA
CBHW032242310726
48973CB00008B/2262